DARKEST THOUGHTS

ALSO BY GORDON BROWN

Craig McIntyre Thrillers
Darkest Thoughts
Furthest Reaches (*)
Deepest Wounds (*)

Charlie Wiggs Thrillers
Falling
Falling Too

Stand Alone
59 Minutes

(*) – Coming Soon

GORDON BROWN

DARKEST THOUGHTS

A Craig McIntyre Thriller

Down & Out Books
3959 Van Dyke Road, Suite 265
Lutz, FL 33558
DownAndOutBooks.com

Cover design by Andrew Forteath

ISBN: 1-64396-013-X
ISBN-13: 978-1-64396-013-5

To Lesley,
for everything.

PROLOGUE

I'm next to a bloodstained wall. Somewhere in Iraq. Cut off from my unit.

It's dark. I'm scared. Someone is after me. I don't know who. I'm cold.

Noises come from the other side of the wall. I sit still. I want the voices to vanish but they don't. My name is being whispered. Over and over. *'Craig...Craig...Craig.'* The accent is American. That should make me feel better. It doesn't.

'Craig.' Close. This side of the wall now. But there's nobody there. *'Craig.'* In my ear. Inches away. I can feel breath. I reach for my gun.

'Craig.' The other ear. *'Craig.'* Both ears. I lift the barrel and point it to my left, then to my right. I can't speak or won't speak. A second voice joins in. *'Craig.'* In stereo. Then three voices. Four. More. The hubbub grows. Hot air and words buzz around my head. The air is alive with people whispering my name.

Then one of the voices shouts. *'CRAIG!'* I wrap my finger around the trigger. *'CRAIG!'*—a second shout. Then they all join in.

Still there's no one there. I try to stand up but the voices force me back to the ground.

Something touches my hair. A gentle brush. My head won't move. It's stuck with Super Glue to the wall. Another touch. Touching and shouting. The touches become strikes. Flicks and

1

hits. I put some pressure on the trigger. Not enough to fire but just short of what's needed.

Somebody or something bites me. A vampire to my neck. Not a nip. A full chunk of flesh between teeth. Ripped from my body the flesh falls to the ground. I pull the trigger and spray bullets around my head. Keeping the pressure on until the clip runs dry.

Blood floods down my body. More bites. Harder. Faster. Tearing my face apart. A tooth touches my eyeball.

Light floods my world.

'Time to get to work, Mr McIntyre.'

The dream is gone and I'm back in the room. Sweat thick on me. A feeling of disconnect clouding my thoughts. The voice from the speakers is the man in the white linen suit. Lendl. *Rise and shine.*

The door opens and Buzz 1 enters. His haircut as sharp as a box-cutter blade.

'Mr Mather will show you the washroom. I'm sure you would like to freshen up.'

Behind Buzz 1 there are two more suits. They're taking no chances with me.

The washroom is heavy on showers. Six in a row. I'm guessing all-night stints are not unusual in this place. I strip off and take the full force of the water.

I finish and towel down. A cabinet reveals some deodorant; toothbrushes in sealed bags along with toothpaste. I scrub and spray.

Buzz 1 times his re-entry to perfection.

A new room. An examination bed against one wall. A table and chair against another. A computer in sleep mode squats on the table. Shelves line the third wall. An oversized TV sits on the space next to the door. Light shines through Plexiglas sheets above.

On the wall next to the examination bed there's a metal panel the length of the bed—about four feet high. It looks like a screen.

The speaker fires up. Lendl's voice fills the room. 'On the bed.'

I obey and sit with my legs dangling. Buzz 1 moves to the room's corner. The door opens. A tall, skeletal man dressed in a white coat enters. He pays me no attention. Sitting at the table he fires up the computer and begins to tap away. A second man comes in pushing a cart loaded with electronic equipment. Monitors, wires, keyboard, small blue boxes—none of which make any sense to me.

'Wire him up,' says the skeleton without looking up.

The second man wheels the cart next to me. He's heavy-set, thick around the gut, sweating freely in the cool air. 'Could you please lie down?'

I wonder what will happen if I say no but even my slight hesitation brings Buzz 1 out of his corner. I lie down.

The sweating man rubs some gel from a tube onto my forehead and opens up my shirt. He smiles as he pulls out a small razor. 'Sorry I've no shaving foam.' With practiced ease he shaves four patches of hair from my chest before attaching wires to the newly-bare areas and my head.

'Is he ready?' asks the skeleton. He doesn't look my way as he speaks.

'Just waiting for the signals to come online.' The sweating man hits a power button and the monitor jumps into life.

'Straps,' orders the skeleton.

Straps? Suddenly Buzz 1 is at my shoulder with another suit in tow. They reach under the bed. Too late I realize what they are going to do. I try to sit up but Buzz 1 whips out his gun and pushes it into my leg. 'A bullet in the thigh won't affect the tests.'

I freeze. Buzz 1 pulls up leather straps and coils them around my wrists and ankles, pulling hard on the buckles to secure them. When they're fastened, he puts the gun away before helping the other suit finish the job. Buzz 1 reappears above my head. He holds a head restraint in his hand and slides the top of my skull into it. With a pull, he tightens the fastening. I'm all but immobile.

'Ready?' asks the skeleton. I can no longer turn my head to tell if he's still looking at the computer.

'Good to go,' says Buzz 1.

'Okay. You two can leave.'

Buzz 1 and the suit exit.

'Open the screen,' orders the skeleton.

There is a click and the sound of movement.

'Okay,' he continues. 'Do the subjects in the next room have any idea what they're here for?'

Lendl's voice rings out from the speakers in reply. *'No. As requested they were picked up from the streets on the promise of drugs and booze.'*

'Have they been given any?'

'Enough to keep them calm.'

'Good.'

'What are you expecting?'

'I don't know. I've a few ideas but we'll see. I have to say I don't hold out much hope. It all seems a little thin.'

'We've seen more from less.'

I'm beginning to lose my grip on the reality of all this. How the hell did I end up strapped to a bed and wired up to the moon? What is it they want?

'Mr McIntyre, please relax,' says Lendl. *'Before we start, I want to ask you a few questions.'*

'Before you start what?'

'A few little tests. Nothing to worry about.'

'If I shouldn't be worrying, why am I trussed up like a turkey?'

'For your own safety.'

'Bullshit.'

'Have it your own way. Now think back to Iraq. To the street outside the brothel. Did anything strike you as unusual?'

4

'Apart from getting mugged?'

'Have it your way. Start the tests.'

'What the fuck is going on?' It's the only question I want an answer to.

Lendl spits a few words. *'Shut him up.'*

The sweating man's dripping face appears above me. He pulls a mouthpiece over the lower half of my face. I'm silenced.

'First scenario.' Skeleton talking. 'Both times the subject claims to have been asleep. On each occasion two people died and on both occasions they killed each other. Would the subject need to know the victims?'

'He did, but let's try it without any knowledge,' says Lendl.

I'm lost. No idea what they're doing.

'Okay.' The Skeleton sounds like he's dictating a memo. 'The subject is now aware we have two test subjects in the next room. Let's put him to sleep and see what happens.'

Put me to sleep. How?

The prick in my arm is a giveaway.

CHAPTER 1

The murder weapon lies a few inches from my feet, hidden beneath a rusting Pepsi can and a blue plastic bag. The broken handle from an axe—thrown from a car three days ago.

The heat forces sweat from my armpits, and my blue shirt—a poor color choice—is stained. A stream flows down my back, soaking my boxers.

The dust is a constant companion. A storm blew through yesterday, leaving a coating on the world. My sunglasses help a little.

Four a.m. Lifeless. Stained cinder-block canyons. This is no place to be caught unawares.

Footsteps. My antennae pop. I size up the approaching man. He's dressed in a traditional Dish-dash-ou. His Shumagg, the white headscarf of the summer months, shadows his face. He shuffles in ill-fitting sandals.

I touch the bulge under my lightweight jacket, feeling the weight of the gun.

The grip is cool but too small. A P99 Rad—a Polish copy of a Walther. At one time it had interchangeable grips. This one came from the back shop of a local merchant apologetic that he didn't have the original packaging and all the optional extras.

The old man pads along the road, head down. I eyeball the handleless, sheet metal door my employer walked through an hour ago. It's sealed tight.

My fingers curl around the top of the gun's slide. I pull it back until the click tells me the weapon is cocked.

I hope it works. I didn't have time to check it over.

The old man stops. Ten yards away. The smell of baking drifts over. Iraqi flat bread—I've grown used to the smell over the last few days.

I take a quarter step sideways to give me a better bead on the target.

He lifts his head and stares at me through cheap Foster Grant sunglasses. I can't see his eyes and he can't see mine. Not good. Alarm bells are ringing in my head. I focus on his hands, which are thrust inside the Dish-dash-ou. He walks towards me and stops a few feet away.

'Masa il Khee,' he says—not the usual formal greeting I have come to expect.

I hesitate while I try to remember the appropriate reply. 'Masa il Noor.'

'Kayf Halak?'

How am I?

I root around again for an answer and come up with 'Qwayysa.'

He tilts his head to one side, as if I've said something wrong, and laughs. 'You mean Qwayyis?' His English is clipped.

'Do I?'

'But of course. *Qwayysa* would be the response were I a woman.'

'Sorry.'

I take a step back. The old man has closed in on me during the exchange. The smell of bread is joined by a sour tang. It's either him or me and I don't recognize the scent.

He coughs. 'You are new to Basra?'

I have a job to do. Any distraction is one too many. 'I'm waiting for someone.'

'What? In this place? My friend, this is not somewhere that you wish to be meeting people.'

He smiles, teeth pure Billy Bob. 'I am only here myself because this is the quickest way to get home. I worked late tonight and am looking forward to some food and half an hour of CNN. Do you like CNN?'

Say nothing. Usually a good way to lay a hint on someone, but it doesn't work on this occasion.

'I like CNN,' he keeps talking. 'My wife does not. She prefers *Extreme Makeover*. That makes me smile. I think she wants the man in the program to come to our house. She likes the houses she sees in MTV's *Cribs*. I like them too, but I am not a pop star—although I can sing a little. Would you like to hear?'

I scan the road and the buildings. He takes this as a no. 'That is probably a good thing. You are American are you not?'

'Look...'

'Ahmed. My name is Ahmed.'

'I'm busy. Could we take a rain check?'

'Rain. Ah, we get a lot of rain here in the winter. Very little in the summer. It has not rained in two months but the waterway keeps the crops supplied. Have you seen our waterway? Impressive, isn't it?'

I back away from him. Trying to keep the smell at a manageable distance. He follows. Behind him the metal door opens.

'McIntyre.' My employer appears. A small man. Small-minded with it. I have instructions to guard him but he told me to stay put while he went inside.

'McIntyre, get the car.' He throws a bunch of keys onto the road and vanishes. I walk over to retrieve them from the dirt.

'Mr Taylor is demanding?'

I spin round as the local speaks.

The old man is picking his nose. 'A member of your government is he not?'

I'm standing halfway between the door and the old man, the keys warm and sticky in my hand.

He takes a step forward. 'Is he your employer?'

I pocket the keys, check the alley once more and walk up to him. 'Will you just fuck off?'

His hands whip out from under his clothes. I see the dull glint of metal as he leaps towards me. I jump to the side but he twists in mid-air.

Metal connects with my skull.

CHAPTER 2

The world returns and I need a box of Tylenol. I try to lift my head, gagging at the pain. I can't focus.

My left hand is pinned under my body and, trying not to move my head, I shift a little to extract it. Pins and needles roll in. I bite my tongue. I reach for my head and my hand finds a sticky mess. Not wet, just sticky. If it's blood, then it's congealed, and that means I have been lying here for a while. I close my eyes, before forcing my head off the ground. Flashes of light replace the dark. Jesus, how hard did the old man hit me?

I open my eyes. The road is empty. The Pepsi can I saw earlier is lying a few feet away. No longer near the storm drain. I pat down my jacket. No gun. To be expected. I pat my hip and can't feel the familiar bulge of my money clip.

I prop myself up on an elbow.

'There!'

The voice is faint. Maybe at the other end of the street. Help? More grief? I turn to look. A freight train crosses my temple. The Diet Coke and kebab I had a few hours before makes a return journey.

I throw my head to one side to avoid my own puke but some of it splatters on my jacket. I want to collapse back to the ground. I take another breath, trying to hold a sitting position.

'See, I told you.'

The voice is closer.

I wipe my mouth, licking the back of my teeth as I do so. I

turn to the sound, closing my eyes, waiting for the dizziness to pass.

When I open them again four figures are approaching. Three IPs and a civilian. I've had a couple of run-ins with the Iraqi Police since I got here. At least it's not the National Police. IPs mean this is a local problem.

The metal door is ajar. Two heads are sticking out. Both locals.

I'm glad the old man took the gun. Iraq might still resemble a war zone but the IP don't take kindly to freelancers.

'Stay still!' The largest of the police officers is shouting. His sandy-colored uniform is straining to hold in his stomach. He's carrying forty pounds of excess fat above his belt. Sweat stains have turned most of his shirt into a dark smudge. 'Lie down. On your front, hands behind your back.'

What the fuck? I don't want to lie down. On your front, hands behind—that's the perp's position. I've done zip—other than getting mugged by a senior citizen.

The fat IP's two colleagues back him up. All three have their guns trained on me. The civilian stands back. He's ripping into his fingernails with his teeth.

The fat IP steps forward. 'Get down. Now.'

I want to stand up, not lie down.

He raises his gun. 'I *will* shoot.'

Shoot? What the hell for? I'm no threat.

'I will not ask again. Lie down *right* now.'

He raises his gun another few inches, then points the barrel to the ground—indicating I should follow.

Maybe they have me mixed up with someone else.

'I'm...'

The discharge of the weapon is a thunderclap. Whatever is going on it's not worth getting killed over.

Instantly my face is back in the dirt. I hear a shuffle of feet. A knee lands in the small of my back. Someone pulls up my hands. My shoulders protest big time. Plastic cuffs are tied off.

A foot kicks me in the side. The restraints cut into my wrists. Fuck. My arms are on fire.

'Up.'

Trying to gain my feet with my hands tied is difficult. I stumble and fall. Road fills my face. I try again. A hand pulls at the cuffs. I scream as I'm hauled to within a finger's width of the fat officer's face. His breath is sweet, mixed with expensive deodorant that needs to be antiperspirant.

My head spins. I vomit again. The fat officer jumps back, cursing. I stagger to the wall for support. I stop retching and look back. Taylor and a young girl are lying in the middle of the road.

The dust around them is thick with blood.

CHAPTER 3

I stare at the bodies. Taylor is face up with the hilt of a pickaxe rising from his stomach. The girl is topless. Her tongue lolls from the side of her mouth. Her small breasts are lathered in blood. Some of my vomit has puddled in one of her shoes.

The fat officer is back in my face. 'Why did you kill them?' Two locals are watching the scene from the door.

I shake my head. 'I didn't.'

'They're dead and you're here.'

'He'—I point at the dead body—'was my employer. I'm his security guard.'

'Easy to kill him then. He would trust you.'

He's interrupted by the roar of a supercharged engine accompanied by the scream of tires digging through dirt. The noise echoing along the walls.

A black SUV races into the road. It kicks up a dust storm as it brakes. The fat officer spins to the noise, gun at the ready. His fellow officers are on the move. Spreading out. Eyes on the new arrival. Trained well.

The passenger door at the back right of the SUV opens and a man emerges, dressed in a suit too dark and heavy for the environment. From the front passenger door a human tombstone steps out. He cradles a semi-automatic machine gun.

The man in the suit walks towards the fat officer. The officer lowers the gun. They meet near the bumper of the SUV and go into a lengthy conversation. At one point one of the locals standing at the metal door is ordered over.

The man in the suit pulls out a laptop, placing it on the SUV's hood. All three look at the screen for five minutes. The suit closes the computer. The man from the door is sent packing. A bit more chat and the fat officer steps to one side as the suit walks towards me.

'Free him!' says the suit. The officer next to me looks to his boss for an instruction. He receives a nod. Reluctantly he reaches behind me and frees my wrists.

'Come with me.' The man in the suit's accent is West Coast. Californian but with a hint of something more southern.

'Why?' I ask.

'Have you seen *Midnight Express*? Trust me, it's got nothing on what they'll do to you if you hang around here.'

'Who are you?'

'Later.'

I weigh up my choices. There are no choices. I walk with my savior.

We approach the SUV. It's pumping cold air into the night. The A/C is on full blast. The driver ignores me. Next to him the tombstone has slid into the passenger seat. In the back a small man with a white linen suit looks out of place in the black interior.

I slide into the middle seat next to him. My savior gets in beside me. As he closes the door, he snaps at the driver. 'Get us the hell out of here.'

The driver selects Reverse and swings the SUV around. He flicks to Drive. He guns the engine just as three more identical SUVs rush past us heading for the crime scene.

'Close,' the man in the white linen suit says before sighing.

I chirp up. 'Who are you?'

'Your friendly neighborhood rescue squad.'

'What in the hell went down?'

'I've no idea.'

'Taylor and the girl are dead.'

14

'Yup.'

'And that's okay?'

He shakes his head. 'Far from it. Now shut up and give us a little quiet. You can talk all you want when we get back to the ranch.'

His voice is a tone too high for comfort. Makes him sound like he's squeezing the words out through a straw. I sit back, the aromatic mix of vomit, sweat and road dirt emanating from me. I rub at my head.

I wish I had some morphine on me.

The ride is smooth. The car's suspension evens out all but the deepest potholes. The blackened windows show little save a succession of lights flicking by. I close my eyes and try to put some perspective on what's going on. I've seen dead bodies before. I've even woken next to them. But I'm surprised I'm in the car. Given the IP had just found the bodies, my first port of call should have been the local station. My rescuers hold some sway.

'Anyone have any Tylenol?'

No answer.

The car hits a set of speed bumps. It slows. The driver's window slides down. A soldier appears with a flashlight. The driver shows a card and the soldier checks us out. His eyes rest on me, then on the blood. He backs out and signals a gate to open. We move forward, only to stop a couple of car lengths later. The gate behind us slams shuts as another opens in front. Twenty yards more and stop. The driver opens the window. Another soldier asks for ID.

A garage door opens and we glide in. No one moves until the door closes behind us. Then, as if choreographed, all four open their doors at the same time to exit.

'Out.' My savior stands clear.

I decide to follow orders.

We are in a gray cube of concrete. Two more black SUVs are parked to the back of the lot. I'm beginning to think that the dealer with the franchise for these things is on a bonus. The man in white linen leads off. We cross to a small door. My savior steps forward, placing his hand on a gray box. A small whirr. A click. The door swings open.

We walk into a whitewashed corridor, me the sandwich between Tombstone and the driver.

The space is barely large enough to hold us. A second door is guarded by another gray box. My savior places his hand on it. Same procedure and we're through.

The room beyond is dark but, as we walk, the ceiling lights spring to life. The place is full of empty tables and plastic chairs. Dust lies everywhere, the walls are unpainted. There's a heavy smell of old sweat.

My savior pushes me towards a chair. 'Take a seat and we'll see about a doctor.'

White Linen and my savior do the box thing on another door. As they vanish, the driver and Tombstone pull up a couple of chairs and sit to stare at me.

I settle back to wait. Tombstone occupies himself by mining his nose. The driver closes his eyes. I touch my head. It's messy. Head wounds can be tricky—I've had experience.

Years ago, I was training in northern Canada. An army exercise to accustom new recruits to the cold. I was buddied-up with a fellow grunt. We were told to find a spot and bed down for the night. It was dark by the time we found somewhere suitable and we decided to pitch the tent beneath an old cedar tree. In the middle of the night I got up for a piss. I walked straight into a branch—knocking myself out. The next morning, I woke up feeling fine. An hour later I collapsed as I packed up the tent. Head wounds can do that.

Tombstone stops mining for a second and I smile at him. He rams his finger back in his nose.

The door opens. A man in a white lab coat walks in carrying a large brown case. He sports a heavyweight beard to make up for the lack of hair on top.

'Is that him?' he says, pointing at me.

Tombstone nods. The lab coat walks over.

'My name's Kelly—Medical Corp on assignment. Head wound, I hear.'

He grabs my head and twists it around.

'I feel a bit faint,' I say.

'Not surprised. Don't pass out on me. I've been told to fix you up. Take these.'

Warm pills, their coating melting from the heat of his hand, are shoved at me.

'Get him some water,' he says to Tombstone without turning.

Tombstone heads for the water cooler. He returns with a plastic cup.

I pop the two pills. 'What are they?'

'Painkiller and anti-nausea.'

He finishes the examination and stands back. 'You should be in hospital. You might have a fractured skull.'

The door opens again to reveal my savior. 'And?'

'Hospital,' says the lab coat.

'Not going to happen,' replies my savior. 'We need him here. Just fix him up.' He exits.

The painkiller is good. The headache is fading. I no longer feel like I'm going to keel over. The doctor cleans the wound and wraps my head in cloth. He hands me a small pile of pills. 'One an hour. Any more and you'll lose the power of speech.'

He leaves. Tombstone stands up, indicating I should do likewise. We walk through the door, into another gray corridor. At the far end he plays with the ubiquitous gray box and we enter a new world.

At one time the room has been a large single entity. Now it's divided into a sea of glass walls. The place is alive with activity. White coats dominate. Computer equipment fills each room. There could be a hundred or more people working.

Tombstone walks through the room, ignoring it all, while I snap my head left and right to take in what's going on. Tombstone stops at another door. 'In here.'

He opens the door and pushes me into a room that contains two chairs and a small table. The door closes behind me.

As interrogation rooms go it's old school. A large panel of mirrored glass indicates the presence of a viewing room. Two CCTV cameras, one facing each chair, sit at the junction of ceiling and wall. The table is bolted to the concrete floor. It has metal rings welded to the underside for feeding prisoners' chains through. The chairs are fixed to the stained floor by heavy-duty bolts. The door to the room has no handle. The tabletop is dotted with cigarette burns. A smell of bleach adds to the sense of menace. I was taught to spray it around for just that reason

My adrenalin is souring and, combined with the painkiller, I'm starting to feel sleepy.

The door opens. My savior enters. 'Coffee?'

'I'd love one.'

He nods at Tombstone who wrestles himself from his chair, feet dragging. He's making it clear he's not happy.

My savior sits opposite me. 'So let's start with the basics. Your name is Craig McIntyre. Ex US military. 1st Infantry Division, 4th Brigade, 2nd Battalion, 16th Infantry Regiment. You spent three months in Iraq in 2003 in Ramadi before being sent home on the Permanent Disability Retirement List. Mental problems.

'Hometown is Los Angeles. Mother's a Brit and father's from New York. Married with no kids and now working for Steel Trap Security. Entered Iraq six days ago. Given the job of babysitting Tom Taylor—now dead, along with an as yet unidentified female. Did I miss anything?'

I shake my head.

'Good.'

Then he punches me.

CHAPTER 4

The blow knocks me off the chair. Tombstone chooses that moment to return, places the coffees on the table and helps me back onto my perch. My savior rubs his knuckles. 'Tom was a friend of mine,' he explains.

I'm still stunned from the punch but I give him my best 'fuck off and die' look. He blanks it.

'So what went down?'

'I was mugged. Woke up to find two dead bodies next to me. That's it. I had nothing to do with their deaths.'

'We know.'

I let my mouth hang loose for a moment. 'And the IP?'

'They also know you didn't have anything to do with the killings.'

'How do they know that?'

He turns to Tombstone. 'Get me the laptop.'

Tombstone vanishes again. He comes back with a laptop, flipped open.

My savior spins the screen towards me. 'Watch.'

A black and white movie fires up. Only this is no early Charlie Chaplain but a view of the road I was mugged on. I'm standing against the wall, the old man approaching. Tom Taylor appears from the door, the keys fly out, I walk forward, the old man approaches and bang, I'm on the ground. The old man rifles around me, lifts my gun and the money clip before vanishing.

I see myself lying on the ground for a few minutes before the metal door opens again. Taylor walks out with the young girl on his arm. He looks up and down the road and spots me sprawled out. The young girl hangs back as he approaches me. A new face appears at the door. I recognize him as one of the local gawkers.

As Taylor bends down to touch me, the young girl walks over to the edge of the road. She reaches down, picks up the broken pickaxe, wanders over to Taylor and taps him on the shoulder. He spins round and she shoves the wood into his stomach.

He staggers forward, latching onto her dress, pulling it down over her breasts. She doesn't seem to notice. He works his hands up, around her neck. They both go down. His hands stay on her throat until she stops moving. He flips on his back, shudders and all is still.

I stare at the blank screen as the video finishes.

My savior plays with the laptop. 'Look closer.' The scene rewinds. My savior fiddles with the controls. He zooms in on her face. 'Do you know her?'

'No.'

'Are you sure?'

'Damn sure. Anyway, why would anyone have CCTV in the back end of nowhere?'

My savior stands up. He digs out a packet of Marlboro. 'Smoke?'

I shake my head and he lights up.

'I'll level with you.' The first plume rises from his lungs. 'Tom was using a brothel and wasn't being too discreet about it. That CCTV has caught a few naughty boys—not just Tom. Our Iraqi friends are not too wild about us lifting you but the CCTV footage convinced them to let us talk to you first. But they'll be back. Not least because the cars you saw pass us on the way here were out to limit the damage. That means the locals won't be happy. They don't take well to us screwing with their crime scenes.'

'So who are you? CIA? Military? Freelance?'

'I work for the government.'

'So does my aunt but she can't remove a suspect from a crime scene, interrogate him and slug him on the chin.'

He smiles. 'So you don't know the girl?'

'No idea who she is.'

Another lungful of smoke drifts to the ceiling. 'Doesn't it strike you as a bit crazy that she would ram a pick axe into his stomach?'

I shake my head. 'Look, figure it for yourself. Your boy Tom got a bit frisky in the club. Forgive me speaking ill of the dead but he wasn't the friendly type. She has a bit too much of the illegal hooch. He pushes it too far. She hits fresh air, then decides she doesn't want to go wherever it was they were going.'

'Don't buy it.'

'Okay. What do you think?'

'I'll have a better idea when my colleagues get through. I'm just the vanguard on this one. If I were you, I'd settle in for the wait.'

He takes one more draw, leaving me to breathe in the second-hand smoke. I pull out a pill and pop it. It's been no time at all since the last one but I need it.

I know the routine so I need to get comfortable. I try lying on the floor, lying on the table, lying against the wall and finally lying across the table again—this time with one leg on the floor, one knee on a chair. It takes another pill to make this comfortable.

Somehow three hours crawl by.

The door opens. Tombstone blocks the view. 'Up.'

I follow him back through the glass maze, into an elevator. We rise.

In the rarefied atmosphere of the higher floors the world has carpet and soft furnishings. Tombstone escorts me to a set of over-polished oak double doors. He knocks—surprisingly gently. A voice tells us to enter.

White Linen sits behind an oversized desk. 'Take a seat, Mr McIntyre.' Then to Tombstone. 'That'll be all.'

I drop onto a leather couch.

He settles back in his chair. 'Coffee?'

'Please.'

White Linen pours from a glass jug sitting behind him. 'Milk?'

'Black.'

He pushes the china cup across his desk and I stand to retrieve it. The closed shutters behind him can't hide the fact that we're enjoying the first rays of a new Iraqi day.

He throws a manila folder towards me. I catch it and find a single typed sheet inside. A brief summary of the events of the last few hours.

'We've arranged for you to take your leave.'

'Not before time. I've a job to get back to—not to mention a hospital visit.'

'You'll be doing neither. When I say you're leaving, I mean you're leaving Iraq.'

'Am I hell!'

He reaches into a drawer in the desk. He takes out an envelope. Tosses it to me. I rip it open. Inside is my passport, a few hundred dollars and a letter. The letter is my dismissal, a simple statement of termination with no references, from Steel Trap Security.

'Your bag's downstairs. There's a car waiting to take you to the airport. Unfortunately, we've had to send you the long way home but it was prudent to put you on the first flight out of here.'

I sit forward in my seat.

'Who the hell do you think you are?'

'Your friend, Mr McIntyre. The IP are looking for someone to hang. You're the perfect candidate. But I'm convinced there's more to last night than you're letting on, so giving you to our hosts won't help me unravel this. You need to go home. We'll pick up on this somewhere more congenial.'

This time I lean forward. 'You have it all on tape. I did nothing.'

He leans back in his high-backed chair. 'We'll provide an escort to see you safely back to US soil.'

I sip the coffee and work through the options. With no job in Iraq and the IP on my tail I think I'm in for Hobson's choice, but I'm damned if I'm just going to roll over. 'And what do I do when I get back? This is the first legit job I've had in years and it took a lot of persuading and a crap salary to get me here.'

'Not my problem. You're the one who screwed up. If you'd been on the ball you wouldn't have been mugged by a geriatric and Tom might still be here. You're lucky we're giving you a way out.'

He hits a buzzer. Tombstone appears.

White Linen points to me. 'Mr McIntyre is leaving. Take him to the car pool. Mr Cameron will join you. I want you to drive and take no shit at the airport. If need be call in our boys, but get Mr McIntyre safely on his plane.'

He turns back to look at me. 'Nice to meet you.'

He lifts a file from the corner of his desk, opens it and begins to scribble some notes.

'What's your name?'

I'm trying to engage Tombstone in conversation as he escorts me through the building. 'Just your name. Come on—how can that hurt?'

'Bo Peep.'

Funny guy.

The car pool turns out to be a high-walled compound with half dozen of the black SUVs parked, nose out, against one wall. Tombstone walks to the furthest, hits the remote and the lights flash. 'Inside.'

I throw my bag over the back seat into the trunk and jump

in. It can't be much past seven but the heat is already a killer. I'm an open faucet of sweat. 'Can you switch on the A/C?'

He ignores me and slams the door. My sweat is already pooling in the seat. There's a clunk as the central locking kicks in. I flip the manual switch but the doors are deadlocked. I try the electric windows. Dead. I'm a fucking US citizen in a US building and I'm being treated like the lead from *Most Wanted*. Who in the hell are these guys? CIA but not CIA—something doesn't add up.

The leather on the seats burns to the touch. To add to the discomfort my headache is back. I reach for a pill. I should have asked for more. There are five left. I pop one but I don't have the spit to swallow it dry and it sticks in my throat.

I scrabble into the front seat. I rifle the glove box and the central console for water but the car is as clean as the day it was delivered. I cough and the pill lodges somewhere near the top of my gullet. I gag and cough again. It won't shift. It feels like it's taking up my whole throat. I grunt to try and help. I inhale hard. The pill slips down a little to wedge further in. It feels like the size of a baseball. I gag and begin to cough.

The door opens. 'What the hell are you doing?'

A new dark suit is looking down on me. Tall, six feet plus, well-muscled-up, my new friend is gym-hardened. His nose has taken a beating at some point. His face holds the pits of long-dead acne. 'Move over.'

'I need a drink. Got any?'

He ignores me. Tombstone gets in the driver's seat.

My new friend slides in beside me. He reaches over and slaps Tombstone over the back of the head. Tombstone spins round. 'What the...?'

I'm surprised at the action. Tombstone doesn't seem like the playful type. The new suit takes a bottle of water from his pocket. He hands it to me.

'What did you hit me for?' spits Tombstone. The most consecutive words I've heard from the walking wall. I unscrew the cap of the bottle and am delighted to find it's cool. I start drinking.

'What?' says the new suit.

'Why did you hit me?'

'What are you talking about?'

'When I got in the car you hit me over the head.'

'Did I hell. Fire up the car. We've a plane to catch.'

Tombstone turns away with a growl. I'm not sure what game my new friend is playing and I don't care. I turn to him. 'Mr Cameron, I assume. What's your first name?'

'What do you care?'

'You're my buddy. If I have to fly with you, I can't keep calling you Mr Cameron. Have you got a first name?'

He circles his head, cracking some bones in his neck. 'You don't need to know.'

The gates unfold in front of us and we exit onto a busy intersection. Cruising past the Indian Market we swing west, away from the crime scene. My eyes close.

When I awaken there's a gun in my face.

CHAPTER 5

The car window is wound down. A blast of heat fights the A/C. The gun belongs to an Iraqi National Police sergeant. The blue and white camouflage clothes a copy of our boys' kit. The man is rabbiting on in Arabic. Cameron is right back at him.

Suddenly the gun vanishes. The window rises as Tombstone hits the button.

'What was that about?' I ask Cameron.

'You.' Cameron leans forward towards Tombstone. 'Keep driving.'

We negotiate some concrete blocks and stop a couple of car lengths further along. Tombstone's window goes down. He flashes his ID. The guard hands him a piece of paper. We drive another fifty yards, we stop, the window goes down and Tombstone hands over the paper. It's inspected and we are waved through.

'Fussy about their security,' I say.

Cameron smiles. 'Wait till you see how many X-ray machines we still have to go through.'

I look out the window. I trace the perimeter fence running into the distance. We're still a couple of miles from the terminal but there's good reason for setting the fence so far away. The Brits used the airport from the get-go. The perimeter was set up to keep the nutters at bay, and the best way to do that was to keep them at a distance.

Tombstone drops us outside the airport entrance. Cameron

isn't joking about the X-ray machines. I count four before we get on the plane. Add in a few more security checks and it takes us ninety minutes to cover less than three hundred yards.

We are in the air twenty minutes later.

Our first destination is Amman—a small airport with basic facilities. We touch down to find the plane to Cyprus is ready to roll and, as I pop the last of the pain pills, we take off. I soon fall asleep.

In Larnaca we have a four-hour stopover. I'm all for going to the bar. My minder is all for avoiding the place.

'Did they really send you just to escort me home?' We're sitting in the airport café. I'm sipping strong coffee.

'I'm being transferred.'

'Promotion?'

'Kind of.'

'Look, I'm not your enemy. We have twenty-four hours of travel left. All I want is a little company. If you don't—fine.'

He drains the cup. 'Another?'

I nod. He has to wait in the line as two women argue over who'll pay. He returns with two large mugs. As he drops into the seat he speaks. 'I screwed up.'

I try not to smile. 'That makes two of us.'

'Yeah, well at least no one got killed on my watch.'

My smile fades. 'What happened with you?'

'I told you. I fucked up.'

'You want to confess?'

'No.'

'Well lighten up and let's have a drink. Nothing you can do about it until you get stateside.'

'I'm a bad drunk.'

'So am I.'

Five minutes later we're in the bar. I'm on a JD and Coke and he's on his second Ballantine's, while telling me who it is that's forcing me to go back home. 'We take on some of the more unusual issues that our government faces. My boss always says,

'*If it don't fit—we'll get it*'. He makes it sound like a rhyme.'

'Unusual. What's the agency called?'

'I'm not going to go into it any more. I can't.'

'So, what's your name?'

'Mike.'

'Where's home?'

'Anchorage, Alaska.'

'Cold.'

'Sometimes.'

'Do you get back often?'

'Not for over a year.'

'Are you married?'

'What do you think?'

'No, but I'll guess you were.'

'We lasted two years and by then she was a stranger. She's moved in with an old friend of mine.'

'Nice.'

'And you?'

I take a breath. 'Married and live in LA. My wife and I went to school together and lost contact. I met her in a bar a few years back. We got married last year.'

'And she's happy you're doing security work in Iraq?'

'It's my first real job in years. We had no choice. It doesn't even pay that well but it was a six-month contract and kept the roof over our heads for another year. She teaches.'

'You're ex-army, aren't you?'

'It was a short affair. Can we drop it?'

'You avoid the department and I'll avoid the army.'

'Deal.'

He drains the whisky and orders another. I'm not halfway through mine. When the waiter returns, he swallows most of it in one go. 'What'll you do when you get home?'

'I'm not sure. It'll be a surprise to Lorraine. My wife. I haven't been able to contact her. Your lot didn't let me take a piss on my own—never mind a phone call.'

'You had them rattled.'

'I did?'

'Tom wasn't just a grunt. He was number two to Lendl.'

'Lendl?'

'The man in the white linen suit.'

'So why didn't you supply Taylor with his own security?'

'This is the twenty-first century. Freelance contracting is all the rage. It means we don't have to put our people in the line of fire. People like you are the new cannon fodder.'

'No shit.'

'Private firms are plastered all over Iraq. It's cheaper than employing your own people, less risky and more flexible. The downside is you don't always get the most competent of operatives.'

I wince. I'm saved from any further embarrassment by the departure board announcing our gate.

Mike glances at the board. 'Time for one more?'

CHAPTER 6

Thirty minutes later and we're sitting near the back of the Cyprus Airways Airbus 320. There are three seats either side of the walkway. The flight is quiet and we have a spare seat between us. Mike orders another two whiskeys as the trolley rolls past. I'm beginning to regret suggesting we had a drink. I decline the stewardess's offer and lean back in the chair.

My headache is growing. I've stocked up on over-the-counter painkillers at the airport, but I'm not sure they're heavy-duty enough. I pop two.

I gather I've dozed off, because I'm awoken by the sound of Mike's raised voice. 'Two more whiskeys.'

The stewardess is standing above him. Her arms folded. She's standing a little further away than would seem polite. 'I'm sorry, Mr Cameron, but I've been told not to serve you any more at the moment.'

'Fuck off. I want a drink.'

I reach over and put a hand on his shoulder. 'Calm down, Mike. She's....'

I don't get to finish my sentence.

'And you can fuck off as well.' His eyes are wide. The whites have hair-streaks of red snaking through them. I've no idea how long I've been asleep but Mike is a good few drinks to the bad side of things. He turns back to the stewardess. 'Get me two drinks now.'

'Sorry, sir, I can't do that.'

He moves to stand up. I place my hand on his shoulder. Again he spins round. 'I told you to fuck off.'

I keep my hand in place. 'This isn't going to get you any-where.'

'It's got nothing to do with you.'

'Keep this up and they'll restrain you.'

He stands up. The stewardess backs off. He turns to face the rear of the plane. 'I'll get one myself. Where's the fucking bar on this thing?'

Mike has the full attention of the people around us. A young couple on the row opposite are leaning away from the inci-dent—as if the plane walls are rubber and will let them gain a little more distance. She's pretty but her face shows fear that diminishes her looks. He's a little geeky and has his head stuck in a book trying to ignore what's going on.

In the row in front of them a head sticks out from behind the back of the chair, level with the stewardess's rear. The owner is in her seventies or has aged badly. Her hair is a tight crop of curls with a heavy rinse of black that makes it look like she's wearing a wig. She shows no fear—just morbid curiosity. The smile on her lips has a little evil twist to it—she probably reads the details of real-life crimes for kicks.

Mike has set off to find some drink. We are only four rows from the rear and he's back double-quick. 'Where are the drinks? It's only fucking restrooms back there.'

The stewardess has been joined by a colleague. I can't read the name badge but the new arrival stands with *I'm in charge* hands on her hips. 'Mr Cameron, will you please return to your seat.'

'Will I hell. I want another drink.'

'I'm sorry but I can't do that. Now can you please sit down.'

'Or what?'

This is going nowhere good. I try one more time. 'Look, Mike. Sit down and we can get you a drink later.'

He takes a step towards the stewardess. She holds his gaze.

'Or what?' he repeats.

I like the stewardess. She's not panicking but she's scared. I'd be scared. She's been trained well and I'd guess this isn't her first drunk passenger. Mike's shoulders are tense. He's leaning forward.

When I was young, I did a little work on the doors of the local nightclub. I know the pose. Mike is spoiling for a fight.

The stewardess opens her mouth to say something but her colleague steps in. 'Sir, if you don't return to your seat I'll have no choice but to inform the captain and arrange for the police to be waiting at Heathrow.'

The stewardess flicks her head round to give her colleague a look that would wither a concrete flower. Her boss is only doing her job but her tone is setting Mike on edge. The stewardess can sense it.

'Fuck off.' Mike takes another unsteady step. An inch or so. Closer to something more violent. He's a southpaw. His left hand is loosely balled up. The old woman with the bad rinse ducks out of sight. The couple have stopped leaning away now the danger has moved down the plane. The geek has his head out of the book and is stretching his neck to get a better view over the headrest of the chair in front.

'Look sir, I'm sure we can resolve this.' The stewardess's voice seems to lessen the tension a little.

Mike eases down a quarter of a gear. 'Just get me a drink.' 'If you could just sit down.'

'Drink.'

'Look, sir,' the boss intervenes again and the tension is back. The stewardess's shoulders slump. She doesn't need help. She's doing okay. I can see it in her face. *Shut up bitch—you're making it worse.*

A grunt comes from behind me. I spin my head. Four people are half standing—trying to get a better view. The grunt is from a man with a triple chin. Rubberneckers.

'Sir,' says the boss.

I need to stop this now. I size up Mike and stand up. He's focused on the two women and I hope he stays that way. I need distance between him and the aircrew. Distance is good.

I take a step. He senses something and does the one thing I'm not prepared for. He lashes out with his left foot—kicking straight back. He catches me in the stomach and I go down.

He backs up and stamps down on my leg. I try to roll away but in the confined space I can do little more than scrabble around. He tries for three in a row. I snatch at his foot. I catch him off balance. He starts to fall, grabbing the nearest armrest. He kicks out again, clipping the top of my shoulder.

The stewardess stops looking at us and turns away to face her boss, pulling her head back as she twists. Her head snaps forward, forehead impacting on her boss's nose. A dull click as bone gives way. The noise bounces off the walls of the plane. The boss reels back and an arc of blood sprays into the air. A ribbon of crimson against the white fuselage.

The boss staggers back, before falling to the floor. The streamer of blood reaches its apex, spraying across the chairs on either side. Shouts go up from the passengers.

The stewardess drops down, landing on her boss. Her hand starts to pump up and down, and I hear screaming.

Mike steps back, struggling to comprehend what he's witnessing.

A few seconds later the stewardess gets up, her uniform splattered with blood. She rotates her head, as if she has just finished a difficult set of exercises, before reaching down to brush her skirt—removing the wrinkles and creases. She swipes at her hair and swings back towards Mike.

Her pupils are dilated. Her face white. Mike puts his hand out to steady himself as he works back along three headrests and shuffles away. I stand up—wary that Mike still has a kick left in him. But he's spent. We both slump into our seats as a woman starts screaming and two more aircrew rush into the cabin.

'Jesus,' one of them shouts. He's looking down at where the stewardess's boss is lying. The other gags and bends over.

'Did you see that?' I realize that Mike is talking to me.

I nod. 'What the hell...?'

The captain appears and pushes the new aircrew to one side. He bends down to attend to the stewardess's boss. He orders one of the aircrew to help. They lift her up and carry her out of the cabin. The stewardess is shepherded by the remaining aircrew to the front of the plane.

Minutes tick by before the captain returns. 'Ladies and gentlemen, can I firstly apologize for the incident that some of you have experienced.'

He closes the curtains behind him. 'We are expecting to land in Heathrow in thirty minutes. The police have been informed of the incident and have requested that everyone in this area of the plane remain seated until they can take some statements.'

There's some murmuring. The captain walks up the aisle, stopping to answer the occasional question. When he reaches us he stops and looks at Mike. 'Mr Cameron. I believe you had an issue with one of my cabin crew.'

Mike keeps his eyes focused on his lap.

'The police want to talk to you. I hope I can count on you to remain in your seat for the remainder of the flight.'

Mike nods.

CHAPTER 7

'Let's start from the top.'

The accent is thick with London. There are two of them—one in uniform and one plain-clothed. I'm in an interview room inside Heathrow airport. It looks much like the one in Iraq but with fewer stains on the floor.

The plain-clothed officer leans forward. His breath could stun a horse. He's two days from the last shave and wrinkles crowd his face, white wisps of hair falling onto gray eyebrows. He taps the table. 'Tell me once more what happened on the flight.'

I rattle off the same story I've been through three times already. I don't vary from the core events. When I finish the cop stares at me. 'Why would the stewardess attack her boss?'

I shake my head.

'Nothing else you'd like to say? No detail you might have missed?'

I shake my head again. 'Can I go now? My flight leaves in just over an hour.'

'I need to check with my colleague first.'

'But my flight...'

'Mr McIntyre, the cabin director is in hospital with multiple facial wounds. Until I'm satisfied you're not involved then you're going nowhere.'

'I want to see someone from my embassy.'

'That I can do—once they have finished with Mr Cameron.'

'Someone from the embassy's already here?'

'They were here in a flash—for your friend. You obviously fall somewhat down the food chain. I'll pass on the message that you want to see someone. The constable here will keep you company.'

Once my interrogator leaves I try to strike up a conversation with my new guard but I'd get more out of the wall. So we sit in silence.

Twenty minutes later the door opens and in walks a dark suit. Not embassy. Agency. Squat, with a bodybuilder's physique, he adjusts his tie. A dark mole dominates a solid face. Definitely agency. I'm beginning to be able to smell them.

'Good afternoon, Mr McIntyre. Please don't get up.'

I have no intention of getting up.

'Trouble just follows you around.'

'Who are you?'

'A friend.'

'I don't need friends. I need answers. I've done nothing wrong.'

'So you say and so you said in Iraq but there are two dead people, a mutilated cabin director and a stewardess who seems to have no memory of her workout on her boss. The only common link in all of this is you.'

'And? I was out for the count in Iraq when the lovebirds killed each other. I was trying to calm your boy down when the airline staff decided to settle a dispute.'

'Still doesn't look good. So here's how it's going to go down. We'll see you safely home. Mr Cameron won't be joining you. He is in need of a little, eh, love and attention.'

'Rehab would be more appropriate.'

'As you say. I think our British cousins are happy to release you into my custody. Your plane leaves in forty minutes.'

'Custody? I've done nothing WRONG.'

'For your own safety, Mr McIntyre. We only have your best interests at heart.'

Ten minutes later and I am being trailed through the back

end of the airport to be deposited at my gate, with none of the nastiness that comes with passport control.

My bodybuilder friend hands me an envelope. 'Your tickets.'

'You wouldn't have anything for a headache?'

He smiles and points to the plane. 'Try sleep.'

As I collapse into the airplane seat I seem to have acquired two more minders. Both have standard-issue dark suits. Both are about five feet ten with identical haircuts—buzz with a hint of a fringe. Buzz 1 is on my left and Buzz 2 on my right. We are coach class again. I down a couple of JD and Cokes with three Tylenols acquired from Buzz 1. A minor Mickey Finn.

New York is still deep in night when we land and the transfer to the LA flight is simple enough. Buzz 1 and 2 keep a respectful distance before placing me as the meat between their sandwich for the last leg.

A new JD and Coke/Tylenol mix doesn't work. The pounding in my head grows as the plane crawls across the Midwest.

I try to distract myself with the events of the last forty-eight hours. Pulling them apart. Piecing them together. Looking for something I may have missed. Trying to makes some sense of the nonsensical.

I fail. Around me the passengers are head down. All trying to get through the flight.

My headache builds. A slow dull pounding that eclipses everything else. Rooted at the back of my skull. Buried. A series of explosions going off, releasing a stream of hot poison that's spreading through my head. Building in waves. Peaks and troughs. Each peak slightly higher. Each trough deeper.

Nausea wells up. I try to focus on the small graphic on the seat screen that indicates where we are. It's frozen over Kansas. As far to go as we have come. I place my head between my knees, gagging as the movement pumps up the pain.

My vision begins to tunnel. The drone from the engines, the few people who are chatting and the odd clink of the drinks trolley are sore noises. Hard noises. Penetrating noises. I'm going to be sick.

I grab for the vomit bag.

Then a cool wave washes down the metal tube. Ice-cold—filling the space around me. Crashing over me. Menthol fresh. I breathe deeply and my lungs shiver as the ice-tinged gas expands into my tissue. I open my eyes. The air is blue. A cobalt haze fills the cabin.

The spitting fire in my head is extinguished. Snuffed out at the source. Forced into a tiny, tight ball. A neutron star forming at the top of my backbone. Wrapped in a blanket of ice. Still there but trapped.

I lift my head. The light-headedness that accompanies the movement momentarily blurs this new, surreal world. I press my eyelids down and wait. Floating in the lack of pain.

I reopen my eyes and smile. The blue is pulsing—a soft, gentle action—between light and dark. Morphing from one to the other.

I turn to look at Buzz 1 but he's iPod-bound, and if he can see the color or sense the chill he's giving no indication. Buzz 2 is reading. He turns to catch my eye. I smile and his forehead creases in confusion. The wrinkles in his skin are the color of a sunny Caribbean bay—the peaks a mountain-high sky blue. He shakes his head as I keep up the smile. I'm on my own in my new blue world.

'Drink, sir?' The stewardess's voice has a light tinkle attached to it. Then she seems to jump forward and her words tumble out with the speed of a DVD on *Skip*. 'Drink, sir?'

I catch the words—but only just. 'Jack Daniels and Coke,' I reply.

She pours on fast-forward, then hands me a midnight-blue version of my favorite fix of alcohol. A jump in time. Now she's all slowmo as she asks my minders if they want a drink. Buzz 1 and 2 decline. I take a sip.

The blue wave washes clear of me: the new world vanishes. My headache has gone but I can still feel the kernel rooted to my brain stem. Waiting.

I contemplate the moment. Trying to figure out what the hell has just happened. There's still the faintest tinge of blue to the world. A hangover from the full effect. It's not unpleasant but it's also something that feels wrong. In the way that a snort of cocaine is both good and bad at the same time. A feeling of elation earned through a substance that will destroy you.

I view the plane's progress on the small screen. We are nearly out of Colorado. An immense leap in distance in a few minutes. I wonder if the system is broken and tap it with my forefinger. Nothing.

I watch as the plane leaves Colorado and, catching the corner of Utah and New Mexico, we enter Arizona. No great leap forward, just a slow progression. How long did the blue world gone on for? Minutes? An hour? It felt like seconds.

The JD is spreading through my system. I suddenly have an irrational fear that the warm alcohol will somehow melt the coating around the headache ball that's squatting in my skull. I clench my teeth waiting for it to explode. An ice cube dropped in a hot-fat fryer. Spitting. But the headache stays buried.

I lean back in the seat and glance at Buzz 1 and 2. Both are still in music- or word-land.

My thoughts turn to home and the conversation with Lorraine that lies ahead. I dump the thought to slug some more JD. I'll deal with it when the time comes.

I close my eyes, bathing in what's left of the blue world.

CHAPTER 8

I should be shattered. It's been over a day since I wasn't on a flight or waiting for one. LAX was the usual. Too busy. Too noisy. Too everything.

I'm now sitting in my apartment. The theme is white with more white and the only thing that isn't white is Lorraine in a red gingham dress. A little under six feet tall, she could have cut it as a model. Dark, shoulder-length hair, a round face, green eyes—she can stop a bus with her smile. She's showing it off now but it's not warm. She's already ahead of the curve, knowing my early return is not good news. When she saw the bandages on my head the smile faded. She has brewed up some industrial-strength coffee and is sitting, hands between her legs, waiting. The pose she takes when bad news is on the horizon.

She leans forward. 'Well?'

I take a breath and offload. I start with the brothel. I work my way through the events. I'm selective. Some of the story isn't for telling today. I skip the blue world. I keep up my sleeve my suspicions that the agency isn't finished with me. I don't share the feeling that I'm not as innocent in all this as I'd like to believe.

I love Lorraine. I should trust her. That's the way it should be. But it isn't. And that hurts.

My lack of trust is my own insecurity playing out. I'm scared of losing her. When we met I never thought she would show any interest in me. It's not that I'm bad looking. I can turn on the charm if need be, but, when we met, I was frazzled from my experience in the army. Mentally in a bad place. I felt Lorraine was too good a thing to be happening to me. The result: I was scared to open up to her. Still am. Scared I'll chase her off. That she will see me for what I am. A burnt-out shell that's struggling to keep things going.

So things that should be shared, husband to wife, are quietly buried. Not a recipe that has much future.

She sits in silence and when I finish she starts to take it all apart—bit by bit. She has a disarming way of asking the most awkward questions. Working with kids has given her an insight into interrogation. Ask the easy questions first. Work up to the hard ones. Keep a few of the easier ones in the background, ready to use, in case things get bogged down. Open questions. *'How did that make you feel?' 'Why do you think that happened?'* Or, in this case, *'So what do you want to do now?'*

It is the question I've been avoiding.

'I don't know. Something will come along. Won't it? I'll contact Steel Trap. This is their problem to sort out.'

'Craig...'

I let my head fall. Her tone says it all. We've been here so often. She met me as a wreck. An ex mental-ward case who had frittered away the last of his parents' inheritance.

She reaches out and touches my hair. 'Craig, this is insane. Murder. Secret agencies. What the...?'

I keep my head down. 'You knew that the job wasn't great. Iraq. Bodyguard. And I did fuck up. Two dead bodies and I was the point man. I got mugged by a man twice my age. It all happened on my watch.'

I lift to find her face is close. She's stunningly pretty. I'm still amazed that she chose me. Amazed and grateful. She once told me that there was something special about me. An energy that she found intoxicating. In the right moment, when we're together, she'll brush my hair and whisper 'I love you' so often that I wonder who she's trying to convince. Me or her.

She strokes me. 'We need to fix this.'

'How?'

'Phone Steel Trap. See what they say first.'

'Now?'

'Now!'

'Can't we do that later?'

'Will that make the call better?'

She's right.

I pick up the phone and dial the number. It's answered on the second ring.

'Dan, it's Craig.'

'Hi Craig.' Cold.

'I take it you've heard about Iraq.'

'No. I never hear when employees fuck up.'

'Funny. What did you hear?'

'You screwed up. Your boy is dead and our name is being trashed. Lot of money to be made in Iraq. So let's make this easy. You're history.'

'And that's it?'

'That's it.'

'Come on. I got kicked out by some black ops agency. Don't you care?'

'Craig you fucked up with the wrong people. They pay well and they don't want you around. What can I say? Most of our work is through them at the moment. They want you out— you're out.'

'That's bull. I'm an employee.'

'Were an employee. We'll pay you a month's salary. And you can count yourself lucky on that.'

'I want to meet.'

'What for?'

'To discuss this.'

'We've been doing that.'

I can see him. Sitting in the tiny room that Steel Trap call their head office. His back to a window that looks on to a grubby alley. Cheap rent area.

'Come on, Dan. It wasn't my fault.'

'Taylor's dead. The client's pissed off and I'm probably not going to see any work from them in the near future. What's not your fault?'

'A coffee. That's all I ask.'

'Craig, it's done. You're out.'

'Just a coffee.'

Silence.

'Fuck you.' I throw the handset onto the sofa.

Lorraine shakes her head. She picks up the phone, killing the call. 'That went well.'

'He's a tosser.'

'Can't you sue?'

'Maybe, but it'll cost money and we aren't exactly floating in cash. I'll ask Gerry in the morning. I need a drink.'

Gerry is an old lawyer friend but I know I'm not going to ask him anything. It's over.

Lorraine leans closer. 'Craig, we need to talk.'

'And we can, but I need out of here.'

'Craig...'

'Michael's.'

'A bar? You want to go to a bar?'

'I need to think, and Michael's is a good place.'

'No, it's not. It's a dump with a leech for an owner.'

'Well I'm going. You can come if you want, but I need a shower first.'

'What's stopping you?'

I tap the bandage.

She shakes her head and walks into the bedroom to reappear with a shower cap.

'Try this.' She throws it at me.

We walk down North Cahuenga. Lorraine has changed into fitted jeans, a tight white T-shirt and a pair of wedges to show off her legs. She's topped it off with a lightweight jacket. I sigh. I'm going to watch guys watch my girl for the next few hours.

We leave a residential stretch and enter low-rise commercial territory. Around us sits the edge of Hollywood. Production companies, agents, marketing companies. We pass the art deco front of the studio that Lorraine pulls extra bucks from. We hit the corner of Melrose where a small shopping mall, a car dealer, a loan shop and a shuttered strip of stores sit. We turn right.

Lorraine keeps her distance. Her hands are rammed into her jean pockets. Her head is down. A sure sign that I'm not Mr Popular at the moment.

To our left, trees hide apartment blocks. We keep to the sidewalk that bounds the shops. We cross Stewart Street, pass the Latin restaurant that sits on the corner and enter Michael's.

It claims to be an Irish pub but it's really a typical downtown, randomly-decorated bar with paraphernalia that might be able to claim some tangential connection to the Emerald Isle.

The bar itself stretches the length of the premises. A platform made of fifty per cent alcohol and fifty per cent wood. The A/C is wound up and the cool air is welcome. Booths sit opposite the bar. The place is dotted with a few customers.

Charlie, the owner (there's no Michael that I'm aware of), is pouring a Bass Ale and smiles when he sees us. Or rather when he sees Lorraine. Weighing in at two-fifty pounds he's a bodybuilder when not juicing people up. Clean-shaven, bald, always on the edge of bursting out of one of his many T-shirts. This one says *I'm Free*.

Charlie is cheer personified.

'One thousand dollars?' he shouts over.

'One thousand and one,' replies Lorraine with little humor.

'Too expensive,' he replies.

I shake my head. Charlie has been offering Lorraine a thousand dollars to sleep with him since the first night we found his place. He refuses to pay more so Lorraine always insists on a dollar extra.

'Are our chairs free?' I ask.

'A little late for the alley.'

'Won't be dark for another hour.'

'Give me five minutes to set it up but don't let me forget you're out there.'

'We won't,' says Lorraine.

'What can I get you both?' He's already pouring our drinks. Me a JD and Coke, Lorraine a white wine spritzer. He places the drinks on the bar and makes for the back door to set up our spot.

I sip at my drink. Lorraine plays with hers. She's not a drinker and one spritzer can last all night if she has a mind.

'I need to pick up something from the library,' she says.

'What. Now?'

The John Freemont Library is just across the road.

'You dragged me out.'

'We need to talk.'

'We will, but Mary Little's doing the Civil War with her kids and wants a book our regular supplier doesn't stock.'

'What's wrong with her legs?'

'Funny.'

'Is she being a nuisance?'

Charlie comes back and stops her from replying. 'Your thrones await.'

We follow the signs for the washrooms and push out the emergency exit into the alley behind. Charlie has placed two folding chairs and a small plastic table against one wall. The alley is deserted and, since it wraps round the block, you can't be seen from the street. On a Sunday there can be ten or twelve people out here, but this late on a Saturday there's no one else.

'Mary?' I say as I sit down.

Lorraine also sits down. 'A real pain. She thinks we owe her big time for letting us stay in Carl's place. Now it's got worse.'

'In what way?'

'The school principal is looking for a new number two. Mary

should be a ringer but the PTA are against it. She's rubbed them up all the wrong way this term. I tried to tell her to ease off. But she doesn't like the chair. They have history.'

'And?'

'The PTA hold a lot of sway. The school was short on funds and the PTA dug us out big time last year.'

'Ah, the old Hollywood C-listers.'

'Don't knock it. Some of the parents take home in a month what we take home in a year.'

'So who do they like for the job?'

'Me.'

'You're kidding?'

'Nope.'

'Fantastic—what's the salary?'

'I haven't got the job yet.'

'But if you did?'

'Another twenty thousand a year.'

'Touchdown.'

'What?'

'I knew coming here was a good idea. We haven't even finished our first drink and we're already sorted for cash.'

'I haven't got the job yet and Mary won't take it lying down.'

'Does she know about the PTA's view?'

'Oh, yes.'

'So what. Forget her. What can she do?'

'Throw us out of our home. Do you know what we would get for a thousand a month around here?'

'Carl won't do that.'

Carl is Mary's husband and a developer. We've had the apartment on the cheap while he's been trying to fill it.

'He will if Mary turns it on. He was round yesterday.'

'What for?'

'Nothing, but he talked about upping our rent.'

'We have an agreement.'

'Not in writing.'

'So now you're her skivvy?'

'No choice. The meeting about the position is on Tuesday—they're drawing up the shortlist. I need to keep her sweet till then. Otherwise she'll think I orchestrated it all.'

She drains a little spritzer. 'It'll take me five minutes to get the book. Then we talk.'

With Lorraine gone, I suck in the alley atmosphere. The door opens. Charlie appears with another drink. 'I thought if I got you drunk you might forget you came with Lorraine and I'd have to walk her home.'

'You can try.'

'What's with the bandage?'

'I forgot to duck.'

He places the black liquid on the table. 'You out of a job already?'

Charlie knows my history—it's what happens when you have a year to sit on the wrong side of a bar.

'Yeah.'

'Careful you don't lose her. She deserves better.'

From anyone else I would have taken issue at the intrusion, but Charlie had become more than the bartender. I'm into him for a good thousand on my tab, and he really doesn't expect me to pay. I think I'm his charity case. I lift the new drink. 'I know. Got a job going?'

'You behind a bar? My profits would vanish.'

'I can be teetotal.'

'And I can run the hundred in less than ten.'

'I'm not that bad.'

'You can be.'

'Could you keep your ear to the ground? I need a job—just to prove I can hold one down for a while.'

'I'll keep a lookout.' He looks up at the sky. 'Thirty minutes and then inside. The sun will be gone by then.'

He's right. It's turning to dusk. I nod.

He pauses before he re-enters the bar. 'There was some trouble last week just up the street. So in before dark.'

He vanishes.

CHAPTER 9

'Sorry.' Lorraine rolls up as the sun vanishes.

'Charlie wants us in. He's having a quiet fit.'

'Tell him to take a chill pill. It's lovely out here.'

Lorraine sits down, a book in her hand.

Silence.

I finish my drink.

More silence.

Suddenly the pub door slams against the wall. Two men roll out and crash to the alley floor. I leap from the chair, grabbing Lorraine and pulling her to one side as the men start rolling around on the ground.

Both are dressed head to toe in leather. One has long hair and the other is a skinhead. The skinhead lands a punch. Their world has no words—just grunts. There's more noise coming from the bar. Shouts, glass breaking—chaos. I need to get Lorraine away, but not through the pub.

I pull at her arm. 'Along the alley. We'll go round the front.' I thrust out my hand. Lorraine takes it and we leave the two leather boys rolling in the dirt.

The alley is short and, as we swing round the corner, we find the exit that leads to the street beyond full of bikes and bikers. Three of them are laying into one guy on the ground. He's taking a serious kicking. One of the bikers is doing nothing other than aiming his boot at the victim's head.

I want to step in. Lorraine senses it. She looks at me, talking to me in silent movie language. Mouth moving—no sound. *Don't go. Leave it. It's not your business.* All emphasized with a flick of an eyebrow.

I look at the scene, my heart racing in anticipation. Two people have died in the last forty-eight hours. I won't stand by and watch another. But I can't put Lorraine in danger.

Lorraine grabs my shoulder as I step forward. Her fear finds voice. 'No, Craig.'

I hesitate. A police siren howls in the distance. The three men stop the attack and run for their bikes. Footsteps echo behind us. I turn round and the two fighters from the alley, shaking themselves down, are sprinting in our direction.

I step in front of Lorraine. But they split like water around a rock and vanish into the night.

The siren is joined by others.

'Back along the alley,' says Lorraine.

I agree.

We jog back to the bar.

'Inside,' she orders.

The bar is a disaster zone. Tables and chairs are wrecked and split. Glass litters the floor. The back bar a wasteland of spilt drink and broken bottles. As we enter, the last of the leather-clad invaders hobbles out of the front door. The front window is gone.

'Charlie?' Lorraine is shouting in the direction of the bar.

Charlie's head pops up. 'Are they gone?'

She nods.

'Get behind the bar with me,' he says. 'Tell the police you ducked down as soon as the first biker came through the door. Otherwise they'll want to know where you were.'

'Charlie, they ain't going to care,' I say.

'And if they do?'

I don't answer as we join him behind the bar. 'What happened?'

The police sirens are close.

'A biker came in through the window and four others followed him through the door.'

'Do you know them?'

'No.'

'Lorraine?' The new voice is out of place. 'Lorraine, are you here?'

Lorraine sticks her head above the bar. 'Mary? What on earth...?'

I pop up. Mary is standing at the door to the washrooms. 'I was looking for you. When the fighting started I hid in the washroom.'

Lorraine stands up. 'How did you know I was in Michael's?'

'I decided to pick up the book myself and the library told me you were here.'

The door to the men's washroom slams open and a biker steps out. His eyes are glazed. He takes in the scene, looks at us. He spots Mary, steps forward and throws his arm around her throat. She screams as he pulls her close.

Mary is small. Four feet ten in her stocking soles. Her hair adds a few inches and is always lacquered with a full can of hair-spray. She wears three-inch heels as standard—five-inch of an evening. She's a touch old for the skinny jeans but they help with the illusion that she's taller. The biker is six feet plus, heavy with stubble. A small skull is tattooed on his left cheek. His dress is top-to-toe leather.

'Let her go.' My voice is loud. The biker ignores me.

'What's going on?' A young officer has arrived through the front door, looking confused. Baby-smooth skin that probably sees a razor once a week.

The biker staggers forward with Mary. He reaches the bar, resting his free arm amongst the debris.

The officer watches him, then looks at Mary. 'Ma'am, do you know this man?'

Mary shakes her head.

'Sir, can you please release the lady?'

The biker looks at the officer. Eyes swimming. High on something. 'No way, man.' His voice is gravel and glass.

A second, older, officer walks through the door. Where his colleague is a fresher, this one is time-served. Gray hair drops below his cap. Wrinkles map his face. A red, blood-burst nose suggests he enjoys a drink or two. The young officer turns his head to the new policeman, looking for help.

There's a click of steel releasing from steel. A crack as metal hits metal. A blade catches the light of the neon Miller Lite sign at the end of the bar. The biker lifts the flick knife into sight, placing it against Mary's throat. She stiffens at the touch of the blade.

'Get backup,' says the older officer to the younger one. 'Tell them it's a possible 207.' He turns to Mary and the biker. 'What's your name ma'am?'

Mary says nothing.

'Ma'am?'

Mary is too scared to answer.

'She's called Mary,' says Lorraine, trying to help.

'What do you do for a living, Mary?'

Odd question.

'A teacher.' A small voice.

'Local?'

Silence.

'King Street Elementary,' says Lorraine.

'Do you hear that, sir?' He's directing his question at the biker. 'Mary here's a teacher. Now you wouldn't want to be hurting a teacher, would you?' He has an Irish lilt to his voice. 'Good people, teachers. We need them. Too few in the world.' He takes a small step forward. 'Mary, are you married?'

She nods.

'Kids?'

Mary shakes her head.

He smiles. 'Enough kids to deal with at school?'

Another step closer.

The biker collapses a little. Mary shrieks as the flick knife nicks her skin.

The officer stops. 'Careful, sir. No one has been hurt so far, and you wouldn't be looking to change that. Put the knife down. Nobody here wants to harm you. Knife down and step away from Mary.'

'No way, man.' The biker turns and rests the small of his back on the bar. Mary is shivering and a trickle of blood dots her pink blouse.

'A knife,' Lorraine gasps. 'In his back.' She's pointing and I follow her finger. A wooden-handled knife is embedded between the biker's shoulder blades. The jacket is black; the light is poor but a large stain is visible. It spreads from the blade and forms a ragged triangle that finishes at the jacket's hem.

That's a lot of blood. No wonder he's leaning against the bar.

The policeman nods at me. He's seen it too. The biker isn't out of his head on drugs or booze. He's losing blood. 'Sir, put down the knife and we can get you to the hospital.'

'No way, man.' He slides along the bar. His blood coating the woodwork. He's only a few feet from Lorraine. All three of us are pressed up hard against the wall.

Mary is sidestepping with the biker, trying to keep the blade away from her throat. With my back against the wall I move behind both of them. Lorraine's eyes widen. I try to pass a silent message to her. '*Stay still.*'

The biker is focused on the police officer. He stumbles again and Mary yelps. The movement takes him another few feet down the bar. I'm now directly behind him. My heart is tripping at triple sixty but my training tells me not to give in to the adrenalin. Use it. Channel it. Suppress the desire for action. Kill any panic.

I take a breath and move, grabbing the biker's knife arm from behind, forcing it forward, away from Mary. He swings round. I pull him hard, away from Lorraine and Charlie. Mary falls forward and the officer starts to move.

The biker wrestles his arm free and I follow up with a blow to the back of his head. He staggers away from me and, without the support of the bar, and too weak to stay upright, he falls. His chin bounces off the edge of the bar as he goes down and vanishes out of sight.

Two more officers run in and the older police officer reaches for Mary and pulls her away. He gestures to the two new cops. 'Make sure he doesn't get up. He's armed.'

The officers drop to the ground to secure the biker.

My breath is coming in lumps, and somewhere inside my skull the kernel cracks and my brain explodes. I collapse to the ground.

Lorraine is beside me in an instant. 'What's wrong?'

'My head. Jesus my head.'

I see a blur above me and Lorraine vanishes as a body lands on her. The biker? I turn to see Lorraine lying on her back, Mary sitting astride her with an empty beer bottle in her hand. She brings it down with a sickening crunch and I shout out.

She brings the bottle down again.

Then the police pile over the bar and Mary is dragged away. I crawl over to Lorraine. Her hands are wrapped around her face. I try to pull them away but I have all the power of an arthritic kitten. 'Lorraine?'

She doesn't respond.

Charlie drops to the ground next to me. We are all wallowing around in a sea of glass and booze. He takes Lorraine's hand. Even in the half-light I can see that her cheek is crushed. Swelling already starting to show.

My head goes supernova. I scream. Then it's gone. The world drops blue. Then light blue. Then we are back to normality. A hand is on my shoulder and I turn to see a paramedic. What the hell is going on?

CHAPTER 10

The hospital is trying its best to be a place of calm, but this is a Saturday night and St Vincent Medical Centre is one of the few local hospitals with a walk-in emergency department. We're only a short ambulance ride from the bar and Lorraine has been taken for emergency treatment. I, on the other hand, have had my bandage renewed, been given a couple of full-strength pain-killers and been dismissed.

I'm sitting in a waiting room with Charlie, reading the plaque that tells me St Vincent's won the 2010 Emergency Medicine Excellence Award, when a doctor walks in. 'Mr McIntyre?'

I nod and he sits next to me. 'Your wife has suffered a blow-out fracture to the orbit. That's the bone that her eye sits in. We may have to put a plate in if the eye starts to sink but, at the moment, we are going to wait and see.'

'What do you mean by her eye sinking?' I ask.

'It can happen when the orbit is smashed. The eye can sink backwards. It may not but we'll need to keep her in for a few days to be sure.'

'Can I see her?'

'Not tonight. She's out for the count. We had to give her some high-strength pain killers.'

'I'll wait for her to wake up.'

'Up to you but I'd say you'd be better getting a night's sleep and coming back in the morning. She isn't going anywhere. There's also a police officer who wants to see you. Can I send him in?'

'What for?'

He shrugs his shoulders and I nod. He leaves to be replaced by a heavy-set man in a crumpled suit. Two-day growth on his chin sits above a dirty shirt collar. He hands me a business card that has been living in the bottom of a drawer. It reads: *Detective Christopher Jones*. He nods. 'A few questions and I'm gone.'

The accent is Midwestern.

He trails me through the events and scribbles a few things down.

'Who were the bikers?' I ask.

The detective stops writing. 'Out of town. As far as we can tell. Unusual as well. Bikers are not given to nonsense like that. The boy with the knife in his back didn't make it, and the others vanished.'

'So it's a murder investigation?' says Charlie. 'Great. That'll bring the clientele flooding in.'

The detective ignores him and keeps his focus on me. 'What gives with the attack on your wife?'

I shrug. 'One minute I'm lying on the floor, head pounding. Next, Mary is ramming a bottle of beer into my wife's face.'

'Any idea why?'

'Not a clue. Are you going to arrest her?'

'Already done. She's up for aggravated assault. We'll need statements from your wife, from you and from you.' The last *you* is aimed at Charlie.

'Now?' I ask.

'Tomorrow morning. Down at the station. We'll come up here for your wife's statement.'

'Can I be here with my wife? We can both give you a statement at the same time.'

'No. I want separate statements. Anyway, you're not under suspicion so just be down at the station for ten.' He turns to leave.

'Detective,' I say to his back. 'What did Mary say about the attack?'

He pauses. 'She claims she can't remember anything. Insists it must be a mistake. I left her pleading her innocence.'

As the door closes behind him I sit back in the chair and let out a long breath. 'Charlie, this is a mess.'

'You're on the pony there my friend.'

I turn to look at the window. 'You go sort out your bar. I'm spending the night with Lorraine.'

'I don't think they'll let you sleep in her room.'

'I'll sleep here then. Now please go.' My words are hard. No argument wanted and the room drops quiet as Charlie leaves.

Creeping through the heavy blinds comes the sound of horns, the squealing of tires, revving engines—all softened by the double-glazing. Voices come and go as people walk along the corridor outside. All whispers and low chatter.

I need a coffee. I find a machine a little way down the corridor and order up a black, extra strong. The machine whirs and coughs until a cup drops and fills with scalding hot liquid. I sip at it and my face creases. Not good.

I wonder where Lorraine is and set off to find someone to ask but I've not gone five paces when I hear voices approaching. I recognise them. Buzz 1 and Buzz 2. I look around for an exit. I'm in no mood to meet them.

The waiting room is to my left and there's another door to my right. I try the handle and the door is unlocked. Diving in, spilling the coffee on the floor, I close the door behind me and listen as the voices stop.

What the hell are they doing here anyway? As if I didn't know. Another murder and I'm on the scene.

The room I'm in is for storage—small and shelved on three sides. Mostly cleaning products. I slide to the floor and wait.

I need to be straight with myself. This is not normal. None of this. Iraq, the plane, the bar, Mary. It's all...

There is a bang and the door caves in. Buzz 1 and Buzz 2 rip me from the floor.

CHAPTER 11

I'm out of the hospital and into the back of an unmarked Regal in less than five minutes. No guns. No arm up the back. Simply Buzz 1 saying, 'Come with us or your wife will suffer.'

I'm not stupid, so I obey.

We wheel north on the I-10. Dodger Stadium appears and a few minutes later we exit the highway. A sign for the Ernest E Debs Regional Park flicks by and we run through the gates into wilderness.

I've been up here a few times with Lorraine. There's not much to it. Mostly trees, scrub and lakes, but it's a nice place to chill and pop a picnic. The car starts to bump along a dirt track before we turn onto a smaller track that leads into a wood.

At this time of night this would be a good place to beat up on someone and dump them.

The headlights pick out branches and bushes. The driver takes the speed down to a crawl. Another turn and we're off the road. The car stops. The engine dies.

'Out,' says Buzz 1.

'What?'

The punch is low. In the gut.

'I didn't say talk. I said out.'

I get out.

'In front. Walk.'

A torch flicks on, picking out a worn footpath. It rises into the trees ahead before bending out of sight. I walk with the two

Buzzes behind me. I hear the Regal engine fire up before it reverses back onto the track and away.

Buzz 1 gives me a push in the back. 'Keep walking.'

The path meanders but, even in the light of the torch, it's clear that it's well used. I need to lean forward as the hill kicks in, my stomach still growling at the punch. A set of wood-and-earth steps appear. Buzz 1 gives me another push. 'Up.'

I start climbing. I count to fifty before the steps stop, and we reach a small clearing. A cinder-block building squats in the corner. It has the hallmark signature of the local power company. It still doesn't explain why the path is so well defined.

'Stop.' Buzz 1 walks forward and I wait for a punch or a kick but he keeps going. He reaches a metal door and I notice a little gray box to the side. I've seen one of those before. He flicks his hand at it. There's a whirr and a click. The door snaps open. No light from inside. Just a dark inkwell.

Buzz 2 gives me a push. 'Inside.'

I hesitate. I don't think they're planning to kill me. Not yet. But they're not preparing my birthday party either. A hand shoves me in.

The inside of the building doesn't hold much promise. Damp, cold—with dripping water. I'm pushed into the cramped space and the three of us stand shoulder to shoulder as Buzz 2 pulls the door closed.

Dark. Complete dark. The rods in my eyes fire at random and my own personal firework display rages and dissipates.

Buzz 1 is to my left. Buzz 2 to my right. Buzz 1 has stale breath. Smoker's breath. Buzz 2 is the Aquafresh kid. I can hear them both breathing. The floor jerks and I can't help but let out a small shout. I hear Buzz 1 laugh. I'm glad somebody's finding this funny.

The floor jerks again and I have the sensation of movement. Down. Another jerk and we stop. The wall in front parts to reveal itself as a pair of elevator doors.

A dim red light shines in.

The interior of the elevator is a cleverly crafted illusion. Walls in fake stone, floor in fake concrete and a small speaker somewhere adding to the effect with a dripping sound. No doubt the damp smell is artificially generated as well.

We step into the space beyond. The doors slide shut behind us. Another gray box and we're into a very different world.

A long corridor stretches out before us. It's as wide as an athletics track and as long. On either side, the walls are lined with doors. Each with a number and a letter stenciled into the wood. The carpet is functional but not low quality. The ceiling is suspended. Hidden lighting gives illumination to the vista. Every wall is plain vanilla and there's the gentle hum of air-conditioning.

There's also something vaguely 1980s about the place. As if the interior designer had reached back to the age of no lunches and power suits for inspiration.

I'm encouraged to walk down the wide passageway. None of the doors are open and, if there are people beyond them, the doors are either soundproof or—and this would make sense—empty, unless there's a night shift on the go.

The corridor ends in a T-junction. We go right and hit another junction. We take a left. All the time the walls are spaced with stenciled doors. I wonder how the hell you keep something like this secret. If all these rooms hold even two people each that's a lot of traffic for a tiny elevator—not to mention the number of cars that would need to access the place via the wood.

We stop at a set of double doors. Buzz 1 steps forward and pushes them open. A corporate conference room lies beyond. A large polished steel table hosts twenty leather-backed chairs. The walls are bare and the carpet is a continuation of the one in the corridor. I'm pushed into a seat as the two Buzzes sit down opposite me.

Time breathes.

A small clock sitting on the desk ticks. Buzz 1 fires up his cell. Buzz 2 cracks his knuckles.

We sit.

I lean back. Close my eyes. Wait.

The doors swing open and a small bald man wearing a white lab coat comes in. He ignores me and makes for the far end of the table. He fiddles around with something underneath. An electric motor kicks in. A large flat-screen TV rises from the table. He waits until it stops rising and swivels it slightly to face me. Flicking the switch, snow appears, the gray and white dancing dots lighting up the room.

Sitting on top of the TV is a camera. He plays around with it for a minute before leaving.

We all sit in the static disco.

'Mr McIntyre. How disappointing to see you so soon. Guys, can you see me?' White Linen appears on the TV. The picture is grainy and flickers a little.

'Yes,' says Buzz 1.

'Good. Can you get Mr McIntyre a coffee?'

The video link is not brilliant. White Linen's lips are out of synch with the image. It has the making of a badly-dubbed movie. I try and dig his name out. A tennis player. It's the same as an old tennis player. Lendl. As in Ivan. 'Mr Lendl, what am I doing here?'

'Coffee first.'

Buzz is mucking around behind me. With a hiss and a spit coffee starts to brew. A phone rings, Lendl reaches forward and he's gone. A few seconds later he's back. *'Things are a bit wild over here.'*

Coffee arrives and I ignore it.

'Mr McIntyre, I promise we haven't put anything in the coffee. So old school.'

He wants me to ask what he means by 'old school.' I don't.

'I hear your wife will be okay. Maybe a little less the beauty but okay all the same.'

I don't rise to the bait.

'So what do we do with you, Mr McIntyre?'

'You could let me go.'

'I don't think so. Not yet. Not before we have a little chat.'

I decide the coffee is a good idea after all. I sip at it. Top-notch stuff. I take a larger slug. Buzz 1 and Buzz 2 watch me. I wonder if I should offer them popcorn and a large Coke.

The phone at Lendl's end goes off again. Another blank screen. Then he's back. *'Sorry.'*

'Not as much as I am,' I say. 'Why the cloak and dagger nonsense? Where the hell am I and who are you?'

Lendl pushes back in his chair. *'Let's discuss you, Mr McIntyre. I read the London and LA police reports with interest.'*

'Already?'

'But a little backtracking first—indulge me. In Iraq we lose Tom and his friend and you're there. On the plane a stewardess takes out her frustration on her boss and again you're there. A biker dies and your wife's best friend tries to rearrange her face—and there you are again. All in a couple of days.'

'So I've had a crap time lately.'

'Nineteen eighty-three, Ramadi, two men hack each other up and the only witness is you?'

'And?'

'Coincidence? You think?'

'Look at your notes, Mr Lendl. I was out of the army on the back of that last incident. I didn't spend nearly five years in the happy farm for fun. I was heading for a breakdown, well before Clegg and Johnston chose to remove each other's limbs. They found me in the corner of the room sitting in my own urine.'

He ignores what I've said. *'All in all, you seem to attract trouble. Or maybe there's more. Maybe you cause it.'*

'Crap. What are you on about?'

Lendl leans forward. *'Mr McIntyre, in my job I don't talk crap. I may deal in it but I don't talk it.'*

I wonder who the hell could get the report from the London police and the LA police so quickly. 'So I was in the wrong place at the wrong time. Sue me. Give me a break. I've lost my job, seen my wife beaten up, been kidnapped…and you think it was down to me?'

'I said it could be. I think we'll take this a little further.'

With that the screen returns to snow. Buzz 1 stands. The door opens and two more suits walk in. Plastic cuffs are dangling from one of the suit's hands. I move to back away but Buzz 2 is behind me. He takes my arm and pushes it up my back. I don't bother to resist. I just want this over.

Cuffs cutting my wrists, I'm frog-marched down the corridor to one of the nondescript doors. With a shove I'm catapulted into the room. I fall to the floor and the door slams shut. I sit up. There's a single chair, bolted to the center of the room. A mattress lies on the floor.

'Lie down, Mr McIntyre. We'll talk in the morning.' Lendl's voice is a disembodied sound with an echo built in. It must be coming from speakers hidden in the walls. The lights go off. I shout out. Then I crawl to the mattress and curl up. I want out. I want my wife. I want food. I want a drink. I want a pee.

I lie awake.

CHAPTER 12

'*Wakey, wakey.*'

I'm back. Sluggish but back. Whatever they injected me with has drained my mouth of liquid.

'Nothing,' says Skeleton.

I'm still strapped to the bed. Unable to move. The mouth gag hard across my lips.

'*Scenario two. Let's inform him on the subjects.*' Lendl's voice.

I try to get my head round what's going on.

'*Mr McIntyre,*' he continues. '*We have two male subjects next door. Both are in their forties. We have David and we have Martin. They don't know each other and are homeless. Bums. David used to be a career banker and Martin has been an alcoholic since college. They live rough. David on Sunset Boulevard and Martin near Santa Monica pier. David is five-ten, gray hair and used to be married to a doctor called Sanya. Martin has never been married and we suspect he might be gay. He's six feet tall with black hair.*'

The tall man talks as he injects me again.

'*Nothing.*' Lendl sounds disappointed as I waken again. '*Scenario three. Stress. The last two incidents on the plane and in the bar were stressful. We'll try stress.*'

Hands grab the waistband of my pants and they're yanked down. My boxers are whipped south and my cock is grabbed. I struggle against the restraints but they're solid. My heart is racing as something cold is placed around the end of my penis.

'Low level stimulus,' is the last thing I hear Skeleton say before I'm hit with an electric shock on my penis. I bite down hard. The pain is a living hot wire. I arch my back. I want to scream. I think I'm going to vomit. Gag to death. The pain subsides and I piss myself.

'Heart rate up to one-forty. Signs are high but no reaction from the two test subjects.'

'Hit him again.'

Jesus no.

This time I bite so hard blood floods my mouth.

'Heart rate one-sixty.' Skeleton sounds like this is something he does every day. 'Signs are very high but no reaction from the two test subjects.'

Lendl clears his throat. An ugly sound through the speakers. *'Okay. Let's take it up a little.'*

I wait for the next shock but it isn't electric.

'Craig?' The voice is soft. Lorraine's voice. In my ear. *'Craig?'* Her voice is distant. A cell phone is pushed to my ear. *'Craig?'*

'Mr McIntyre, we have lifted your wife from the hospital. She's in this complex. You're being uncooperative and we need you to work with us. We have wired her up to the mains. I'm going to have to give her the bad news.'

I want to shout. To scream. To tell them I don't know what it is they want. *Please don't hurt Lorraine. Please.* Take this fucking thing from my mouth. What the hell can I tell gagged?

'Heart rate one-seventy. Signs are still very high but no reaction from test subjects.'

'Hit her.'

The howl from the phone is terrible. Lorraine. God what are they doing. Lorraine!

Skeleton speaks. 'Heart rate one-eighty. Signs are maxing out. Still no reaction.'

'*One more time.*'

I throw everything I have into getting free but my muscles collapse at the sound of Lorraine screaming again.

'Heart rate still one-eighty. Signs still maxed out. Still no reaction from test subjects.'

'*Shit. Wheel him next door.*'

Buzz 1 and Buzz 2 grab the dolly. The ceiling moves as I'm transferred to the room I spent the night in. None of the restraints are loosened.

This needs to stop. What do they want? Why do that to Lorraine? She could die. She can't take it. Not in her state. What do they want? What in the hell do they want?

The pain around my groin is deep and feels serious. There's the smell of burning flesh. A smell you don't forget once you have been exposed to it. I wasn't in Iraq long the first time round but you didn't need to be around that smell too often to pick up the scent.

I have to take control of this. I need to figure what it is they want.

'*How are you feeling, Mr McIntyre?*'

I want to rip the speakers from their roots and ram them down Lendl's throat.

Click, footsteps, fumbling and my head restraint is removed. 'You fucking bastard. When I get out of here I'll kill you. I swear to fuck on everything that I can fucking think off. I WILL kill you.'

Silence.

'Do you hear me?' I shout. 'I'll rip your heart out through the end of your dick. Do you understand?'

Silence.

'Are you there?'

'*Are you finished?*'

'No. What do you want? Just tell me what you want.'

'*I will.*'

'What?'

'*Nothing.*'

'Fuck off.'

'*True. Nothing. I'm not sure there's anything we want. I may have been wrong about you.*'

'About what?' I'm straining at the leather restraints. Still trying to tear them from their mounts.

'*About you.*'

I quit the struggle. 'Please just speak plain English.'

'*I am, Mr McIntyre. I thought you could be of some use to us. I thought you might have some ability that could have proved a useful aid to our agency but I'm probably wrong. It would seem that you are just one unlucky son-of-a-bitch.*'

'Then let Lorraine go.'

'*Lorraine? Mr McIntyre, we don't have Lorraine. She's still in St Vincent's.*'

'Then that wasn't Lorraine on the phone?'

The relief is unbelievable. I'm almost pleased. These people have just wired my privates to the power company and I'm almost pleased.

'*Yes, it was,*' says Lendl.

My heart skips.

'*We just recorded it all in the hospital.*'

'Fuck you.'

The background hiss that accompanies his voice falls away and I'm back on my own.

I lie churning events over in my mind. What do they want? Or do I know what they want?

Do I?

Iraq in 2003, Iraq a few days ago, the plane and the bar. Violence and me in the background—or is it me in the foreground? Five dead, two badly injured and I was there. Coincidence? It has to be. I knew the first four casualties, but I was asleep each time it all went down. I didn't know the aircrew and the biker was a stranger.

OK, I know Mary. Know some—don't know others. Would

it have all happened if I had been elsewhere? Probably. Tom and the prostitute. He was beating up on her in the club. She was out for revenge. The plane? Clearly the aircrew had some history. You don't try and rip someone's face off without good reason.

The biker? I don't get that one. I wasn't even in the building when he was stabbed. Mary? Well she has history with Lorraine and the sort that was getting worse.

Clegg and Johnston in Ramadi? They had bad history. Everyone knew that. Clegg had been back to the US on leave and decided that Johnston's girlfriend was a better bet than his own wife. All because Johnston had shown Clegg some fairly explicit picture of his new girlfriend. It had been a mistake. Clegg was a nasty person at best. Rape or consensual—it didn't matter. What mattered was that he happily told Johnston all about it on his return.

Oh, they had history all right.

But I didn't know them. It was my first patrol with them and I only found out the backstory after they killed each other.

So where does that leave me?

Nowhere. None of this makes sense.

Buzz 1 and 2 return.

They circle me a few times and slip my bonds. I sit up and take stock. My groin is on fire but I'm not looking at it while Dumb and Dumber are at home. I get off the dolly and drop to the bed. Buzz 1 and 2 move to stand either side of the door. They are going nowhere.

I curl up, facing away from them, and check for damage. My foreskin is burnt and it hurts like a bitch. I cover myself up and sit up. Buzz 1 and Buzz 2 are staring at me. I stand, they tense. I sit and they ease off. I could probably take one of them. Maybe even both if I got lucky, but then what?

'Any chance of a drink?'

I might as well be talking to the wall.

CHAPTER 13

There's a vibrating sound. Buzz 1 stares at his cell phone. He nods to Buzz 2 and they leave. I get up and try the door. Surprise, surprise—locked. I walk round the room. Four walls, a door. All solid. I'm sure there'll be a camera to back up the speakers. I walk back to the door before slamming my fist on the metal.

I feel something go in my head. The breaking of the kernel. A flash of light. I want out. I want out now.

I drop to my knees as my head rips open.

Hell's teeth.

Crack. I slam my head into the wall. Somebody is cutting into my skull with a hacksaw.

Head to the floor. Head to the wall. Scream. Scream.

The door bursts open. The Buzzes barrel in.

Screaming. I'm all scream.

'*Tie him down again.*' Lendl's voice echoes around the room. Buzz 1 reaches down to grab me. He stops, surprise written into his face as Buzz 2's arm appears around his neck, launching him backwards. Buzz 2 takes Buzz 1's weight on his chest, throwing him into the air. As Buzz 1 smacks back to earth Buzz 2 is on him, fists pounding at face and chest. Buzz 1 does a poor job of defending himself. Buzz 2 is going into overdrive.

Then the world drops blue.

Headache gone, I stand and walk towards the open door.

'*Stop him!*' shouts Lendl.

The Buzz twins have no interest in me. Buzz 2 is head-

69

butting his colleague.

The blue is pulsing again. Slow and sure. Serene. Calm.

An alarm begins to howl. But in the blue world it's a far away thing.

I turn into the corridor and try to remember the way to the elevator. A door next to me opens and three men exit. No jackets and no ties but still the same white shirts and black pants. They size me up. One of them smiles. His left front tooth is gold. He steps in front of me and pulls his arm back to throw a punch. Slow motion kicks in, kicks out, kicks in and disappears again. A strobe effect that throws the man forward in fits and starts.

His smile widens as he winds up for a punch. Then the gold tooth is obscured as a colleague rushes him, taking him in a football tackle around the waist. The two of them bounce off the corridor wall and go down. The third man looks on, bemused. He scratches at a dark mole that dominates his face.

I keep walking.

Another door opens, two more men fly out. They take in the fighting on the floor behind me. They look at each other. One is a redhead. His colleague is six feet six with broad shoulders.

'Get him!' Lendl's voice screams from hidden speakers.

The ginger drops his shoulder to charge me, but his friend sticks out a foot and trips him up. I watch him go down, side-stepping his outstretched hand. His friend uses his height to great effect and drops on the redhead, driving his knee into the small of his colleague's back.

I keep walking.

Two more doors open. More bodies tumble out. A man's head swivels in my direction with the handle of a letter opener where an eye should be. A woman with short blonde hair is locked to his ear—trying to bite it off.

There's a howl from behind me and, in the stop/start world of blue, I turn.

One of the suits—the man with the mole—is hammering to-wards me.

The speaker bursts into life again. '*Someone get him and get him* right fucking now!'

The man with the mole has his eyes fixed on me. He has a couple of yards before I'm going to act as his personal airbag.

'Jim!'

The man with the mole flicks his eyes towards the sound. A young woman has just emerged from a door to my left. She's holding something in her hand and, with the wind-up of a major-league player, she heaves it at mole man. We hit slow motion and I can pick out the shape of the missile. Swirling patterns in glass, tumbling in the air. The paperweight catches the man high on the forehead. He stumbles, hands flying to his skull. He staggers towards me. I step to my right, he crashes past, landing on the man with the letter opener for an eye. I hop over the two bodies.

The speakers burst into life again. '*What the hell is going on? Stop him. Stop him, right* fucking *now.*'

I turn into the next corridor. Maybe thirty people are crammed into the space in front of me. They are fighting. A mass brawl. No one has any interest in me. I decide to walk through the chaos. Two men, one squat and fat, the other thin as sin, catch me on the arm as they fight. The thin man is driving an industrial staple gun into the fat man's gut, pumping the trigger in wild excitement.

I keep going.

A woman stands up in front of me. She's a looker. Long dark hair. Deep purple lipstick. I try to sidestep her. Blood spurts from her mouth, spraying my face. She falls forward. Behind her a man is holding a smashed and bloodied laptop.

The alarm continues to blare. Lendl's voice is lost in the chaos around me. I dodge more bodies and reach the next corridor. There are only two men ahead. One has his head buried in the other's lap. He's shaking his head like a dog drying itself. Blood spraying in the air around him. He lifts his head clear, revealing flabby cheeks and a double chin. I don't need to know what he

71

has in his mouth.

I keep on moving. I reach the closed doors of the elevator. I look at the gray box. I try waving my hand in front of it but nothing is going to happen soon. Behind me the castrated man is gurgling, hugging his legs, blood pouring onto the carpet. The double-chinned man is running away.

I breathe in a lungful, stepping towards the man on the floor. I grab him by the shoulders, hauling him to the door. He leaves a trail like a snail.

A howl and Buzz 2 rounds the corner. 'McIntyre.'

I pull the castrated man another foot, lifting his hand to the gray box. Buzz 2 closes in. I look at the doors that line the corridor. Why the hell doesn't one open?

A click from behind signals the elevator doors are about to part. I drop the castrated man's hand. He looks up at me. Silently pleading for help. I shake my head, there's nothing I can do. He goes back to hugging his groin. I jump into the elevator.

Buzz 2 is closing fast.

There are three buttons on the elevator wall. None has markings. One for this level, one for the top, one for emergency? Maybe. I hit the top one. The door starts to close. Buzz's hand reaches into the gap. The doors stop and open again. Buzz stands square in the door. I charge at him, shoulder first and we both fly out of the elevator. I grab the edge of the elevator door to stop me arriving back into the corridor. Buzz 2 trips over the castrated man. I scrabble back into the elevator and hit the button again. Buzz 2 tries to get up, but the castrated man grabs his wrist. 'Help me.'

The doors close. With a sigh the elevator heads up.

The smell of damp and the sound of dripping take over. I lie against the wall. The blue world provides all the light I need. Instant night vision. I spot a small camera in the corner.

'Mr McIntyre. *Stay where you are.*' Lendl's voice springs from the hidden speakers.

'Fuck off, Lendl.' Not my most articulate response.

The elevator stops and I press myself against the side as the door opens. Morning air rushes in, but it's unaccompanied by suits or bullets. No one standing outside waiting for me. I sprint out into the sunlight. My eyes blinking.

I start to jog down the trail. If my captors are going to be anywhere, they'll be on the road at the end of the path. I change direction to push into the bushes on my right, fighting my way through the foliage. The blue is fading. Still there but thinner. Less obvious.

I pop out of the undergrowth to find myself standing at the top of a small rise. Dodger Stadium and the freeway are maybe a half mile away. Beneath me is scrub and more bushes. I start down the small hill, keeping my eyes open for the suits.

A couple are out walking their dog. They see me and turn to head in the opposite direction.

I've been up here a couple of times with Lorraine, visiting a sick friend in a nursing home that sits on the edge of the park. I know if I reach the perimeter I can try and lose myself among the buildings that surround the far end of the park.

I hear a roar of an engine and spin round. A motorbike is bearing down on me. I start to run but the bike changes direction and cuts me off. The rider pulls it to a halt, revving the engine. He's wearing a black, full-face helmet but his T-shirt doesn't look like something the suits would wear.

The biker pulls his helmet off. Long blond hair falls to his shoulders. 'Hey, man. What ya running for? You wouldn't have a stick, would you?'

He can't be more than eighteen years old. The bike he's sitting on is a battered trail model of some vintage.

'A stick?' I say.

'Cigarette, man.'

A second engine growls in the distance and a black SUV bounces into view.

'A cigarette for a shot of your bike?' I say.

'Eh?'

'You heard.'

'No, man.'

'I've eighteen left in a packet. You can have them all for a go on your bike.'

'Nah. I just want one. Don't need that many.'

I move forward. The SUV is putting on speed.

'Okay. Here.' I reach into my jacket. He involuntarily leans forward in the seat. I pull my hand from my jacket and reach out to offer him a cigarette I don't have. As he puts his hand out I grab it, yanking him towards me.

'Hey!'

He falls and the bike throws him clear. His helmet lands at my feet. I snatch it up and ram it on my head. It's a snug fit but it goes on. The young man is trying to get up. I look up, the SUV is bearing down on me. I turn and kick the biker in the guts and he folds up. I take the handlebars and heave. The bike is no lightweight. I don't recognise the logo. Probably an old communist-bloc make.

Some dirt explodes in a puff next to the front wheel. It takes me way too long to realize that I'm being shot at. I double the effort to pull the bike upright. I get on.

I haven't been on a bike since college. I pull in the clutch, feeding the gears back to neutral. I find the kick-start and slam my foot on it. The engine coughs but doesn't burst into life. A bullet pings off the rear mudguard. The SUV slews to a halt with a suit leaning out of the passenger window, levelling his gun for a body shot. It's Buzz 1. His face is swollen. Blood cakes his face. The young man is trying to get up. I plunge my foot down once more on the kick-start. With a roar, the engine explodes into life. I flick up into first, letting out the clutch, slowly, listening for the note-drop—willing myself not to stall it.

The engine bites, the bike starts to move. The door of the SUV opens. Buzz 2 rolls out. He steadies his gun. A spurt of air just above my hand tells me that Buzz 2 isn't trying to warn me. He's trying to kill me.

Dirt spits up from behind me as the bike shoots forward. I haven't the skill to wheel the machine away from the SUV the way I've seen dirt bikers handle their machines. Instead I gun it, heading straight for Buzz 2. He dives out of the way.

I'm gone.

I point the bike down a worn track, winding up the throttle. The roar of the engine drowns any other sound. The situation demands speed.

I reach a bend in the track and flick my head round to see if the suits are following me. The SUV is much closer than I would have thought possible. I cut off the track, heading in what I hope is the direction of the exit.

I crest a small ridge, spotting the entrance we came in last night. It's about a quarter of a mile away. Next to it, nestled on a small hillock, is a red brick building—Broadview, the Christian Science nursing home that Lorraine's friend was in.

Another SUV slides into view, blocking the exit gate. I swing left, aiming for the red brick.

The second car sets off after me once it's sure I'm not going to double back.

I reach the grounds of the nursing home and feed the bike onto a well-tended path that leads to the gardens beyond. I have to slow as I roll along the path.

Passing a pond and a flagpole, I swerve to avoid ploughing into a man pushing a wheelchair. I keep vertical and spin the throttle to maintain speed. The man's mouth is moving. I'm not sure they are very Christian Science words.

The place is a maze of paths. Designed to help you to lose yourself. I'm doing a fine job of that.

The main building finally appears through a gap in the trees. I aim for it, cutting over newly-mown lawn and leaving deep tracks. A group of people stand chatting on the lawn edge. Their heads all turn to me as I fly by.

I catch sight of a car moving beyond the building on what has to be the main road. I spray gravel as I round the structure and vomit into a blacktop parking lot. Squirting through a pair of six-feet-high gates, past the gatehouse I wheel to my left. Low-rise detached houses start to flick by. I slow down to turn my head. No sign of the SUVs.

The freeway is to my right but I would be too easy to spot if they caught up with me. I'm conscious of my speed as I spit along the road. The last thing I want is the police stopping me.

I hit a junction with an ATM at the corner. I need cash but not here. The road falls away in front of me. I try to balance legal and illegal on the speedometer.

I take lefts and rights at random. I don't know this area in any depth. I could be heading for a dead end, but I can't stop. I have to give myself some breathing space. Some thinking space.

I pass under the freeway, before skirting the Dodger Stadium. A strip mall appears. It has a parking lot hidden from the road. Ideal.

I park the bike next to a pickup—checking it can't be easily seen from the road. I walk to the front of the shops and enter a mom and pop diner.

The world seems to slow down. I've slipped back thirty years. To a time when the planet spun a little less frantically. To a place where people spent their days with coffee and pie.

The restaurant is empty. Gingham cloths decorate the tables. I think of Lorraine's dress. The waitress wobbles up to me as I sit down. I choose a seat with a view of the parking lot and road. I order a coffee and slice of apple pie. I need the caffeine. I need the sugar.

Much more than that, I need Lorraine. I have to see her. I have to know she's alright. She could be dead. The screams on my cell haunt me. What did they do to her? I look around. The payphone in the corner is in use. A rare object. How many pay-phones now exist? How many are ever used? A slim woman is in gab mode. I stare at her. Willing her to put the receiver down but she's in full flow. I wait.

I let my mind look back at the carnage that unfolded as I

escaped. The blinding headache, the blue world, the violence. I'm beginning to get a sense of what Lendl is after. In some way I was responsible for the spontaneous brutality back there in the agency hideout. As I was in Iraq the first time, Iraq again, the plane, the bar. Me as the common link. What am I? A victim of circumstance? A catalyst for destruction? A freak? Or is there something else?

Lorraine would wrap some perspective around it all. She's good at that. I need her gentle voice. I need her wisdom. I can't take it all in. There has to be a simple explanation. How can it be me? If I *am* some kind of freak, I would have suspected something long before now. These things—whatever these things are—don't just creep up on you. Or do they?

The thought continues to scuttle to the front of my frazzled brain. What if I really am the cause of all this? Look what it did to people. Look what it did to Lorraine. Hell, it could happen again. How would I know? I could be my wife's executioner-in-waiting. Sitting in the wings. Never knowing when I'm going to bring harm down on her.

Stupid. Just stupid. It makes no sense. But it does—just a little. Just enough to make me think twice about visiting her. Just enough to make me think about never seeing her again. God no! Not an option.

The waitress asks if I want more coffee. I nod.

Never seeing Lorraine. The words are painful. I can't accept them. I'm making more out of this than there is. I need to calm down.

First things first. Lorraine. The talker on the payphone has finished. I root around to make change. I ask the waitress for the directory. She pulls it out from beneath the counter. She has to blow the dust off it.

I retreat to the payphone, flicking through the directory to find the medical centre. I dial.

'*St Vincent's. How can I help?*' The voice is bright and cheery.

'I'm trying to find out how Mrs Lorraine McIntyre is doing.

I'm her husband. She was brought in last night.'

'Please hold, sir.'

Light music fills the earpiece. The door to the diner swings open. Two guys in jeans and T-shirts enter. They sit at the counter. Before they've sat down the waitress has poured coffee. Regulars.

Time ticks by. The music keeps pumping.

Ten minutes later I'm still on hold.

I tap the phone against the wall. Lorraine tells me I do this all the time with the cell phone—as if it'll speed up the person on the other end.

The Bontempi organ player on the phone decides to give the Bee Gees' *More Than a Woman* a hammering. Food arrives for the two guys. I see a black Buick Regal slipping into a space in the strip mall parking lot. No one emerges from it. Then a second black Regal stops in the middle of the lot.

A third Regal edges into view.

For Regals, read SUVs.

Suit cars.

Shit.

God, I'm dumb.

I slam the phone down as the doors to all three cars open. Suits pour out. Buzz 2 is leading from the front. I leap the counter. The waitress shouts as I push through the swing doors to the kitchen.

They'll be out the back. The thought skids across my brain.

The short-order cook freezes, knife in hand, as I enter.

I throw my hands up. 'I'm not trouble. Is there any way out of here other than through the back door?'

He looks through the serving hatch to the front door, as it flies open. At the same time the door behind him bounces off the wall. A pincer of black suits is on.

Buzz 2, straddling the counter, shouts for me to stand still. The chef lifts his finger and points to a closet door next to me. 'In there. Through the window.'

I spin. I see the door. I grab at the handle, praying it's not locked. It opens.

Once inside, I slam it shut. The closet is a storeroom racked with shelving units. I grab the nearest one and pull. It comes away from the wall in a waterfall of tins and jars, crashing to the floor in front of the door. Someone reaches the door and tries to open it but the unit stops it travelling more than a few inches.

A fly-screened window sits about four feet off the ground at the back of the closet. A chest freezer sits below it. I jump on to it and push open the window. I stick my head out, expecting to see suits. The window opens onto the side of the mall. The parking lot is on one side and the back of the mall on the other.

There are no suits.

I scramble through the gap, falling to the ground. I land on dusty grass. Up and I'm sprinting into the bushes in front of me. Out of the corner of my eye I spot suits, just as they round the corner from the parking lot. A shout goes up. Spotted.

I emerge from the bushes.

I put my head down and run.

The street ahead is bordered with single-story detached homes. Mid-market abodes with two- and three-year-old cars peppered along the sidewalk. I jink to my right, up the first driveway and into the backyard.

An old lady is sitting sipping a glass of something. I throw her a smile as I leap the fence into the next garden. A sun-tanned old man with a deeply wrinkled face and a faded Dodgers sweat is tending a patch of dirt. I give him the same smile, cutting right to jump over a back fence into the alley beyond.

I'm faced with the rear of what looks like a small church. I skirt round it.

I have no plan. I just need to keep running.

A Regal screams into the road ahead. I leap into the yard directly across from the church and enter another backyard. This one is empty.

I hurdle up through the next four yards. At the fifth fence I place my hand on a post for support, launching myself into the air. I come down on a woman lying on a sunbed. She screams and we both roll onto her lawn. I push to get up. She's wearing a bikini. My hand slips on the grass. I grab at her to stop me falling back to earth. I get a handful of breast and she yelps.

'What the fuck?' The man of the house emerges from the back door. He's wearing boxers and nothing else. I ignore him, heading for the rear and into a back alley.

I can't keep this speed up for long. I'm not as fit as I need to be. I jump into another yard where a young boy in shorts and a striped shirt is washing a Toyota Hilux. The driver's door is open. The boy is on the other side waxing the hood. I jog up to the open door and look in. A set of keys dangle from the ignition. I jump in. Slam the door. Turn the key. Select drive and plant my foot.

The pickup jumps forward. I have to stand on the brakes to make the turn into the road. In the rear view mirror the boy is standing—jaw hanging open. I hurtle down the road and hang a left. A sign for the I-10 takes me onto the freeway. I stay on for a couple of junctions, slip off and start to weave my way across town.

I have one destination in mind. The hospital.

CHAPTER 14

St Vincent's sits across from me. I've parked up the Hilux oppo-site the main entrance and I've already clocked four suits. Another Regal rolls up. I start the engine and cruise away. Circling to the back of the building brings another Regal into view.

I drive round once more. Another SUV has joined the party. Buzz 2 gets out. I drive away. My focus is on Lorraine but get-ting myself caught won't help.

I head for Charlie's place.

The pub has boards across the main window. I see Charlie through the glass front door. I keep back into the shade of the bushes that guard the library. I dropped the car a few blocks back, parking it in an office lot. I've been watching Charlie's place for an hour. If there are suits around they are well hidden.

It sums up my life that the only person I can turn to is Charlie—a man who sells oblivion to people. Friends are thin on the ground these days. They peeled away as my time in the hospital stretched. The odd visit was the best I had. Even then it was little more than the army liaison team.

Charlie is tidying up. Amazingly—despite the devastation—he's still open. A couple of regulars seem to be earning beers by helping out.

I wait until the late afternoon light is gone and circle round to the back alley. There's no one here. Good news.

I push open the back door and slip in. There's noise from the bar but, before I enter, I check out both washrooms and Charlie's office. All are empty.

I stick my head into the bar, checking out the booths. There's a man in one but he's all T-shirt and jeans. Two more customers are sitting at the bar enjoying the reward for helping with the clean-up. Apart from the boarded window, Charlie has done a remarkable job on the place. There are fewer tables and chairs than there used to be, and the front of the bar has a crack in the woodwork running half the length, but the gantry behind is clean and tidy, the floor is swept and even the jukebox seems to be working—*Chirpy Chirpy Cheep Cheep* by Middle of the Road.

Charlie spots me. 'Craig?'

I wave for him to come over. The three customers look up and dismiss me. I point to his office. He nods and we vanish into the cubbyhole.

'What the heck is going on?' he says, dropping into a battered leather office chair.

'I'd like to know the answer to that question too. Has anyone been asking about me?'

'Two men in suits have been in. Three times so far. Each time I tell them the same thing. I haven't seen you since last night. Each time they say they'll be back. Who are they?'

'I don't know. Not police that's for sure. Some agency.'

'FBI?'

'No. Not CIA either. Something else.'

'What do they want with you? Is it to do with Iraq?'

'Partly. I'm struggling to make sense of it all.'

A voice shouts from the bar. Charlie tells me he'll be back in a second. I look up at the battered picture that hangs above Charlie's desk.

Stripped to a pair of leather briefs, Charlie is in full-pose mode. All oiled up and flexing muscles. A certificate underneath announces his first place in a competition held in San Diego.

Charlie returns with a grimace on his face. 'Craig McIntyre, you're an expensive son-of-a-bitch. I had to double up the rounds for free or we wouldn't get five minutes to talk.'

'Shit happens.'

'So what gives?'

I'm not sure what to say to Charlie. I could do with another brain on this one and Charlie is smart. Far smarter than he makes out. Lorraine is also convinced he has a share in a few other places. She overheard him talk about a place in Florida one night. I asked him about it once, but he just laughed.

I need to make a call. I flip a coin in my head. It comes down heads. 'How much do you want to know?'

'All of it. I'm a barman remember. Gossip is my trade—or rather keeping gossip quiet is my trade.'

'I'm being serious. Whoever these guys are this is not a kid's game. They've tortured me and Lorraine already.'

This brings a silence.

'Lorraine. When?'

'Thanks for the concern for me.'

'I can see you're okay, but isn't Lorraine in hospital?'

'Yes, and they pushed a few hundred volts through her while she lay in her sick bed.'

'Fuck. Really?'

'I think so. So you see I'm not kidding. I sure could do with some help.'

'Hang on.'

He's gone for five minutes and I'm left with the Charles Atlas picture for company. I lean back in the chair. I can't get Lorraine out of my head. I'm considering whether I should return to the hospital and leave the chat with Charlie until later when he returns. 'I just closed up. My regulars aren't too happy but I promised them a free night on the beer and they saw sense.'

The lights are out in the bar. Charlie pulls the office door shut. He reaches out to the small wire-meshed window that faces onto the alley, yanking a thick strip of material across the glass. 'That'll make the place look empty but if someone is listening in the alley they'll still hear us.'

He's whispering. 'Okay, Craig. Shoot.'

I give him what I know. Even the bits I missed out for Lorraine. Charlie asks the odd question. When I get to my escape from the park he whistles.

'Either you have the best imagination since Raymond Chandler or we're in a whole new land of hurt. Do you want a drink?'

The question catches me by surprise.

I think about it for an eighth of a second. 'Yes.'

'So do I.'

That surprises me. Charlie is all but teetotal with the odd exception—his birthday, the odd celebration—like the time he won fifty thousand on the lottery. Once more he vanishes, this time to return with a large pitcher of Coke, a bottle of Jack Daniels and a bucket of ice.

He pours two drinks. Mine's a triple, his a single. I polish off half of mine in one go.

'So?' He looks at me while scratching at the side of his head. 'Three choices. Either all of this 'stuff' that went down is just coincidence. Or, someone is out to mix you up in something that makes no sense at the moment. Or...'

'Or?' I ask.

'Or you have something about you that has its rightful place in the Twilight Zone.'

'And where would your money lie?'

'The first two if I was being realistic. The latter if I was a betting man.'

'You think I'm responsible for all this?'

'I should say no, but look at it. Unless you've just made it all up or got the facts way wrong, it sure sounds like it.'

'How could I be?'

'Oh don't be so stupid. Listen to what you've just told me. Look at what has happened. Violence, headaches, a 'blue world', secret agency, miracle escapes.'

'I could be delusional.'

84

'True, but that wouldn't explain the bikers last night or Mary sticking a bottle in your wife's eye or the two suits that keep asking after you.'

'Do you think that's what the experiments were about?'

'Run through what they did and said again.'

I sip at the JD. 'They tied me down and told me there were two subjects on the other side of the screen. Then they mentioned that I had been asleep or out for the count when Clegg and Johnston and Tom and his girl had been killed. When I woke up they talked about me being stressed. That's when they wired me up and ran the mains through my dick. Then they talked about me knowing the subjects, ran a spiel on the two down-and-outs, did a Frankenstein on me again. Then they did the same to Lorraine. After that they called it quits.'

'Sounds like they were trying to trigger whatever it is they think you do.'

'You figure?'

'Don't you?'

I take another slug, finishing the glass. The JD is getting to work nicely but I don't want it to take over. It would be too easy to take that path. 'No, it doesn't make sense, but it's one explanation.'

Charlie leaves his drink untouched. 'Did anything ever happen like this outside of the last few days and the two soldiers back in '03?'

Another slug. I root around in my head for a minute. 'Not as such but...'

'But what?'

'Have you ever felt that there was something else going on around you that you didn't know about? That things weren't all they seemed?'

'All the time. When people are drunk they tell you all sorts of weird crap and sometimes, just sometimes, it rings a bell.'

'Well every so often I've been in places where I feel the world is operating without me. I'm there but I'm not.'

'Lost you.'

I decide a refill won't do any harm and pour a small one. 'I'll give you an example. I was witness to a car crash a year after I left the army. I was on day release and an RV broadsided a battered old Camaro. The RV shot a red. The Camaro had no chance. I went over to help but the passenger and driver in the Camaro were at each other's throats, as were the two in the RV. Neither were in the slightest interested in the crash. I tried to intervene but it was as if I wasn't there. Every so often stuff like that happens, but nothing like the last few days.'

'Have you talked to Lorraine about it?'

'No way. She has to deal with the fact I was once an extra from the Mad Hatter's tea party. She married me and thinks I'm okay now.'

Charlie smiles.

'What?' I ask.

'Lorraine knows you're not okay. She's not stupid. Five years in the loony farm and you're going to flip to Mr Alright? No way.'

'It wasn't a loony farm.'

'Sorry. Anyway, how long has this stuff been going on?'

'Since Iraq the first time.'

Charlie takes a sip of his drink, licks his lips and drains the glass. 'You know you can't go back to Lorraine.'

I drop air from my lungs in one lump. 'What?'

'If these guys really want you they'll stop at nothing to get you. You need to vanish.'

'And what if they use Lorraine to get to me?'

'Leave that to me.'

'Look, I'm going to get Lorraine and that's it.' I fiddle with my drink.

'And then what? You can't move her. She'll be in need of care for a good few weeks. Didn't you also say they have the hospital staked out? They know you'll go for her. Come on, Craig, these guys want you and want you bad. You try and get her and you're a dead man walking. Leave Lorraine to me.'

'You? How?'

'Well for a start I'm going to tell the police that the men in suits have been sniffing around. I'll mention they've threatened me and told me to tell you that if I see you they'll harm Lorraine.'

'I don't think the police will bother these guys.'

'Maybe not, but it might make them think twice about hurting Lorraine. I'll drop a note to the local paper. Men in black suits, vague threats, bikers ripping up my bar—they'll love it.'

'And the fact your brother is the editor doesn't do any harm.'

'That as well.'

'Then?'

He pushes his glass to one side. 'Then I set up shop at the hospital and when Lorraine is on the mend we get the hell out of there.'

'Hell, Charlie, they'll come after you. After both of you.'

'And they won't come after you?'

'Maybe, but she's my wife. I'm not running.'

'And what if Mary was just the start of the pain you bring to her life?'

'What else can I do?' I lean back in the chair and stare at a picture of Gary Cooper on Charlie's wall. Charlie loves *High Noon*.

'Hide.'

'And just leave Lorraine?'

'Hanging around for the men in black suits to pick you up isn't the best idea on the planet.'

'Hiding isn't going to solve anything.'

'Might give you some space to figure a solution. If the men in black suits catch you and you're to blame for all this, then I can think of a hundred uses for a ticking time bomb. But then again maybe it's not you making people flip out. Maybe, even if it is, it can be fixed.'

'Who by?'

'Try *Ripley's Believe It or Not!* website—they have a phone number.'

'Funny. Where do I go? I can't just hit the road. I need to have a plan—somewhere to stay—an objective.'

'You also need to act quickly.'

'No shit.'

'No, I mean it. Listen.'

The sound of a single footstep bounces off the wire-meshed window.

CHAPTER 15

Charlie throws the light switch, plunging us into near-perfect darkness.

A second step. Soft. Not someone out for a stroll. Someone trying not to be there.

A voice, so low it's a murmur. No words. Too indistinct. Then a second voice.

Charlie whispers, 'Time to go, Craig. We can finish this later.'

'How do I get out?'

'Female washroom. I'll draw them in and then you go.'

I stand up and feel my way round the wall to the door. It opens with a soft squeak and I wince at the sound as I cross the corridor. A shape blocks out the light in the doorway to the alley. I duck, pushing into the ladies' washroom.

It smells far fresher than the gents. The light from the alley casts shadows. There are two cubicles and a single bowl, with a hand dryer pinned to one wall.

The voices are talking again. Still too low to make out the words. The cold faucet on the sink is dripping. A single drop every four or five seconds. The extractor fan, built into the window, turns as a gust of air flows through the alley. I move behind the entrance door. Unless someone slams it open, I'll be hidden if they do a quick check.

Someone is trying the back door. It clicks as the handle lowers. I can feel the change in air pressure as the door opens and the outside air slides in. I stiffen.

Light spills under the door and Charlie's voice booms out, 'I have a gun.'

The door clicks shut again. Charlie has changed plans on me. No one is going to come in with a gun waiting for them. The sound of retreating footsteps suggests they're leaving. Then the washroom door opens. Did one of them make it in? My eyes burn as light floods the room. I try to keep still but the door opens wide and catches my toes.

'Craig?' Charlie's voice.

'Are they gone?' I'm whispering.

'No. I had a peak through the drapes. There were four of them. All suited and booted. I figured that inviting them in might not be the best idea. If there are four out back, there will be more out front. We need a plan B.'

'Like what?'

'This way and keep low.'

I follow him out of the washroom.

He grabs my hand. 'Keep your head down.'

I do as I am told.

We enter the bar. Charlie points towards the far end. 'There's a trapdoor behind the bar. The stairs go straight down.'

I quickly find the handle on the floor and pull up the cover. The trapdoor is heavy, awkward to move, but it finally gives. I swing it up and drop it to the floor.

Charlie follows me over and whispers. 'There's a small door at the rear of the cellar. The key is on a nail to the left. When you go through the door you'll find another trapdoor that's used for dropping in beer and spirits. It comes up under the fire escape in the alley. In this light you might get out without being seen. It's the best I can think of.'

'Thanks, Charlie.'

I start to drop down and he grabs my shoulder. 'Here. It's not much but it will get you out of town. I wouldn't go using any ATMs or swiping credit cards in the near future.' He hands me a fistful of notes and I stuff them in my pocket.

'Charlie, I'm still going for Lorraine.'

'Don't be stupid. I'll take care of it. Trust me.' Charlie closes the hatch. I fumble around until I find the door and the key.

The lock is tough to open. When it frees itself the door flies inward. I stumble into the space beyond. My shin cracks against a beer keg. I curse in the dark. Waving my hands around, I find the hatch. I undo the catch, all by feel, and lean upward, shoulder against the metal.

The plate lifts into the alley. Catching it with my hand, I put my head to the crack. I've seen the hatch often enough as Lorraine and I have lounged near the pub door. It sits hard against the wall, under a metal fire escape.

I can't see anyone but my view is restricted. I listen for any telltale sounds but the rumble of traffic and the sounds of the city are all I can hear.

I heave, catching the metal handle before the hatch bangs on the ground. I haul myself up and close the hatch. The alley rolls into view. Clear.

For a second.

A suit rounds the corner, then another. I turn to find the other end of the alley blocked by three more. Buzz 1 leads them. He smiles. I think about diving down the hatch but I'd be trapped. The bar door is an option but I'd be back where I was. I stare like I've been caught in a car's headlights.

'Okay, Mr McIntyre, don't make this any harder than it needs to be.' Buzz 2 starts to close in.

I look up, more for inspiration than for any outreach to a higher authority. Either way it works. The fire escape. Jumping up I grab the pull-down ladder. It rattles down as my weight triggers the release mechanism. Buzz 2 starts to run as I start to climb.

Charlie's premises are part of a three-story block and I gain the platform for the first floor as the suits converge at the bottom of the ladder. I try to pull it up but Buzz 2 is only feet behind me. I wait until his head is level with my feet and stamp down hard on his face. He twists to avoid the kick, but he's too slow. My foot catches him a side blow, he loses grip, falling into the suits below.

I fly up the next twenty feet and at the top I'm faced with a flat roof. There are no other exits. I sprint to the far side and look down onto the street. Two suits are standing at either end of the alley. Three more are standing at the front door to the bar. I duck back as Buzz 2 makes the top of the fire escape.

I run to the far end of the building. Looking down, I can see the alley below. Across from me is the next strip of buildings— all two-story. The roof beyond is flat, with a doorway about halfway along. The door is ajar and I can see stairs leading down.

I look back. Buzz 2 is on the roof and bearing down on me. I judge the gap between my building and the next at a good twelve feet with a ten-foot difference in height. I'd never make the distance as a regular long jump but with the fall I might.

I need a long run-up but Buzz 2 will be on me in seconds. I have no choice. I run at the edge and leap, knowing I'm not going to make it. I'm too slow and my leap too weak.

The far wall looms. I throw my hands up. The edge of the roof digs into my palms. I grab hold of it to stop me plunging to the alley floor. My chest hits the side wall, followed by my legs. It hurts. My hands find a grip and hold. I scrabble with my feet for some purchase. I feel something jutting from the wall. I put my left foot on it and push.

'Jump! After him!'

'No way.'

The voices are coming from the roof I've just left.

I plant my other foot on the protruding object, shoving myself onto the roof. I don't look back. I just run for the door.

Crashing through, I fly down the stairs. There are two flights, then another door. I open it and fall into an empty space. It looks like a storage area. I scan the surroundings. A

92

gap at the back leads out onto what looks like a balcony. I head for it.

I hear glass breaking from below, then voices. These guys are not for giving in.

I reach the balcony only to find it's glassed in. This is no storage area. Someone has laid this out as a loft-style apartment. Three glass sliding doors protect the metal balcony. I try the sliding doors one by one, but they're all locked. I look around for something to break the glass with, but there's nothing. The voices are closing in. Rising from below.

I run back to the stairs. With heavy legs I return to the roof. Sprinting to the edge where the balcony sits, I drop myself onto the metal structure. Through the glass doors I see suits pour into the space beyond. One of them sees me. His mouth moves but the double-glazing stifles the shout. He raises a gun. I place my hand on the balcony railing and leap over.

There is no alley below—just a stretch of scrubland. I fall ten feet, roll forward and I'm up and running again.

A muffled shot rings out, followed by the sound of one of the glass doors exploding. I keep running, entering a small parking lot at the back of a commercial row of buildings at the other end of the scrub. I run into the gap between two buildings and out onto the street beyond.

Across the street there's a movie lot stuffed with cinema equipment. Flats, lighting covered in tarpaulins, a couple of trucks and range of props. I enter the lot, grab a handful of the tarpaulin from one of the lighting rigs and pull it over myself. Underneath the rig is a crisscross of aluminum tubing. I climb up a few rungs, settle myself into the nest of steel and try to stop breathing.

There is no point running further. I haven't the strength. This might be the most obvious place to hide in LA or it just might fool them. I just wish I didn't need air.

Breathing makes so much noise.

CHAPTER 16

'Did you see him?'

It's Buzz 2. He's only a few feet away.

'No, but he can't have gone far.'

'You try that way. I'll try this way.'

They're talking too loud. You don't yak like you have just come out from a rock concert when you're hunting someone. You do it by signs, not words. Not unless you want the prey to believe they are close to freedom.

I'm cramping up. The cold of the metal is creeping into my bones. Don't move. It's all I can do. Not to move. My ears are my defense. The slightest noise. Any sign that I'm not on my own. Anything. I start to count. Backwards from one thousand. If I get to zero with no sign, then I'll move.

A car drives by. Chat and laughter and the car slows.

'Is he watching us?' A girl's voice. Then she continues: 'He is.'

'Hey!' Now a man's voice. 'What are you looking at? You dressed for a funeral? Because it'll be yours if you don't fuck off.'

I'm guessing one of the suits is hanging around to see if I re-appear.

'Let's go.' The girl sounds drunk. 'Maybe he likes to watch. Is that it—you like to watch?' The last few words are shouted.

More laughter as they move away.

I've lost count so I start again.

1,000-999-998...

I hit zero and wait for another count of one hundred before

starting to unfurl my legs. The blood rushes back. I bite my tongue and clench my fists as the pain kicks in. The pins and needles are extreme. I flex my joints to try to ease the throbbing. My foot hits the ground as I drop down. I'm still inside the tarpaulin tent. Leaning my head to the ground, the smell of damp concrete in my nose, I stretch my hand out and lift the corner of the material to reveal a slice of the road.

I crawl forward, lifting the tarpaulin a little more. No one— but this is like shining a torch for light in a desert. You can see a few feet but someone a mile away can see you. I lift a little more and push my head into the gap.

No one.

I roll out, waiting for the pins and needles to ease before standing.

Still no one.

Time to walk—not run. No need to draw attention. Anyway, I'm out of running at the moment.

There's no cover to be had on the street but the next corner is only yards away. I hold my breath as I walk round it and exhale as I put my hiding place out of sight behind me. I cross the road and enter yet another alley.

As I exit the alley I spot a cab sitting at the end of the next street. I walk up and jump in. The cabbie looks surprised to find he has a fare.

'St Vincent's Medical Centre,' I say.

The driver takes off. I try to look behind in a manner that doesn't suggest I'm being followed. There's no one in sight. I settle into the seat as the driver takes an on-ramp to the I-10 and heads downtown.

We hit the off-ramp with St Vincent's a block away. Two SUVs sit at the next corner. I duck as we pass them. Two more sit at the entrance, with three suits on the door.

'Take me round the back.'

The cabbie nods.

An SUV, a Regal and two suits sit at the back.

Fuck.

The cab stops.

'Not here,' I say.

'Where then?'

'The nearest payphone.'

Two blocks on, the cabbie pulls up at a phone.

I jump out. 'I'll be two minutes.' The phone is working and I dial Charlie's pub.

'Michael's, can I help you,' Charlie answers.

'Charlie, it's me.'

'How are you?'

'How am I? How the hell do you think I am?'

Silence.

'Charlie, are you alone?'

'I...'

I slam the phone down. Stupid. Just stupid. Of course he's not alone. A car burns rubber. I turn, expecting to see an SUV or a Regal, but it's an old Taurus pulling away from the lights too quickly.

I jump back in the cab. 'The Greyhound Bus Depot.'

I'm no use to Lorraine here. It's me they want. A little distance and figure things out. Then back for her when things have cooled off. I pull the bundle of notes that Charlie gave me from my pocket but it's not enough. Charlie has given me fifty dollars. I need to get more cash.

Shit.

I lean forward. 'Can you pull off the freeway and find an ATM?'

The driver doesn't look happy but I don't care. I have to get cash now. If I draw it out at the bus station it will be a giveaway as to where I am. And I need money. Once I'm on the road I can't access more.

There's an ATM at the bottom of the next off-ramp. The machine only lets me draw four hundred dollars. I jump back in the cab and we take off again.

Twenty minutes later the taxi driver pulls up at the bus depot. The complex lies on a side street fronted by chain link. The buses are parked rear in. It's quiet, it's late, but there are still buses pulling in and out. I strip forty bucks from my cash and pay the driver.

As I enter the depot I keep an eye out for suits. The good news is that they'll stand out a mile in here. Two-piece and ties are thin on the ground. The ticket office has a queue of one. I approach it trying to figure where I'm going.

Two police officers walk into the depot and, with the eyes of the well-practiced, scan the concourse. They stop when they see me. I look away. When I turn back one of them is on his walkie-talkie.

Can't be for me. Can it? The suits have some reach if the beat cops have me down pat already. I wander to the coffee machine and order up something to keep me awake. When the cup pops out I risk a glance at the cops—they're gone.

I swallow most of the liquid in two shots. Time to leave town.

I approach the ticket booth. 'When is the next bus to New Orleans?'

'Ten to twelve tonight, sir.'

The ticket man looks bored. His shirt is stained and his badge tells me his name is Helmut.

'Helmut, how long does the journey take?'

'You arrive at ten to eight on Monday night. Change twice. Tomorrow morning at six-fifteen in El Paso and then again at Houston at eleven fifteen on Monday morning.'

Long trip. I reach for my money. 'A single to New Orleans.'

The man hits a few buttons on his screen. 'One hundred and ninety dollars.'

I step back. 'That the cheapest fare?'

'Book on the web and you'll get some off.'

As if. I start to count out the cash. 'Okay. I'll go with it.'

He prints off the ticket along with a receipt.

'Do you have a list of the stops in between?' I ask.

He plays with the screen again before a printer spits out a list of towns.

'Thanks.' I scan the list, counting off the states. Arizona, New Mexico, Texas and Louisiana. 'How far is it?'

Helmut shakes his head and punches some more. 'Just under nineteen hundred miles. Most of it on the I-10.'

I sip at the last of the coffee and screw my face up at the taste. 'Last question. Will it be busy?'

This time he smiles. 'There are a few on board but if you're looking for company'—he winks as he says company—'you may be disappointed.'

The phone next to him rings and I'm dismissed.

I check out the café and load up on doughnuts, candy and Coke. There's a small stand selling travel aids next to the cafe. Inflatable headrests, non-drip cups and the like. A shiny Leatherman hangs from the top of a small carousel. I'm a Boy Scout at heart. I cough up for the tool and slip it into my pocket. I ask where the nearest liquor store is. I'm directed a few blocks away. A bottle of Jack Daniels and I'm back at the depot with ten minutes to spare before the bus departs.

I'm not sure I want to go all the way to New Orleans, but I need distance and there will be plenty of places en route to stop off if I change my mind.

It's as good a plan as I can come up with.

The bus is waiting on the last but one stand. There's no one out front of the vehicle but the back seats seem heavy with people. I flash my ticket at the driver. The rear is noisy. At a guess I would say we have entered 'little old lady' land. The chatter is loud and friendly. I count twenty women. Halfway down the bus two older men sit on their own. I choose a seat a few in front of them and flop. Then I'm bolt upright. No cup!

I jump off the bus, order another coffee I don't want from the machine, tip out the liquid, leaping back on as the driver shuts the door to pull out.

As we leave I scan for suits but it seems clear. Suddenly I feel trapped in the metal shell. This is such a dumb thing to do. How easy will it be to figure where I have gone? Why am I leaving with Lorraine still in hospital? I decide to exit my head. I mix up a drink and tip it down in one go.

What is the plan? I mix a second drink. Who are the suits? What do they want? I slug half the second drink.

What do I do next? Do I stay on the run? For how long?

I finish the drink and pour another.

CHAPTER 17

'We stop here for an hour.' The voice cuts through the fug of booze and sleep.

'Sorry?'

The driver is standing over me. 'We stop over for an hour. You can stay on board if you want, but you might want to get a coffee.'

I rub my eyes before looking out of the window. There's a six-lane highway outside and little else. The bus is sitting in a double-height concrete shell.

'Any good restaurants around?' I enquire.

The driver shakes his head. 'Depot café or nothing.'

An hour later I'm back in my seat, two coffees to the good, three doughnuts light from my bag of six. The gaggle of women is back on board. They're a little more subdued than when we left. The two older men have moved to the row behind me.

'You on your own, son?' One of the men is talking to me but I'm not in the mood for chat.

'We don't bite,' the second man joins in. I still ignore them.

'You had a nice gab with Jack last night,' says the first man. His bright blond hair is an award-winner in the bouffant category. It sits atop a suntanned face with more wrinkles than could be cleaned out with a pipe cleaner. He's wearing a cardigan, purple with 69 picked out in stitched panels. His teeth look store-bought.

'Jack?' says the second man, and points at my bag. He smells of expensive aftershave. I smell like crap. 'Jack Daniels?'

They both laugh.

'Up for sharing it?' he asks.

I shake my head.

'Long journey if you are going all the way to the Big Easy. Pays to be friends with people on a bus. You never know when you'll want company.' The second man is as bald as his friend is hirsute. He's equally as tanned and is top to toe in black—a roll top hiding his neck.

I turn away.

'Company.' The Bouffant King rolls the word around his mouth as if he's chewing hot candy floss.

'Company,' repeats the Man in Black.

I lean against the window as the bus pulls out. Thankfully they lose interest in me.

At Tucson I crash the restroom for a quick wash.

We cross into New Mexico around midday and the driver pulls over and tells us we have a half-hour stopover in Lordsburg. There's a McDonald's on the opposite corner to a gas station. I decide to risk a Big Mac.

The place is busy. The little old ladies are ahead of me and have all decided to tuck into calories. The only spare seat is in the booth next to the Bouffant King and the Man in Black. I sigh, pick up my dead cow and take a seat. Thankfully they are too engrossed in each other to bother with me.

'So who's left?' The Bouffant King is talking.

'For me, Mary, Caroline and Jenny. You?' says the Man in Black.

'Caroline, Deborah and Enid.'

'Oh you'll love Enid. Kinky if you push it.'

'Really?'

'If you persuade her. Know what I mean?'

They're looking at the women as they talk. I'm not sure I want to hear this.

'Caroline is the real money,' says the Bouffant King.

'Hard nut to crack. Hell, I've been on the case for over a year.'

'Worth it though.'

'No doubt.'

'How was Jenny?' the Man in Black stage-whispers.

'Dull as dishwater. I think I was the first man in her pantyhose for a decade. It smelt that way anyway.'

They both laugh.

'So who's next?' The Man in the Black leans out of the booth. He catches me listening. 'You looking for some old tail?'

I duck back in.

'Young man there fancies some aged pussy I think,' says the Bouffant King.

I slide out of the booth, taking my meal into the morning heat. I'm followed by two of the old ladies. They sit down next to me.

'Hi, I'm Enid and this is Tanya.'

The 'kinky' one and friend.

'I see you were talking to Bert and George,' says Enid.

'Is that the man in black and his friend?' I munch as I talk.

'That's them.'

'Can I ask what you're all doing on the bus?'

'Sure,' says Enid. 'We're off to a mystery convention in New Orleans.'

My look of confusion spurs her on.

'Mystery novels—you know, detective, crime. We go every year.'

'By bus?'

'Three of us are scared of flying. Anyway, we're all retired. We're in no hurry. What are you doing on the bus?'

'Going to see a friend.'

'You should join us. Bert and George aren't much company.'

'Not unless you pull your knickers down.' They're the first words Tanya has spoken.

'If you don't mind, ladies, I'd rather grab some sleep.'

'JD will do that to you.'

I'm not as anonymous as I thought. 'I'll take that on advice.'

'Well, any time you want a chat we'll be at the back—you can't miss us.'

They get up and head for the bus as their friends troop out to join them. Bert and George are laughing as they leave.

El Paso comes into view at just after half-past five. We need to transfer buses and there's forty minutes to kill. I avoid the Mystery Mob.

The bus leaves carrying the same passengers who've been on board since Los Angeles. The last of the hop-ons left us at El Paso. It's just the Mystery Mob, the Bouffant King, the Man in Black and me.

The light is dropping. Outside, the land has a bad case of dry brushwood acne on either side of the highway. The odd oncoming headlight breaks the monotony but, as the light dips, there's little to see.

A broken shell of a shack flies into view. A long-dead Dodge, rusting back to the earth it came from, guards the shack's front door. I check the printed itinerary that the ticket man produced. We're not far from the next stop. My Jack Daniels is burning a hole in my bag.

The laughter is like a gunshot in my ear.

'Bert, fuck off.'

Bert is laughing as Enid shouts after him. He returns to the seat behind me to sit down next to George.

'What did you say?' asks George.

'Asked if her ass was available for rent.'

They both laugh.

Bert hangs over my seat, his bouffant moving of its own accord. 'Want to split that bottle three ways? We're dry.'

'No.' Direct usually works. Only this time it doesn't.

'Too good to drink with us old fogies?'

'No. I just want a quiet drink.'

'So do we son. I'll get you a fresh bottle at the next stop.'

'No thanks.'

'We insist.'

It dawns on me that he's drunk. They both are. George adds his two cents' worth. 'We only want a drink.'

I shake my head. 'Might have had one too many already.'

'You tellin' us how much we can drink, son?' Bert has an edge to his voice.

'No. I just want a quiet time.'

George taps me on the shoulder. 'Look, all we want is a drink and we'll be off your case.' His words are loud. A mean drunk. I seem to attract them.

'Look, I'm just going to slip down to the front of the bus and leave you two alone. You can pick up a bottle at the next stop and drink till you fall over. Okay?'

George pushes Bert to one side. He exits onto the aisle. 'Look, son. You ain't going to down that bottle on your own— so just divvy up the fair way.'

I stand up. 'The bar is closed.'

George is a few inches shorter than me. I have earned-muscle on my side, but he's drunk and running on brave pills. He stands his ground. I place a hand on his shoulders. I lean forward.

He tenses. 'Get your hands off me, son.'

'Or what?'

He tries to step back. I grip him.

'Or what?' I repeat, leaning in close. I don't want trouble. But he's drunk enough to do something real stupid.

The scene has the attention of the bus now. The Mystery Mob are fixed on us and George knows he's on a loser. He might get a punch in but I can take him, and he knows it. He can back down, but his future sexual conquests are watching and his chances of bedding them are slipping away. He rocks a little from foot to foot.

Bert wades in. 'George, you old fool. Let the boy be.' He turns to the Mystery Mob. 'Now ladies, has anyone squirreled away a little drink they would care to share?'

George backs off, glad of the exit. I slide down the bus, choosing the seat behind the driver. I twist the cap on the bottle to settle down for a drink.

An hour later and the noise from the back of the bus is akin to a school kids' outing. It sounds like Bert and George have mined some drink from someone and are winding up the Mystery Mob. The driver glances in the rear-view mirror.

'Noisy for an old bunch,' I say, cup to my lips.

'Always the same,' he replies. 'Teenagers and the gray brigade—as bad as each other. I'll need to warn them though. Other passengers won't be happy.'

I am the only other passenger. 'I'm okay,' I tell him.

'Yeah, but there will be others to get on and that's when it won't be okay.'

I think there's a suggestion that I might like to go have a quiet word. I'm having none of it. I sip at my drink.

A horn blast from a rig grabs my attention. My window lights up as a truck flicks its full beam at a car riding beside us. The car lays an inch of rubber on the blacktop as it's forced to duck back and fall in at our rear.

The light revealed, just before it slid back, a black SUV. The alarm bells go off in my head. The headlight had briefly picked out a man in a suit in the passenger seat. I think he might have been looking up at me. I think it's Buzz 2.

I cross the bus, sit on the other side and wait. A few minutes later the top of the SUV glides up again—matching the bus's speed. It doesn't overtake; instead it hangs there—on the wrong side of the road. Another truck approaches. This time the SUV accelerates, pulling in front of the bus. The bus driver hits his horn, swearing at the SUV as it accelerates before slowing down fifty yards in front.

The SUV's rear window is lit up by the bus headlights—but the tint is heavy and I can only make out two shapes. My mind goes into overdrive.

I flick open the itinerary and look for the next stop. Van

Horn. I've never been there.

The SUV keeps ahead. Gaining none. Losing none. I check my watch. We're scheduled to arrive in twenty minutes.

I weigh up the options and don't like any of them. Waiting for the next stop is bottom of the list. It will be suit city. Getting off early is a poor choice. It's still scrub desert outside. I won't get far on foot. There might be a chance to get off as we enter the town and make a break for it but, for all I know, the bus stops at the edge of town. I wonder why they showed their hand early. Why not wait for the bus to pull in?

I lean forward to talk to the driver. 'Do we come off the highway for the next stop?'

The driver turns slightly to answer. 'Yes. Not long now.'

A second SUV drifts alongside. I shift back to the seat behind the driver. 'Don't leave the highway at the junction.'

The driver turns round. 'What?'

I point at the road. 'Don't stop. Keep your foot on the gas and just drive.'

CHAPTER 18

The SUV in front begins to slow down.

'Kill the internal lights and keep up the speed.' I slide to the edge of the seat to get a better view.

'What?'

I slap him hard over the back of the head. I need control. 'Lights out. Foot down.'

He reaches down. He flicks a switch and the bus descends into darkness. There's whooping from behind as the school kids think it's recess.

'What the hell do you want me to do?' The driver's shoulders are tensed up.

I yank out the Leatherman's blade, jamming it into the back of his neck. Hard. 'Just drive.'

'We should turn off soon,' he says.

'No. We just keep going.'

'Where to?'

I have no idea. I look around the driver's seat. 'Do you have a map?'

'No. GPS.' He points to the small unit sitting on the dash.

'Pass it here.'

He pulls it off the dashboard and passes it up.

The SUV is less than ten yards in front.

'Pull out and overtake,' I order.

The driver signals. Almost immediately the SUV swings to block us.

I push the blade into his skin a little more. 'Right up his ass. Get the bus up his tail.'

The driver doesn't respond. I push the blade deeper and his skin splits. A drop of blood spreads down his neck—black in the light of the instruments.

He plants his foot. The bus surges forward. For a second the SUV doesn't react; then, with only feet to spare, it accelerates.

I try to play with the GPS, but I can't work it with one hand holding the rail and the other on the knife.

'I'm going to remove the knife. If you piss me off, I'll stick it in your ear and slice open your eardrum.'

The GPS is touch-screen. I flick around the area we're travelling through. I whizz by something and back it up. A small airport. It's marked up as Culberson County Airport—a three-runway triangular set-up. One of thousands across the country. It's less than a mile beyond the town, three-quarters of a mile from the highway at its nearest point.

We pass the exit for Van Horn as two SUVs speed along the on-ramp to join us. We are now four to one.

The GPS shows a road running parallel to us, the Old Bankhead Highway. It runs out just beyond the airport with the turnoff leading to it just ahead.

'Slow down. Right down,' I say.

The driver obeys. Two of the SUVs pull up beside us. A window winds down on the nearest one. Buzz 2 waves at the driver to pull over.

'Ignore him.' My heart rate racks up as I weigh up my options. The speed at which the two new SUVs joined in suggests they have the town loaded up. They still want me bad.

My head starts to thump but I shake it to try and concentrate on what I need to do.

A shout goes up from behind. The Mystery Mob seem to be having more fun.

Then my head explodes. I want to curl up, but I need to keep my mind on the job at hand.

A shout from behind. 'What the…?' Then a scream. A man's scream.

'Jesus, what are you fucking doing?' Bert is shouting.

The driver turns round.

'Keep your eyes on the road,' I yell. My head is splitting down the middle.

'Fuck.' The word hammers down the length of the bus. 'Get off me you stupid cow.'

A muffled *thwump* and another scream rises from the back of the bus.

One of the new SUVs tries to cut in front of us, forcing the driver to brake. I lean forward, planting my hand on his foot. I push down. The bus leaps forward, catching the SUV on the inside rear. The car flips to the left. The other SUV has to stand on the brakes to prevent ploughing into it. They both vanish from view, leaving a lone escort out front.

I clip the driver's head. 'I told you not to stop.'

Another scream from behind. 'How do you like a little persuasion? A little kinky, eh?' Enid's voice is strong. 'He talks dirty. I don't like it when he talks dirty. I tell you what, Tanya, I've got scissors in my bag. Be a good girl and get them for me.'

What the hell is going on back there? I turn round but there's not enough light to see by. My headache is starting to blind me.

'No. Noooooo!' The scream from behind is desperate.

'There, got it,' says Enid.

'It's so gooey,' says Tanya.

George shouts out. I can't be sure what is going down but I can guess.

'You shut up. You're next,' cries Enid.

'I got his cell and he has KY in a tube. Maybe George would like to see if it fits,' says Tanya.

I get back to the job in hand. I suspect that Bert and George are on the receiving end of a bad night but I can't cope with the headache, the suits and the nonsense on the bus.

I tap the driver on the shoulder. 'I want you to take the next turn-off. Don't indicate; wait until the last minute. I'll tell you when. Do you understand?'

The driver nods as another SUV pulls up beside us. The tinted window is down. This time there's a gun pointing at the bus. The driver sees it. He eases off the gas. I reach down, pushing his foot again. 'They're not going to shoot with a bus full of passengers. But they will shoot if we stop. It's up to you.'

The driver stares ahead.

The junction emerges in the headlights of the SUV. It's unmarked.

'Now wait until you are on the junction—then hard left. Once you're round give it as much gas as you can.'

The white lines are no longer a blur as the driver eases off for the turn. Each line looks like a stepping stone over a black sea. The SUV passes the junction. The bus looks like it will follow suit.

'Now,' I shout.

The driver pulls hard down on the wheel and we swing across the oncoming highway. I'm flung hard against the chair. I look back at the road. The following SUVs are caught out and miss the turn.

We are slewing to a halt. I smack the driver's head. 'Foot down.'

The road we are on is no more than a dirt track. Seconds later we're bouncing across a set of railway lines. There's still commotion from behind and, as we leap the lines, I step out onto the aisle to try and look back.

My foot slips and I fall onto the chair. I try to stand up. I slip again. I put my hand on the floor. It comes up wet, sticky...and warm.

What the hell?

I lift my hand into the light cast by the instruments in front of the driver. I realize that Bert and George are having a very, very bad night.

Car lights appear in the giant wing mirrors of the bus. They gain at speed, but the road is too narrow for the SUVs to get past and the terrain either side is lethal.

I haul myself back onto my seat. 'Another half mile and then take another left. There should be a road.'

The driver is hunched in concentration. He's driving too fast on a road that's not designed for the behemoth he's trying to control. Add to that the chasing cars, the nonsense going on in the rear, my knife, and his shoulders are rods of iron under his jacket.

One of the SUVs pulls out into the desert in an attempt to overtake. I reach out, grab the steering wheel and pull it towards the vehicle. The bus lurches off the road. The driver yells, pulling the wheel back. I hear a crunch and headlights spin away to our left.

I strain to see ahead. I haven't got this all figured out but action is better than inaction. The road twists and turns. Every so often a pair of white eyes flick out of the dark as the headlights hit the back of some nocturnal beast's eye sockets.

We crest a small rise. There's no sign of the road promised by the GPS. I play with the machine. 'Where the hell is the road?'

'What road?' the driver responds.

'It says on the map there's a road—the Old Bankhead Highway.'

'It's nothing but a dirt track. Gone long ago.'

'How would you know?'

'I live nearby.'

Shit.

Somebody grabs my leg and I leap. Twisting round I bring my fist down on an arm holding the material of my pants. Bert looks up at me. He tries to talk but it's muffled. His tongue is gone. I want to lash out. Push him away. Get him the fuck out of my face. His bouffant hair is a matt of blood. The 69 cardigan is ripped and torn. His mouth opens. A dark hole. 'Mmmphhh.' Jesus.

I step back. We hit a large pothole, flipping Bert over. His pants are gone, as is his manhood. No tongue—no dick. There is a scream from behind. George is receiving the attention of the

Mystery Mob. I push Bert's arm away. The Mystery Mob are getting their revenge big time and I'm sure I'm the catalyst.

My head is pounding, a steam hammer, making it hard to think. My skull is in a vice, as if someone is turning it tighter notch by notch. The bus staggers to the left. I'm thrown sideways. I grab the rail to pull myself upright. The driver is staring at Bert. I slap him on the face. 'The road. Look at the fucking road.'

He turns back but we're off the track. The bus bounces out across the desert floor. Then, suddenly, another dirt track flashes into view at right angles to the way we're travelling.

'That must be it. Get on it!' The driver's shoulder gets a thump as I say this.

The driver hauls the wheel. If this is the Old Bankhead Highway then the GPS is having a laugh. The driver was right. This is no better than the road we were on.

My head is fit to split. I can feel bile rising in my throat. 'Open the door.'

The driver reaches down, flicks a lever and the doors slide apart. A light above the entrance flicks on. I take my knife, driving it into the light to kill it.

Mistake.

The driver spots the tiny blade.

'I can still kill you with it.' I need to shout over the noise coming through the doors. 'Listen carefully. Those guys out there are not your friends. If you stop here, they'll take you out with me. Do you understand? They will kill you. You need to get back to town. This road runs back into Van Horn. Drive to the depot. Make sure there are plenty of people around before you stop. If you don't, they WILL kill you. Do you understand?'

He nods.

'Good. What's in the bag?'

There's a sports bag sitting in the well next to him. He glances down at it. 'A change of clothes and my snack.'

'I'm taking it.' I reach down and lift the bag. Heavier than it looks. 'Swing right and slow right down. I'm jumping. As soon as I'm clear, get back on the road. With luck they'll follow you and not notice I'm gone.'

A last scream from behind and I turn. It's too dark to see but I don't fancy George's chances. Bert is lying at my feet. He isn't moving. I turn back to the driver.

'Do you know if there's a hospital in Van Horn?'

He nods.

'Change of plan. Go there instead of the depot.' It's the best I can do for Bert and George. 'Now—swing off.'

The driver hauls us out into the desert, slowing down. I jump down the steps. The ground is rushing by. I throw out the bag. In my head I pull up the training manual for landing after a parachute jump, and leap. As I do, the world drops blue and the headache vanishes.

I hit the dirt and roll. The rear of the bus flashes by. I hear the driver gun the engine. I lie flat. The SUVs scream by feet from my head. I count to ten and look up. Four sets of tail-lights are chasing the bus. The road is keeping them back but they are swinging left and right trying to find a way past.

The blue world brings my own personal night vision. It could be midday. I search for the driver's bag and pick it up, cross the dirt track before heading in the direction of the airport.

I look back. The bus is still rolling—good news. The longer it keeps moving the more distance I can gain.

I start to jog and the bag clinks. I stop and unzip it. A fresh shirt and pants are rolled up on top along with a plastic lunch box. Beneath there are bottles. I pull one out. Wild Turkey bourbon. It has five more brothers to keep it company. Not my favourite brand but good stuff. Not the sort of luggage that inspires me with confidence in a driver though.

I break back into a jog.

I'm amazed to see animals dotted around. A coyote stands not ten yards from me. Watching. Its eyes follow me. I smile at it. It's so clear I could draw it.

I chink my way down to a fast walk, flicking my head to check that the SUVs aren't on their way back.

The noise of the wild has replaced the noise of engines; the vehicles are out of sight. My breath is ragged. It occurs to me that this place isn't on sea level. I'm grabbing for air. Mexico lies not far behind me. I wonder if I would be safer trying for a foreign country.

I stumble onto concrete and realize that I'm standing on one of the airport's runways. In the middle distance a small group of buildings are huddled together with some planes parked on the apron. A taxi-way leads to the planes. Beyond them another clump of buildings squat in the blue light.

The place looks deserted but that would be normal—most of these local airports are dawn-to-dusk affairs. I cut across the runway and begin to walk up the taxi-way, listening for any signs of life in front or behind me.

The main buildings are shut tight, the two planes sitting on the taxi-way the only sign that the place is in use. As I circle the buildings the sound of a radio falls from the light breeze.

I freeze.

Baseball. I can't hear the words but the cadence and the rhythm suggests commentators going through a game. A few steps and I've located the source. Behind the buildings an RV is parked up. The window is all but blacked out but a slip of light is escaping from the corner. I walk round the vehicle. Two men are talking inside. The conversation seems to revolve around planes.

A car engine hums in the distance. Probably traffic on the highway but the suits could have it figured by now. The blue world is fading and darkness is returning. I hit the door with my fist.

It opens to reveal a bald man with a beer gut hidden beneath a faded Texas Rangers sweat. 'What?'

Nice greeting. Beer fumes mixed with cigarette smoke rush into the night. I back off a step as I gag on the cloud. 'My car packed in a few miles back. Do you have a phone?'

'Who is it?' comes a shout from within.

'His car broke down.' Baldy turns to look into the RV as he says this.

'Does he have any booze on him?' the voice comes back.

Baldy looks at me. 'Do you have any booze on you?'

I step forward a little. 'I might.'

'He says he might.'

The voice inside warms up. 'Then invite him in. I'm as dry as a buzzard's ring-piece.'

Baldy steps back, beckoning me to go in. I step up.

The RV is a tip. A dozen Miller Lite cans are spread on the floor. Three empty pizza boxes lie on the table. Ash lies thick on the carpet. My host sweeps a pile of porn to the floor to let me sit down.

'So, do you have booze?' The other man is thin. He has wisps of long hair. The last vestiges clinging to his liver-spotted pate. He burps and points to the can in his hand. 'Last one.'

'Either of you a pilot?' I ask.

'I am.' Baldy drops to a chair as he talks.

'So, is one of the planes yours?'

'The Skycatcher.'

'Not all his,' says the thin one. 'Part share.'

'Still mine and less than six months old.' Baldy rubs his belly and smiles.

'How many does she seat?' I ask.

'Two. Pilot and passenger. Why? You looking for some lessons?'

'No, a ride.'

'Where?'

'Just a ride.'

'Come back tomorrow.'

'No, tonight!'

They both laugh.

'No way, San Jose,' says Baldy. 'It's dark and, in case you haven't noticed, we've been on the juice.'

The thin man stands up. Unsteady. 'Federal Aviation Regulation 91.17 prohibits pilots from flying aircraft with an alcohol level of 0.04% or more, and/or within eight hours of consuming alcohol. Isn't that right?'

Baldy nods as the thin man falls back to the seat.

I think I can hear engines. Too loud to be from the highway. I reach into the driver's sports bag and pull out a bottle of Wild Turkey. 'Would this change your mind?'

The thin one's eyes light up. He reaches over to grab the bottle.

I pull it away. 'A ride first. Ten minutes. No more.'

'Ain't going to happen,' says Baldy.

I pull a second bottle out.

'Cornbread,' says the thin one. 'Matt, just give him the once round. Ain't no one going to know.'

Matt eyes the bottle. 'Chip, it's not worth it.' I dip my hand in once more and pull out a third. 'Ten minutes,' I say.

Engines.

Matt's eyes are fixed on the booze.

'Come on, Matt. Up and down for three bottles. How hard can it be?'

Matt rubs his gut again. 'Okay, but no crap. Up and down.'

'You're the pilot,' I say.

I stand up, wondering how bad your drink problem must be to agree to fly a stranger at night.

'Leave the booze here,' says the thin one.

I throw one to him.

Matt grabs one of the others and leads the way out of the RV. I drop the third bottle on a chair as I leave.

We circle the buildings. Matt is swaying as if the earth is trying to shake him loose. He's slugging hard on the Wild Turkey. We reach the aircraft. Matt points to the passenger door. 'Jump in and strap up.'

Louder engines.

Matt walks round the aircraft and gets in the other side. 'Up and down.'

116

I smile. 'Up and down.'

He starts to play with the plane's controls. I hear the note of a gear change. The cars are close. Matt fires up the prop.

To my left I can see lights bouncing towards us. Matt is flipping and checking. I want to gun the throttle for him. He flips some more, then the plane jerks forward. I hope he doesn't notice the headlights. My luck holds as he swings the nose of the plane away from the building and the advancing cars.

We taxi back to where I entered the airport, at the junction of the two runways. One runs parallel with the taxi-way and the other tracks at forty-five degrees. Both start at the end of the taxi-way. If Matt takes the parallel runway, he can't fail to see the cars.

We wheel left and he advances onto the further-away strip. He looks at me. I pray the buildings hide the cars. He pushes the throttle and we zip forward.

It's clear that the silence from Matt, since we got in the plane, is down to sheer concentration. I wonder again at how much he wants booze that he'll risk a flight rather than the drive to the liquor store.

A double bounce and we're airborne. Airtime. I look over my shoulder and see four cars converging on the airport.

'Where to?' Matt's first words since we started up.

I point away from the airport, keeping the tail towards the brewing trouble.

'So are we good?' Matt starts to bank the plane. 'Ten and down.'

'We can't go back to the airport.'

'What?'

'You'll be grounded.'

'Who by?'

'FBI.'

The plane takes on a swinging motion as he tries to look at me and steer at the same time. 'FBI?'

'Back at the airport. Lots of them. Have a look.'

He nudges the plane round a few degrees.

The airport is lit by a collection of car lights. We're far enough away for them to be a single burning flame on the ground.

Matt straightens the plane. 'You a wanted man?'

'Sort of.'

'Bad deal.'

'Go back and your license is history.'

He buries the bad news in another slug of bourbon. 'Bad deal. Bad deal.'

'How far can we fly?'

'A few hundred miles—the tanks aren't full.'

'Is there anywhere you can set down?'

'Maybe.'

'You can park the plane, spend the night and fly back tomorrow.'

'And what do I say when they come asking about you?'

'Whatever you want. Just leave out the bit about the booze and your willing participation. You took me up because I threatened you. I forced you to land. You didn't want to take off again in the dark. You waited until the morning before flying back.'

'Won't wash. Chip will have blabbed. He has a mouth like a motor about to throw a rod.'

'Blank it. Let him tell his story and you say when we got outside the RV you were going to change your mind and I got heavy. Puts you in the clear.'

'And the fact I have one hundred per cent proof running in my veins?'

'Quit drinking now and don't go back until you're sober.'

His eyes are darting from me to the windshield. I think the story works and I think he thinks it works.

He dips the plane and we head for the ground.

'What are you doing?'

'Getting below radar. There is a plateau up ahead. If we hug it they won't be able to pick us up.'

I'm about to go low-level flying with a drunk.

CHAPTER 19

The desert is a smear, picked out by the moon hanging in a clear sky. We top a hundred knots. Close to the plane's maximum. We're so low we're in danger of clipping the cacti. For a while the highway is company but Matt waits until it's clear of cars before crossing it and swinging south.

'Where are we going?' I try to keep my eyes from the hypnotic conveyor belt unfolding beneath us.

'Fort Davis.'

'Where?'

'Middle of nowhere. It's a ways from the highway but there are roads leading south to the border or you can try to make the coast at Corpus Christi.'

'How far is it from Van Horn?'

'As the crow flies maybe fifty miles. Sorry I'm not going any further.'

'It'll do. Do you have a map?'

'In the back.'

I reach over and pull out a large map. Fort Davis isn't the best choice for someone on the run but it'll give me a head start. I stuff the map into the holdall. 'Where are you going to land?'

'There's a disused landing strip to the south of the town. I use it when I spray crops. There's an old barn at one end. It has a bunk. There's no lights so it'll be tricky but it's far enough from town that no one will hear us landing. After that you're on your own.'

119

Matt nudges the plane a few degrees further east. We suddenly twist in the air. He shakes his head—trying to clear the bourbon. I can see the lights of the town to the right, we're circling to avoid the built-up area.

Matt's head starts to do a nodding dog. I thought he was just drunk. I now think he's wasted. We're flying on Matt's personal version of autopilot.

The plane skirts the town. Matt dips us a few more feet and I grip the door handle. The ground is a smudge.

'Could be rough,' Matt says. 'Hold on.'

He pushes us down a little more. I can't see anything but wasteland. Then we zip over a fence and there's a rough strip of ground. The wheels hit the dirt.

I might know shit about planes but we seem to be going way too fast. We rise back into the air before bouncing down again. A barn rises from the dark as we take to the night air once more—there's no way that we are going to stop in time.

Matt is fighting the plane. His reactions are slow. The barn too close. I lift my hands to my face. The plane bounces, tries to lift once more and we plough into the building.

The world is alive with noise as the prop rips through the barn's wooden door. The engine roars, dies, and the plane continues to career forward. The nose dips, burying itself in the ground. The planet flips forward—slamming us to a halt. Windshield fills my face. The seat belt bites. Matt shouts.

Outside the barn is a whirlwind of dust, wood and shredded hay. It spins a cloud around everything as the night tries to reclaim some calm.

Matt is still shouting. My gut tells me to get out of the plane. I fumble with my belt, push at the door and fall to the ground. Staggering away from the wreck, I climb over the shattered door to squeeze out into the field beyond. I walk a few yards before falling to the deck.

To my surprise the sports bag is in my left hand.

Matt follows a few seconds later. 'This will take some explaining,' he coughs.

A mild understatement.

'Somebody will have heard that,' I say.

'Don't count on it. We're a good few miles from civilization.'

He's wrong. A pair of headlights are sliding across the field toward us. I jump up. 'I need to go.'

It's hard to believe that the suits would be here but I can't risk it. I pat Matt on the head and sprint for the rear of the barn. If I'm not turned around, the town is a couple of miles along the road the car has just left.

I watch the vehicle bump across the field. It pulls up beside Matt. I cross the road and start to walk against any oncoming traffic. Ten minutes later the car flies by. Matt's face in the window. He looks less than happy. I pray he's not on the way to the police.

No other vehicles pass as I reach the edge of town. When I hit a crossroads voices attract my attention. I walk to the far side of the intersection, approaching a low-roofed, clapperboard house.

A large truck is sitting in front of the garage, rear door open, headlights on. A man walks into view, his arms full of what looks like wood. He's large. Bulked up. A pair of dungarees and heavy boots catch in the light. He jumps into the truck's rear and re-emerges empty handed.

As he walks out of view I jog up the driveway to look into the back. In the dark it's impossible to see what the man is loading but there's a heavy smell of freshly cut timber coupled with the scent of wood stain. I duck out of sight as the man approaches again.

'Graham, you've left one.' A woman's voice, soft.

'I know. I'm putting it in the front. I promised Muzzle that I would drop it off on the way.'

More stuff is loaded before he retreats.

'Long way, honey,' she says.

Graham sighs. 'I know, but the buyer has four people lined up. I can move all of this in one trip. It will get us through winter easily.'

'But Tampa's so far.'

'No choice.'

'Where are you going to stop on the way?'

'Probably Mobile. Depends how I'm doing.'

'I'll miss you.'

'I'll be back before the party.'

I jump into the back of the truck before he reappears.

It's full of wooden boxes, all securely fixed to the floor. I crawl across them before hunkering down at the back. In daylight I would be spotted easily but in the dark you would need to be standing on me to know I was there. Graham pulls down the shutter. A minute later the engine fires up.

Mobile sounds as good a destination as any. The suits would have to be psychic to know I had jumped in the back of a truck heading that way. Unless of course they thought me important enough to spring road blocks across the south of the country. But that's all a bit too 'most wanted' for me.

I crawl forward to sit down in the space between the rear door and the last of the boxes. Mobile has to be a good eighteen-hour drive.

We've hardly picked up speed when the truck turns sharp right, stops and the engine dies. I crawl away from the door but it stays closed. The engine fires up again. I figure Graham has just delivered Muzzle his package.

I crawl back to my seat. Graham picks up the pace. I'm in for a few hours of rock 'n' roll.

Out of curiosity I reach into the nearest box, root around and pull out a wooden carving.

It's about a foot long, a few inches wide and feels like the wing of a plane. I run my hands along the surface. Smooth and curved. One side swoops in, while the reverse sweeps out, giving the wing a fat belly. A small rod protrudes from the bottom. I scrabble around in the box and find a clutch of bases, each with a hole in the middle. I put two and two together and slot the rod home.

The carving is a superb tactile experience. Along the edges it's carved in small waves and the whole item rotates twenty degrees or so from top to bottom. It's too dark to see it properly but I find myself turning and stroking the object.

I lie my head against the truck wall, rubbing the carving, and try to sleep.

CHAPTER 20

I wake to the sound of the engine winding down as the gentle deceleration of the brakes being applied kicks in. Check my watch. Midday. I've been out for eight hours. I scramble towards the cab, away from the door.

We rumble to a stop. I wait for the door to open. Nothing happens. I wait a further five minutes before crawling back over the boxes.

A little light creeps through the seal on the doors but I have no idea where I am. I do some math. Eight hours at sixty would put us almost five hundred miles west. San Antonio or maybe Houston.

I need a whizz and I don't fancy relieving myself in the truck. The thought of sloshing around in my own urine lacks appeal.

Reaching out, I pull on the handle of the truck door and the catch gives. The door starts to move up. I hold it an inch from its home. A breeze blows in. Bathing my face. I open the door a little further, roll under and drop to the ground. As I stand I find myself facing a brick wall. Reaching back, I grab the sports bag, push the door down and twist the handle to lock it. The sports bag is lumped onto my shoulder as I walk round the truck.

The skyline of Houston dominates the scene. My math was spot on. The driver has pulled into a truck stop a few miles short of the city. Semis and trucks are spread around like discarded toys in a kid's bedroom. A low-slung building with plate glass ground-to-ceiling windows holds a diner. To the right there are signs for the washrooms. I choose the latter and a few seconds later I'm emptying my bladder.

I pop the sports bag on the toilet lid and rifle through it. Wash kit, fresh white shirt, boxers, jeans, socks, a lightweight blue rain-jacket and a baseball cap. I pull them all out. The bus driver matches me in height but not in girth. There are pay-as-you-go showers at the back of the washroom. I repack the bag, pay the attendant, grab a towel and scrub myself raw.

The driver's wash kit is small but on the money. Toothpaste, toothbrush, mouthwash, deodorant, aftershave, mini shaver—the works. I dry myself before putting on the driver's clothes, wincing a little at using someone else's boxers.

A shave and a splash later and, with the help of my belt pulling the oversized jeans tight, I'm feeling a little more human. I check my reflection—if the suits have a description of me it isn't in a white shirt, jeans and blue jacket. I ram the baseball cap on.

I'm no longer the me that walked into the washroom.

Now for some food.

The diner is busy. I spot Graham in the corner tucking into some serious cholesterol. I order up coffee and a meatball sub, paying with my dwindling money supply. A slip of paper falls from between two tens, drifting to the floor. I pick it up.

'*2234 Irondale Lane, Fairway Oaks, Hudson. Key in the pelican's beak.*'

It's written in Charlie's scrawl. I take my food to a window seat and check that there are no black SUVs before eating. I study the piece of paper. The address is alien.

The first bite of the meatballs floods my mouth with taste. Rich and thick. Just the way mother would have done them. I slug some coffee, letting the caffeine get to work.

I finger the index on the pilot's map.

The only Hudson I can find is about forty miles north of St Petersburg on the Gulf coast. If Graham is Tampa-bound, he has to skirt the town. If he takes US 19 he'll almost pass through it. If he opts for the freeway, he'll pass about five miles east of it.

Maybe my luck is changing.

I weigh up the piece of paper. If the suits have decided to ride Charlie, he might have given up the address. It's no mistake it's bundled in the cash though. Charlie's giving me somewhere to hide out.

The meatballs give way to sweet onion and I wonder if the suits will have leaned on Charlie. A few questions, sure, but would they get heavy? Maybe. If so, Hudson is a no-go. But I need a destination and Charlie's address is the only place I have at the moment.

I swallow the last of the sub, then drain the coffee. Graham is reading *USA Today*. The waitress is refilling his coffee. My lift seems in no hurry to get back onto the road.

A small shop sits at the entrance to the diner. I go inside to stock up on chips, Coke and a large bottle of water. It'll get warm in the truck. I need something to drink and something to piss in if we're in for a long drive. An inflatable neck rest, a blowup cushion, a packet of Lifesavers and I'm set.

The Houston sun is on bake mode. I've no desire to cook in the rear of the truck before I have to. A coffee refill sounds good. Graham has yet to pay for his food.

Outside, the drivers are playing Tetris with their vehicles in the parking lot. My eyes keep a lookout for SUVs or Regals. More than once a black car catches my eye, but when Graham stretches and pays the bill there's still no sign of the suits.

I'm in the back of the truck and crouching at the rear before he has left the building.

As the engine fires up I blow up the cushion and neck rest. I have a thought. I clamber to the back and, as we start to move, empty the sculptures from one of the boxes into the others. Once it's clear of wood I get in. I'm fairly sure that I can't be seen from the door if someone looks in. It's too cramped to stay in for long but it's a better hiding place than crouching at the back.

I crawl forward and lie down, letting the rocking movement play over me.

* * *

Bang…

My head hits the side of one of the boxes and I'm awake. Despite myself, I've been out for the count again. We've either hit something or come close. The truck has stopped moving. I sit up to check my watch. The luminous dial tells me it's gone four.

The heat is intense. I crawl to the back and get into my box. Once settled, I pop a Coke, downing it in three gulps.

The sound of a siren cuts in.

The police.

My heart lurches into the starting blocks. I try and bury myself deeper in the box. I can hear talking before the door rattles up and light floods in.

'See,' says Graham. 'Wooden carvings.'

The vehicle rocks as he climbs into the truck. I hear him root around in one of the boxes.

'Okay, sir,' says a voice used to giving orders. 'Do you mind if I take a look?'

'Be my guest.'

The truck moves as another body gets on board.

'Look, officer,' Graham adds, 'I just lost concentration and slipped onto the meridian. No big deal. There's no damage.'

'Could you jump out, sir?'

The truck moves again.

There are six rows of boxes in the truck, from back to front. I hear the police officer dig into a box followed by the click of wood on wood. Then the truck rocks and I realize that he's crawling over the boxes to get at the ones in the back. Something has wound up his radar.

He stops to check a few more boxes before crawling a little nearer. I can smell stale sweat and long-since applied antiperspirant. His breathing is labored. I imagine a gut hanging out over the police-issue gun belt.

'Fuck.' The word spits out as the truck rocks again. It sounds like he's fallen into one of the boxes. He's onto the last but one row. I know what he's after. If the driver is hiding anything it'll be at the back.

I wait for a face to appear over the lip. I grab at my breath, holding it tight, burying my head in my lap. But that won't prevent me from being seen. I tense my legs. If he appears I have one choice. Up and away. I just hope I can take him by surprise.

More rooting and he's in the box next to mine. My muscles are starting to ache with the tension, ready to leap. My hands get ready to grab him. Click. He drops one of the carvings back into the box.

'Anything?' A new voice.

'No.' The police officer's voice is so close that I jump a little.

'We have a call,' says the new voice. 'A 10-67 on Starling Street. We're the nearest.'

'Okay. Coming.'

I let go of the breath as the police officer moves back to the door. There's some chat, then the door slides down. A few more minutes and the truck starts to move again. We bump and grind to exit the meridian before smoothing out as the road takes over. I climb from the box. My back clicks. Bones find other bones to play with. Once back at the door, I place the cushion at my head.

I try to settle down again. There will be no sleep this time.

CHAPTER 21

The dim light from the gap in the door is gone as day drops to dusk. The driver is on a mission. No stops, foot down. He's smooth as well. No sudden turns and since the incident with the meridian we are, if anything, moving faster. I had expected him to pull in after the bump with the grass but he's on his second wind.

The truck slows. We swing to the right, tumble over something rough and come to a halt. I crawl into my box. Nothing. I crawl back, flipping the door handle. The air outside floods in. My sweat dries in the coolness.

A Holiday Inn Express sign lights up the parking lot around me. I jump out and spot Graham at the reception desk, checking in. One of the comfy beds inside could be mine too. But I've no idea when he's likely to set out, and rides to Hudson could be thin on the ground.

I really don't fancy spending a night in the truck though. An hour slips by before I approach the check-in desk.

The sign over the door informs me that I'm in, or near, Mobile. Graham's not hanging around. A young lad, maybe a couple of years past the peak of his acne, is manning the desk. He's neat in the company uniform but his hair is a mess or, more likely, it's his way of rebelling against the corporate world.

He looks up as I approach. 'Can I help you, sir?'

'Sure can. A friend of mine checked in an hour ago. He's driving the small truck.' I point as I say this. 'I've to meet him in the morning but I don't want to disturb him tonight. Will you be on in the morning?'

The change of direction with the last bit of the question throws him a little. He nods. 'Eh. Yes.'

'Good. I'd like to check in but I'd also like a wake-up call when my friend is ready to leave. Would that be possible?'

'What is your friend's name?'

Good question.

'Graham.'

'Graham what?'

Good question. I don't answer. 'Do you have a room?'

He checks with the computer and it confirms what is obvious from the lack of cars outside

'Yes, sir. Will that be one night?'

I nod.

The phone next to him rings and he picks it up. 'Certainly, Mr Laidlaw. 7.00am and Mr Laidlaw, I have a friend of yours here...'

I violently shake my head as he says this. He looks confused as hell. 'Eh...Sorry, Mr Laidlaw, my mistake. 7.00am. Have a good night.'

He replaces the phone.

I lean forward. Trying to make it look friendly. 'It's a bit complicated but I don't want to see him right now.'

He nods. 'Do you still want me to call you when Mr Laidlaw checks out?'

'You know what, just leave it. I'll phone him in the morning.'

The young man finishes checking me in and doesn't blink when I take the cash option for paying.

Once in my room I strip, placing the bus driver's clothes on a hanger. I run the faucet to hot, fill the basin with water and take out my own boxers to give them a wash. I do the same for my socks. I throw in the shirt for good measure.

Once washed I wring them out as best I can before hanging them over the shower rail. Change my mind and hang them over the TV to take a shower. Change my mind and fill the tub for a bath. I make myself a coffee. Change my mind. I slip on my trousers and old shirt. Skipping to the lobby I empty the vending machine of three Cokes. Return to the room, strip and slip into the tub with a glass, a bottle of Wild Turkey sitting on the floor next to me—cola cans at the ready.

The tub is a touch too small for me to spread out in but it's luxury compared to the back of the truck. As the hot water works its magic on the outside of my body some Wild Turkey does the trick inside. I'm hungry but, despite the sleep I have squeezed in today, I'm too tired to get dressed and hunt down food. Breakfast will have to be a big one.

The constant roar of traffic makes me wish I had flipped on the radio but now that I'm up to my chest in water I'm not for moving.

It dawns on me that I don't know where I am. It also dawns on me that no one else knows either. Of course the smartass suits may have me all figured by now. SUVs rushing to the scene. Plastic cuffs at the ready. Waiting outside the door as I lie in the tub. Metal battering ram at the ready or, to be less dramatic, a master key from the receptionist. Six of them—me dragged naked into the parking lot and back to Lendl.

I hear a bang from the corridor. The water chills around me. I strain to catch another sound. A man and a woman laughing. I try to relax. How the hell could the suits know I'm here?

But the relaxed mood is gone. I climb from the tub and towel down. The bed is inviting but I do the good boy thing and brush my teeth first, only to undermine the action by pouring another drink. One more and I'll call it quits. I don't want to miss my ride in the morning.

I prop up a few pillows, lie down and wonder how Lorraine is. I want to call but can't figure a way to do it without giving away my location.

Not for the first time I'm left wondering at the lack of people I can turn to. LA is a desert as far as friends go. My old army colleagues are few and thin on the pond. My mom and dad are long since gone. My brother could be on the Moon for all I know. I laugh. He really could be on the Moon. He works for NASA—a trained astronaut. Home boy made good—unlike me.

I let my head wander over recent events.

The truth is something I don't want to face. Am I a catalyst freak of nature? An emotion engine driving people to commit acts of random violence? Or could it all still be a wave of coincidences. An unprecedented set of episodes. Unrelated. Unconnected. A mathematician's statistical nightmare.

The last of the Wild Turkey slides down my throat. I pick up the phone and put in for an alarm call to the receptionist for 6.00am.

Perspective is difficult when you have no one to talk to. My head has no fresh place to go. It drags up the same old, same old. Playing it out in a disjointed order. Lendl. Who is he? Why is he? The deaths. The alley in Iraq. The plane. The 'go for it' stewardess. The underground office. The sheer mass of people trying to maim and wound. The Mystery Mob. The fate of the Bouffant King and his friend.

How many days since Iraq? Four? Five? A lifetime of events for anyone. Yet it's not going to stop soon. How can it if I'm the architect of my own downfall?

I shuffle the pillow, willing sleep.

My head is ready for sleep but my body isn't. I scramble around the bed like a lovesick spider. I move my drying clothes, flick on the TV and find CNN, expecting to see my face above a caption telling the nation: *Do not approach this man. He's dangerous. If you see him inform the police immediately.*

The top-of-the-hour headlines slide into view. As usual the world is in a shit state. I wonder when it wasn't a turkey shoot. I kill the TV, get up and pull back the drapes. The parking lot sits beyond my window. I can see the truck from here. Beyond it a strip of badly rutted road leads to the highway. A car pulls in, U-turns and exits. A run of trees blocks out any other view.

I'm pulling the drapes shut when I catch sight of movement. Two men pass under the Holiday Inn Express ad sign, both dressed head to foot in black. They walk to the front of Graham's truck. They're too far away for me to make out much detail but both look short of six feet and skinny with it. One of them flips at the handle of the truck. His friend tries the other door, before they wander back to the hood. A chat and they're off to the rear.

Shit.

It never rains but…I can't let them do the truck over. My little ruse with the receptionist is stacking up to be a bad idea. I see what's coming. The two thieves raid the back of the truck. The next morning my driver discovers the break-in. The police are called. They interview the receptionist and I appear on the police note pad. The police ask after me. I'm gone. On the run. They have a description and I'm wanted. If the suits are worth their salt, then I'll pop up on a screen somewhere and they'll know where I am.

Strike that. Scenario two. The two thieves raid the back of the truck. The next morning the driver doesn't do a check. Somewhere between here and Tampa he checks the load. He calls the police, mentions his stop in Mobile. A phone call and I'm there again. The suits close in and know I am somewhere around.

Scenario three. Same as scenario two but my driver doesn't check until he reaches his destination. I'm history as a stowaway but he calls the police, mentions Mobile and there I am once more. The suits close in and know I'm somewhere between Mobile and Tampa.

Whichever way, the truck getting done over is not going to help me stay on the run. How difficult can it be to just vanish? Don't thousands of people do it every year? Why the hell is this so hard?

Because there isn't some black ops agency tracking those people down!

I flick off the light, throw on my pants and my old shirt. I'm pulling on my shoes as I return to keep a watch on the parking lot.

They're gone. I breathe a sigh of relief, but swallow again when I see the truck rock. They're inside. Why the hell didn't the driver lock it? Stupid question. I was the one who left it open.

I grab the room keycard. I could use the fire escape but it will be alarmed. The receptionist looks up as I walk out. I realize that I'm wearing the same shirt I left LA in.

Too late to do anything about it.

I pull up a tuneless whistle, slapping my feet on the wet concrete as I walk towards the truck. Trying to scare them off. The tail door rattles down as I approach. The front of the truck is bathed in light but the rear is in shade. I slide along the vehicle. No whistling now. No slapping. Either they're gone or they're still inside.

Rain starts to fall. Light drizzle works down my neck collar. I'm halfway along the side when the truck moves again. Enough to suggest that at least one of them is still inside. Basic training one-o-one would be to riddle the truck with bullets and then go in.

Get real.

I scan the bush behind the truck for any sign of movement. Nothing. I back off, circle round to the other side and then back to the front.

Dropping to my knees I crawl under the truck—aiming for the rear. A large puddle has formed in a dip halfway down. I have no choice but to crawl through it. My pants soak up the water, followed by my boxers, my shirt, my shoes and my socks. I grab at my belt, tightening it a notch to stop the water-heavy pants from paying a visit to my ankles. I grind out the next few feet, keeping my eyes fixed on the gap between the truck rear and the ground. A wet sponge belly-flopping forward.

I stop short of the tailgate.

Time to wait.

Raindrops bounce a few inches in front of my nose. The night is warm but the rain is cool. Heat starts to seep from me. It's uncomfortable but hardly life-threatening. The truck vibrates as a scrape echoes down through the drive-shaft above my head.

The latch is being turned.

I tense, hearing the roller lift a few inches. There's still no movement from the bushes. The door winds up and a leg drops over the edge. The heel swings back. I roll to the side to avoid being kicked. A second leg appears. One of the thieves drops to the parking lot. A third leg appears. They must have bedded down in the back when they heard me coming.

The fourth leg drops into sight.

'What in the grease bucket is this?' The accent is heavy southern.

'Ain't nothin' but lumps of wood.' Another deep south drawl.

'Worth anythin'?'

'Who knows?'

'There's enough of it to fill ma ma's barn.'

'Let's dump it all in the pickup and go. We can figure for it later.'

'Go get the wheels.'

I watch one of them walk off. The other lifts his leg to jump back in the truck. I wait until he's inside and I slide out from underneath.

Standing up slowly I find the man in the truck with his back to me. I check that the other one is out of sight. I reach in, grab the thief's jacket and pull. He catapults from the rear, flying over my shoulder. I turn to jump on him but find empty air. Something slams into the side of my head. My head lights up and he's on top of me.

He drops his knee onto my chest as I hit the ground and lets me have some good news with his right fist. I roll my head with the blow. The second punch is already incoming. Boxer-quick. I snap my head to the right and he grazes my chin. A third blow. I whip my head back and to the side. The strike misses. He uses the ground as a punch bag. He howls, pulling his hand back. I push up and dislodge him from my chest. As I try to roll free, I lash out with my foot and, more by luck than design, I catch him high on the hip. He screams.

I roll onto my front, raise my backside in the air and I'm hit from behind with a kick that dead-legs me on the thigh.

Shit but he's real quick.

He follows up with another kick. I think he has just separated two of my ribs. My breath vanishes. I'm back on the floor. I feel his weight as he drops from a height, driving his knee into my side. I try to spin away but he catches me on the back of the head with the side of his fist.

The rev of an engine suggests his friend is back. A flash of headlights illuminates the ground as another blow slams my head off the parking lot black. Another hit and sparks fly across my vision. My hearing dulls. My ribs are throbbing. I'm losing the battle to stay conscious.

A door slams. 'Corey, what the hell?'

The attack stops. Corey stands up. 'He jumped me.'

'Need a hand?'

'Nope.' Corey bends down. The blows start again.

I curl up to minimize the target. It is all I can do.

Corey gets bored, jumps off me, stands up and lands a kick in my stomach. 'What should we do with 'im?'

His friend strolls over. Casual. 'Get the duct tape outta the pickup.'

Another kick from Corey as he leaves.

One too many. My head explodes. Above my neck, below the centre of my head, a small bomb goes off as the kernel cracks. A grenade spreads shrapnel. I cry out. The pain comes in waves. Deep, deep pain that caves in my vision, my thinking. I'm flicking in and out of the dark. I pull up as tight as I can. Corey's friend looks down at me but with little more than mild interest. I'm battling to stay here.

Corey returns with a roll of tape. 'He's seen us. Maybe we should take care of him a bit more permanent. Make it look like an accident though. You know—like Carl.'

'Over some bits of carved wood?' Corey's friend says.

'He's seen us,' says Corey.

'True.'

Not good.

I place a virtual hand in my skull and try to get a hold of the chaos. Amidst the pain I have a single thought. If I really am that catalyst who can set off people—*mano a mano*—why isn't it happening now? When I need it. Why aren't the attackers tearing lumps out of each other? Iraq, the plane, the agency, the bus—why not now? Screaming hot metal is flowing through my head.

Corey bends down to tape me.

I shout over the noise in my skull. My voice is loud in the parking lot. '*Now. Why not now?*'

Corey stops at the outburst. He stands up, rocking his head from side to side. His friend looks at him. 'Whatcha waiting on?'

Corey rolls his head back and forth for a few more seconds before stopping, his skull at an angle. His eyes are narrowing. Slits against an invisible wind. Then they snap open. His head straightens, a twist around the horizontal, and settles side-on to me.

'Get on with it!' Corey's friend senses something is off kilter.

Corey turns on his heel, dropping the tape on the ground. It bounces twice, before rolling under the truck, coming to rest on the same spot I had been lying in not five minutes ago. It tips on its side. Corey's friend watches it vanish from view, trying to figure what's going on.

Corey takes a step towards him, pivots: left foot planted, right foot trailing. He crouches, only a few inches, priming the spring. His shoulders recoil and his head goes down. He swings on his hip, his trailing foot lifting from the ground, the supporting knee bent, hip leaning out, keeping the centre of balance, working his muscles to build momentum, keeping the movement smooth. The trailing foot overtakes his body, rising as it does so, turned inwards, knee still bent. His eyes are fixed on his friend. The right hand swings out to counterbalance the flying leg. His hand is less than a foot from the ground. Bending at his stomach, his flying leg unfurling, he drives forward, gut muscles pulling tight, foot now extended, supporting knee springing straight.

His foot connects with his friend's face. Heel to chin. A powerful blow. Practiced. This is no amateur attempt. His friend's head bounces back as far as his neck will allow. No time for surprise in his eyes. They are blank. He starts to go down, his feet flying from under him. His arm flies out. A reflex action but he's close to the rear of the truck. Too close. His hand misses the edge of the loading strip and he keeps falling.

Corey is still spinning. Unwinding the attack. Using the kick to make a three-sixty. Before he can complete the circle there's a sickening smack as his friend's head meets the metal edge of the truck. His body tries to keep going—gravity pulling it to the ground. His head is a brake.

Corey watches as his friend's head bounces hard—the light gone from his eyes, his body a rag doll's as it tumbles onto the wet asphalt. Corey settles from the roundhouse kick and has to squat to stop the forward motion.

'Nick.' Single word. Quiet. From the back of Corey's throat.

Nick's head lolls to one side, his tongue pushes between his lips. A single drop of blood squeezes through the space created by his tongue—evacuated by his last breath.

My headache vanishes as the blue world takes hold. My night vision is acute—bringing everything into perspective with a flash of stage lights going up. Corey is still rocking from the kick as Nick's left foot twitches. The final act of a man with no future.

The roar of the traffic from the highway fades. A gentle twist of the volume dial and it's background noise. The pickup is kicking out exhaust. Dirt black/blue—suggesting the engine was due for a service in the late '80s. The driver's door is open—the interior light a cobalt wash. High above, a silver blue bullet glides by with a wink of wing lights.

Corey has stopped rocking. His shoulders have slumped. His body giving way to the recognition of what he has just done. He lets go at the knees, dropping to the ground—reaching for his friend.

Cold, unmoving eyes tell him the truth of his actions but still he reaches, unsure what else to do. He touches Nick's neck, looking for a pulse because that's what they do in *Law and Order*. Then the wrist because he's seen it on *The Wire*. Now he's at a loss.

I watch him fall to his backside. I realize that the man on the ground is dead because of me. Not by my hand. But by my mind.

The blue is becoming a bruise then a blood clot, then dark.

And now I need to act again. To take control. To figure out what to do. I want to run but I can't leave. The chain would kick in. Police, death, interviews, the driver and then I would appear—courtesy of the receptionist.

I stand up and place a hand on Corey's shoulder. He doesn't react. I bend down. He turns his head towards me. His eyes are vacant, uncomprehending. I point to the truck and he gets up. I grab his shoulder, indicating towards his freshly dead friend. 'In the truck.'

Somehow I know he'll obey. No questions.

He sighs. A sound out of place. He sighs again and reaches down to grab his friend by the arms. I check that no one is watching before grabbing Nick's feet. Three steps and he's in the back of the pickup.

I step back. 'As far as you can. Just drive.'

Corey nods at my words, gets in and, with the speed of a snail on dope, drives from the parking lot.

I return to the truck to pull down the door. I check the lip of the loading strip. A small clot of hair and blood lies near one end. I wipe it with the arm of my shirt and head back to the hotel.

The receptionist is missing. For that I'm grateful.

Once back in the room I take off the shirt and scrub it until my hands hurt. I do the same for the pants and fall on the bed.

An hour before my alarm call I'm still awake.

CHAPTER 22

The phone rings. I knock it from the cradle and let the automated voice talk to the carpet. My eyes can't have been shut for more than ten minutes.

I try to sit up. Pain enters my life as the kicking from last night stacks up a range of options for my brain to focus on. Top of the charts is my jaw. Not broken, I don't think. But sore from the punches. A shower doesn't help and putting on damp clothes doesn't improve the situation.

As I exit the hotel I decide to make sure that we're police-free—that the pickup driver hasn't been picked up.

Turning away from the truck—just in case someone is looking—I start to circle the building. A grass vista of neatly-mown yard rolls in front of me. I pass ground floor bedroom windows. If anyone is looking out, I'll be a bit of a surprise.

Reaching the far end of the hotel I stop, pushing my head round the corner. The truck is sitting quietly. There's no swarm of police around it. No CSI team. No SUVs. No suits. Of course they could be hiding, waiting for me. But taking me in my room would have been a far more sensible option than waiting until I was in the open. You can't run when your hotel room has only one exit.

I make my way back round the hotel again—just in case—approaching the truck from the other side. I check for any blood and hair I may have missed on the lip of the loading strip. It's clean. I examine the ground where Corey's head lay. Clean.

Another quick look round and I yank up the roller door. As I climb to the back to settle into my box, I roll the night's events over in my head.

The implications are massive. Charlie was right: I'm not only a freak, I'm a dangerous freak.

Last night I *wanted* it to happen. Wanted the grinding head pain to appear. Willed it to happen. Screamed for it to happen. And it did. Wasn't that the way it went down? Wasn't that the way it all rolled out in front of me? My own red carpet to a new world. A bad world. An incomprehensible world—because these things don't happen. Can't happen. People don't reach out through thin air and turn others into killing machines. They just don't.

But I did. And, just when I needed it. Stressed to high heaven. When I was stressed...and there's the rub. Is that when it happens? Stress?

Iraq. I was on the ground. A blank to the planet. Both times in Iraq. First and second time. So that's that. It's not stress. We're back in the good old world of coincidence. None of this is explainable in the everyday world. So what in the hell is the blue world? Where does that fit into the new life that I am coursing through?

My thoughts are interrupted by the sound of Graham getting into the cab. The engine fires and we are back on the road to Tampa.

I wonder what has happened to Corey. Maybe he's still on the road. On a mission to nowhere. But if he is—why? If this is all coincidence then why would he get in his pickup, dead friend in the back, and drive off?

The heat in the truck is already building. I clamber from the box, lying down at the back of the truck. The motion suggests that my driver is in a hurry. He sees his destination and wants to be there today. No more layovers.

Hours begin to sew together like long tough strips. Each one stretching to join to the next but never far enough. Always a little further to go than would make sense. Time as a rubber band. Snapping together when I drift off to sleep. Moving forward in leaps and fits. Awake, a minute is an hour.

My mind turns to getting off the truck. I have no intention of finishing the journey with Graham in Tampa. Charlie's house in Hudson is worth checking out. It's either that or a few nights in a hotel before my cash runs out.

I'm hoping the driver sees US 19 as an option. Traffic lights will make it easy to jump off. If he chooses the freeway I'm in for a long trek back from Tampa.

A few more hours crawl away before we leave the endless drone of the freeway and start to ride out a start/stop motion. I twist onto my front to grab the release handle for the door. My ribs bitch but I ignore them. I hope there's no door alarm in the cab. If there is, I need to be ready to run.

I pull the handle up, releasing it from the catch. I let the roller take hold and push up, keeping my weight behind the action in case the door springs wide. The road is vanishing into the distance—unwinding beneath me.

The six-lane highway is bordered with a succession of stores and businesses. Through the buildings on the right I can see the sun starting its journey into the Gulf of Mexico.

We hit a set of lights. I lean out for a better view. There's a road sign but from this angle I can't read it. I wonder why Graham has left the freeway. Are we in Tampa already? I do some mental math but reckon we are still a good few hours away.

I'm caught napping when we hang a left and I let go of the door. It hangs for a second, then slams down. I grab the handle again and lift it. Once more air rushes in but this time it's slower. We're off the main road; in a backwater estate. The houses are typical Florida for the less well-off—all board and peeling paint. Streets creep past. There's no indication as to the area we're driving through.

The truck slows at the next four-way stop and crosses it at a crawl. Brakes are hit. We stop. I jump back, climb over the boxes and dive into my hiding place.

A few seconds pass then I hear the door fly up, followed by the noise of a box being scraped across the truck floor. Graham grunts as the box drops to the ground. The door stays open.

I wait before sticking my head up. Hold or go? It's an age-old problem in the field. Hold or go? I go. If I'm caught now I'll need to bullshit my way out.

Dropping to the ground there's little sign of life. The area shows lots of wear and tear. Pickups and ten-year-old SUVs out-number cars three to one. Every third house has a flag waving on the front yard. We are deep in Schlitz and Old Milwaukee land.

My driver is staggering up the driveway of a house that has had some out-of-the ordinary TLC applied to it. The paint is fresh, grass covers the front yard, mowed into neat lines. The small fence that borders the lawn is white and unbroken. An oasis in a *Homes and Gardens* desert.

The front door opens. I duck out of sight.

There's chatter but nothing I can make sense of. Laughter and the door closes. I jump back into the truck—waiting for Graham to return—but ten minutes later and I'm still on my own.

I get out again, wondering at the man's attention to security. Not only does he not lock the truck door but he also feels it's okay to leave the thing open in an area where even the packing boxes could be used to turn a buck. I almost feel a duty to stay, to play guard to his goods.

I nip round the truck, keeping it between the house and me. The passenger door is open. I reach in and pull out a battered Rand McNally road atlas—no GPS for my boy. The pilot's map I have is useless for up-close detail.

I saunter to the cross walk. Trying to look as if I belong here. Christine and 2nd. I flip through the map and track down the possibles for the two road names. I come up with only one town with both: Shady Hills. The good news is that I'm not much more than ten miles from Hudson.

A young man appears on the sidewalk opposite, he walks up to me, jeans so low it's hard to tell if he's lost ten pounds in the last ten minutes or is just too lazy to pull them up. His ears are full of white as an iPod pumps music intravenously. Hair hides his eyes.

He yanks one ear bud free. 'Dude, got a flame?'

I shake my head.

'Know where I can get one, man?'

Hippy meets Hip Hop. He's white with a black voice on Haight-Ashbury lyrics. Go figure.

I shake my head again. 'Sorry.'

'Bummer. You sure, man.'

'Positive.'

'Bummer.'

He likes the word.

I turn back to the truck but he isn't finished.

'Could you get me one, man? You know, ask one of the homes.'

I start walking.

'Hey man, no need for the rude walk, man.'

I keep walking.

'Bummer. Could you tell me what I need to do next?'

The question stops me in my tracks. I don't want to turn round and re-engage but I'm intrigued.

He keeps talking. 'Could you? My life could be better. Much better.'

The down in the grit accent is slipping. A southern lilt of a well-educated boy creeping through. I still don't want to turn. Turning will mean speaking and speaking will mean I might miss my ride. Although I'm already thinking my time with the truck is done. My driver will head for the Suncoast Parkway, bypassing Hudson—the bible according to Rand McNally says there is no other choice that makes sense.

The boy steps towards me. 'Could you? I mean you kind of look like you might know about these things.'

My driver exits the house. A man with a neatly trimmed goatee waves him goodbye. There's no way I can make the back of the truck now even if I want to.

I feel sad. I had intended to take one of the sculptures as a memento. Leaving twenty bucks of course. Assuming they were worth that much or maybe that would have been too little. Graham slams the truck door shut and he's history.

Shit.

My bag. My clothes. The Wild Turkey.

Shit.

Fingerprints. DNA.

Shit.

'Excuse me, sir? Can you help? My life seems to have gone wrong somewhere.' The boy's voice is close.

What the hell is this kid on?

There is enough in the truck to tie me to the Greyhound bus and from there to the plane and from there to the truck and from there to Florida.

Shit.

The boy keeps going. 'I did very well at school. I did well at college but I met up with some cool guys. At least they were cool when I met them. Now I think about it I'm not sure they were cool. Too many drugs. Too much of everything really.'

I turn. I don't want to but I can't see the downside now. He's standing a few feet away. Head down. 'My ma is worried sick. She thinks I'm going to end up in prison. I think I might. What do I do?'

The boy is a little different to a few minutes ago. His pants are up round his waist. His shirt is tucked in. His hair pulled back from his eyes. He's holding it in a ponytail with his left hand. The false accent is gone. He stands straight—the street slump gone.

'Look,' I say. 'I'm not sure what you need but if you want a bit of advice—smarten up, get back to college and work hard. Get a part-time job and knuckle down. Will that do?'

His face lights up. 'Wonderful.'

He screws round on his heels. A military turn and he marches off—whistling.

What in the hell was that all about?

But I know something. At least I know he's going to march all the way home. He's going to walk into his house. Up the stairs. Into his room. He's going to throw off the street clothes and pull on an Izod polo shirt, a pair of chinos and a set of Payless brogues. He's going to flush the smack he has hidden in among his childhood Lego. He'll go to the barber's, get a number two. He'll walk to the college, wait until the doors open tomorrow and sign up again. Then he'll go down to McDonald's, ask if they need anyone to flip burgers or clean the john. After that he'll try and ace the first year at college.

How do I know this? I don't. Somehow it's the only thing that makes sense and that in itself doesn't make sense.

I feel good about it. Real good. Like I've just saved a life. A One Republic moment—only I didn't have to stay up all night to do it. I turn west and look to the dipping sun. Hudson lies ten miles that way. Ten miles is a three-hour walk. A walk I am looking forward to.

The bag is history. The truck is history. The nonsense around me is history. For a bit. It may not go away but for the next three hours it can sit on the shelf. I may even blow a few dollars on a beer or two.

CHAPTER 23

The neon bar-light wraps a warm welcome around my shoulders and carries me in. It has echoes of Charlie's place but heavier with locals, although, thankfully, there's no brushwood moment as I cross the threshold. No one cares.

Two barmen are on call. The younger asks what I want and I ask for a Coors Light. JD is too heavy for the moment. He cracks one from the cooler and pops the top. I decline the frosted glass, necking a third of the contents to get me on my way.

The feel-good sensation is still lingering. So much so that I made a point of looking for waifs and strays on my walk. A walking Oprah-meets-Jerry thing. I found none.

I sit on one of the stools guarding the bar, relaxing into my drink. Cool time. The first real cool time since the back alley at Charlie's place. This brings up Lorraine and the cool moment passes.

I can see her lying on the bar floor. Face pouring with blood. Mary being carried away screaming. I look at the payphone on the wall. It's heart-achingly hard not to get in touch. Not to pick up the receiver and dial the hospital number. Not to listen to her voice telling me she's fine and, by the way, what are you talking about—electrocution—me?

'New boy?'

The question comes from my neighbor—a checked-shirt-and-tartan-tied man with slicked-back hair. He has a faint air of decline about him.

I half smile at him. 'Just stopping for one.'

'I used to say that. He returns the smile and flips a hand at the nearest barman for another. 'Where are you from?'

'New York,' I lie.

'Never been. Kind of a Florida State man me. Tim Askovitz.' He reaches out a hand. I shake.

'Paul Dearham.' Paul was my medical liaison officer when I was discharged from the army.

'Knew a Dearham once. In the army I think.'

I think he notices the double take on my face.

'Really. Never been in the army,' I reply.

'Me neither. What do you do?'

'Freelance security. You?'

'Anything that pays.' He laughs. 'Used to be the sales director for a big software company but I got canned. Downsizing. Recession—you know the drill.'

'And now?'

'On the road. Sales. Bag in hand. Hand on bell. Foot in door. Mostly cleaning stuff.' He points to a sample case squeezed between his legs and the bar. 'You don't happen to need a couple of hundred gallons of Mr Kleen—Number 1?'

I shake my head.

'Same story everywhere.'

My good mood has evaporated. I want to be out of here. The change is sudden, dramatic. I slug the Coors but there's too much to finish in one go.

'Your face looks a little familiar.' He's leaning towards me.

'Can't think why,' I say.

'Bit like a friend of mine. You have that look. Lost. Not sure of what's going on.'

I make the effort, draining the bottle before standing up. 'Time to go.'

'You just got here!'

'A quick visit. Nice meeting you.'

'Have one more?'

'I can't.'

'Why? Where do you need to be?'

'Somewhere.'

'No you don't. You don't have to be anywhere. You don't need to be two yards from here in the next week.' His voice has an aggressive edge.

'Yeah, well I'm off. Nice meeting you.'

'No it wasn't. You think I'm a waster.'

I get up.

He stands. 'Can see it in your eyes. Waster. Used to be big time—now a waster.'

'Tim. Leave the man alone.' The barman is on his shoulder.

I push open the door. Tim shouts out. 'Ain't no waster. I know where I am. Where are you? Where are you?'

The door cuts him off and I regret going for the beer. I walk out into the parking lot. US 19 hums along in front of me. I begin walking and if I have my directions correct it can't be more than a couple of miles or so to Hudson.

The day is closing off and the traffic winding up. I cross strip mall after strip mall. Parking lot after parking lot. The sign for Hudson appears—now I'm looking for Hudson Avenue. I find it. A Regions Bank on one corner, a Walgreens on the other. There's a Winn-Dixie in the mall, behind the bank. I cross to walk in. I enter the world of A/C and ask where Fairway Oaks is.

'When you hit two gas stations keep going—it's on your left.' So says the man stacking the trolleys.

I exit, wandering along the road. I find the gas stations sitting next to another mall. I start to hunt down Irondale Lane.

The whole name thing is a giveaway. Golf course development. I enter the estate, glimpsing a golf hole in between the homes. The area is nice. Large, well kept, stand-alone houses. Each stands in its own plot and most are in good condition. The odd house sits in an overgrown garden but since the credit crunch nowhere has got off. Probably repossessions that won't sell.

A sign telling me to beware of golf buggies signals a crossing point between green and tee. After a few false starts I find the street I'm looking for and finally the house.

I walk by—trying, once more, to look like I belong where I don't. There are no SUVs. No Regals. No suits. I walk up the blockwork drive. A large stone pelican sits next to the front door. I take a look round. Clear. I put my hand in the pelican's beak. Nothing. I dig a little deeper and feel metal, grasp it and pull it out.

The front door opens onto a sitting room. The house is well kept. To my right is a dining area and, beyond this, a large open-plan kitchen sits next to the TV lounge. In the corner of the lounge, sliding doors lead out to a meshed-in pool. A quick wander and I count four bedrooms, three bathrooms, a walk-in changing room in the master bedroom to back up the sitting room, dining area, kitchen and lounge.

The decoration is neutral. The smell suggests it's been uninhabited for a while. Although someone is keeping the garden neat and the dust off the furniture.

I flip the fridge. Empty. I spotted a Publix in the mall next to the gas stations. I do a fly round once more and leave. Pocketing the key, I head for the supermarket, stock up on chips, chocolate, a bottle of JD, Coke and something for breakfast.

On my return I slump into a large corner unit that's wrapped around the TV. I crack a packet of Lays. I add in a Hershey. I flick on the TV. The Tampa Bay Devil Rays are at home to the Toronto Blue Jays; the first of a three-game series is into the bottom of the second inning. I watch the game unfold, switching it off at the top of the fifth with the Devil Rays two to zip and looking good.

I enter the master bedroom and strip off. My clothes are fit for the trash but I search out the washtub to load everything I have into it. I tip in some powder that might or might not be for washing. As the machine kicks in I walk back to the bedroom and through to the shower.

Fifteen minutes later I'm lying on the bed. A JD and Coke in one hand, my dick in the other. I'm not doing anything with it—just a comfort thing. There are paperbacks stacked in a display unit. I pull down a Stephen King I haven't read and try and give it some attention. I fail.

I go for another wander. I see a red light flashing on the telephone. Pressing the play button brings Charlie's voice into the house.

'Each day at ten o'clock in the morning. I'll phone each day at ten o'clock until I get you.'

There are two more of the same messages on the machine. Each timed at ten o'clock. Twelve hours before the next one. Time for another drink and maybe bed.

Three drinks later, bed is still a distant objective. I fire up the TV again. The Rays win four to one and the late-night news doesn't have my face on it. I think about a dip in the pool, but I have no costume.

I lie on the bed and drain another and another and—good night.

The phone cuts through. I roll over and lift it.

'Craig?'

'Charlie?'

'You made it okay?'

I'm trying to clear my head. 'Yes.'

'Everything all right?'

'Where are you calling from?'

'A cell. Prepaid. Fresh out of the wrapper. Don't want the men in black listening in.'

'Lorraine. How is Lorraine?'

'Fine. I saw her last night. She's a bit groggy. I think your boys gave her something to keep her quiet.'

'What?'

'She doesn't have much recollection of the last few days.'

'But she's okay?'

'She's as okay as you get when you've had your face caved in by a beer bottle. But the doc thinks it will heal well enough. She might need a minor op to correct the breaks but all in all she's a lot better than she could have been.'

'Thank God.' I roll back on the bed. The sense of relief is stunning. Simply stunning. 'When will she get out?'

'She hasn't been told.'

'The suits?'

'Nowhere to be seen at the hospital.'

'Do you think they'll leave her alone?'

'How the hell would I know, but it would be hard to get to her. She's in a busy ward.'

It didn't stop the bastards electrocuting her.

'What are you going to do now?' asks Charlie.

'I don't know. Lie low?'

'You think that'll work?'

'No idea but the suits are serious. Deadly serious. Where are you?'

'Down on Santa Monica pier. Only place I could think of where I can get a clear view of everyone. I had a hell of a job losing the tail they put on me.'

'They're following you?'

'Craig, I haven't always been injecting alcohol into the needy. I can tell when someone is playing my shadow.'

'And you're clear of them?'

'Not for long. How are you for cash?'

'Busted. Won't last another few days.'

'I can't send you cash. Too easy to trace. But I might be able to get you a job. A bouncer. Private club. Not on the street. Discreet. Interested?'

'Charlie, I can't. Whoever the suits are they'll find out.'

'They won't. There's no connection to me. Trust me. Okay, if they tie me down and slice off my testicles a ham slice at a time I might talk, but if they're that desperate you're fucked anyway.'

'Where's the job?'

'Tampa.'

'Let me think.'

'I'll call tonight. Seven o'clock.'

'Okay.'

'I need to go.'

'Do me a favour?'

'What?'

'Pop in and see Lorraine for me.'

'Deal.'

The line drops dead. My first thought is a vision of Charlie standing in a ring of suits, the man in white linen nodding, telling him how well he has done. How clever he has been in tying me to the house, while they arrange to have me lifted.

Only they would have been here by now. This is not a game. I pull back the blinds. At least it's a quiet road with no SUVs.

I'm going to take the job. I knew it as soon as Charlie mentioned it. I need the time to think. I need the cash. Lorraine is okay. For the moment. It's a risk keeping the tie with Charlie—house, job, phone calls—but I need a line to my wife. Also, the world is a crap place when you have no cash.

Tampa is straight down US 19. I'll need to figure the public transport system. Not that I'm a fan. The Greyhound was my first bus in ten years but public transport is as anonymous as you get. And it's cheap.

I take a trip to the washtub. I forgot to take the stuff out and dry it. I put it in the spin dryer to give it twenty minutes.

While waiting I use the door that leads to the garage. Here it's a great place to dry stuff. Always hot and no chance of a sudden Floridian downpour.

The garage would hold two cars and a party if need be. Much to my surprise, there's a vehicle taking up some of the space. It's wrapped in a white tarpaulin with just the wheels jutting out. I pull the cover off to reveal a late-'90s Toyota Corolla. White, a little dented, it's the perfect runabout. If the keys are around I could be mobile. I have to assume that it's Charlie's. Insurance is another thing altogether.

I try the car doors. Locked. I search around. Behind the wheels. On top of the tires. I do a scan of the garage but it's clear of junk and there are no keys hanging up.

I return to the house, beginning a systematic search. I start with the master bedroom, checking all the drawers and cupboards. I work room by room, striking lucky in the kitchen. Beneath the light switch there's a key hanging on a hook with the telltale Toyota bull sign embossed on it.

The remote is working. The car's lights flash at me as I press the tit. I flip the driver's door. Heat barrels out. I let the interior equalize with the exterior before getting in. Sticking the key in the slot I find I have a full tank. It's a stick shift but I'll get by. I start her up.

She fires first time.

I'm still naked. I know my wardrobe is limited. I saw a sign for Walmart back at the main junction on my way in. Back in the bedroom I dig out a pair of shorts, an old T-shirt and a pair of flip-flops that are lying at the bottom of a drawer. Not exactly de rigueur but it will do until I can get to the store. I hit the remote on the garage door and I'm away.

The journey isn't far but it's a little bumpy. Not down to the lack of road maintenance. More down to me trying to work a stick shift in an unfamiliar car. I kangaroo for the first few turns, stalling at every light. I park a country mile from the front door of the Walmart. Too scared to try and park anywhere near other cars.

I'm a cheap shopper. Ten-dollar jeans, a pack of three white T-shirts for seven dollars, unbranded trainers for fifteen bucks. The rest of my cash goes on a cheap suit, a shirt and a tie, a look I finish with a pair of leather-look shoes. Along with boxers and a few other essentials it all but cleans me out. I'm taking the car for the job interview. I haven't the bus fare left.

On the way back I hang a left rather than a right at the main intersection. I slide down a road bordered on either side by houses backing onto row after row of canals. A boatyard appears and the road circles round on itself to meet the road coming in. A small beach borders the road, with a bar as a full stop. It's a wooden affair and sits with its face towards the gulf. The sign above the door tells me it's called Sam's. They're advertising meals with a spectacular sunset over the sea.

Twenty yards from the beach a boat is exiting one of the canals. I eye the bar and wish I had a few more bucks in my pocket. A couple of beers watching the boat people do their business sounds fine. I pull into the parking lot that lines the beach, leaving the engine running to power the A/C. On a whim I root around in the glove box with visions of finding a few dollars squirreled away.

Nothing.

I reach into the back and flip down the split seat. The trunk has a black jacket lying on the floor. I pull it out. Rifling the pockets I find Andrew Jackson is crumpled up, hiding in an inside pocket. Andrew is worth a couple of beers of anybody's money. Well, Sam, let's see how good the view is.

I stuff the twenty-dollar bill into my pocket. I rip open the T-shirt packet to remove one. Jeans, T-shirt, boxers, socks and sneakers in tow, I enter Sam's washroom and emerge as Steve Austin's poor cousin, the thirty-dollar man.

The bar opens out to an area corralled by a low fence. Colorful pictures of fish are fixed to it low down, and an outdoor bar sits to the right. I choose one of the cut benches that border the fence. A narrow boardwalk flows from the fence to the water and then it's liquid all the way to Mexico.

A boat cuts through the swell to meet the main channel—a series of markers points the way to the sea.

A waitress bounds up. I ask for a Miller on draft. She smiles, vanishes and re-appears with a glass fresh out of the freezer, froth bubbling from the top. Ice cold and just perfect for a day like today. I lick at the white bubbles, inhaling a few inches of the beer. With a satisfied sigh I lean back to fix my eyes on the departing boat.

The bar is quiet but I suspect that at night this will change.

A second boat cuts through the channel and falls in behind the first. A third and there's a convoy heading for a day of fun. I compose myself at the wheel of the boat in my mind. I take a few minutes to suck in the salt air, to feel the sea spitting in my face. I close my eyes and drift, the sun as my personal heater, the shallow breeze a pre-ordered cooler.

'Craig McIntyre?'

I snap out of the daydream, twisting round to locate the voice.

'Craig. What on earth are you doing here?'

CHAPTER 24

The girl is small. Five feet max. Short blonde hair. Tight white T-shirt and tighter jeans. She's rocking on high heels. Maybe a few inches short of five feet. I have no idea who she is. Pretty though.

She flicks her hair. 'You don't remember me?'

'Not really.'

She laughs. A friendly 'me I'm likeable' laugh. She sits down across from me. A little too premature for my liking.

'Can't say I'm surprised. Hatch Roll?' she says.

'Hatch Roll?'

'Sharon. Sharon Davies. Day nurse?'

Hatch Roll. Not a great time in my life but I still can't place her.

'A good few years ago. When I left you were still under observation.'

'You worked there?'

'Yip. Nurse. Do you mind if I sit a while? Huh. I'm supposed to be meeting someone but they're running late.'

I wave my hand and she settles in. She flicks her hair again. 'How have you been?'

'Good.'

'When did you get out?' She makes it sound like I was in prison.

'A few years back.'

'You look good on it.'

I know she's lying. My clothes might be bright and shiny but the person inside is dull and muted. 'What are you doing here?'

She doesn't answer at first, her eye drawn to the departing boats. She looks back at me. 'I moved down here after I quit at Hatch Roll. You?'

'Taking a break.'

'On your own?'

I don't want to go there. She's a link to a past I want buried. She's also a connection to a world that the suits know all about.

'Yes,' I say.

'No girlfriend?'

Strange thing to ask. 'I need to be going.'

'You've hardly touched your beer.'

'I've been feeling a bit off. Thought this was a good idea. It isn't.'

'Where are you staying?'

I shuffle in my seat. Feel like I'm being interrogated. 'Hotel up the road. Days Inn. Just for last night. I'm moving on.'

'Where to?'

Give me a break. 'Don't know.'

'You have a car?'

Hells teeth. 'Yip.'

'Which one?'

'Sorry?'

'Which one's yours?'

'What is it with the twenty questions?'

'Just being friendly.'

She looks put out. Her face screws up. A pretty sort of screw-up.

'And what are you doing these days?'

'Same old, same old. New place though. Not far from here. Straight up the road and across the 19. Huh. You can't miss it.'

I'd seen the signs for the hospital on the way to the house. 'And I take it you stay local?'

'Fairway Oaks.'

Shit.

'It's not far from my work. Nice place. My boyfriend owns

it. Huh. It backs onto the golf course.'

I have a sinking feeling as I speak. 'What street?'

'Twenty questions.'

'Sorry?'

'Your turn. Twenty questions. It's Irondale Lane. Why?'

Double shit. 'No reason.'

A sun-filled silence descends. Count to twenty and still no talking.

'I thought you had to go?'

I can't. Unless I leave my car and walk. Sharon will see me get in and later on could spot the car when I get back to the house. 'You've cheered me up. Maybe I'll finish my beer.'

The waitress appears. Sharon orders an orange juice. 'So you feel Hatch Roll is in the past? Huh.'

She fixes her eyes on me as she speaks. There's a sparkle there that gives her real warmth.

'Yes and no. A lot of the time was a haze but when it was bad it was bad.'

'How long were you there?'

'Three years and then a few more on weekend release.'

'Long time. What are you doing now?'

'This and that. I'm surprised you remember me.'

'When you've changed a man's clothes, cleaned him up and spoon-fed him you've done more than most wives ever do. Huh. My boss used to call you the hurricane.'

'Why?'

'You had a way of being at the centre of a storm. Usually when you were out of it on the meds—and you had some heavy meds at times. Fights on the ward, arguments—we even had a couple of stabbings. All in your ward. We moved you around to see what the heck was going on and you just kept being the eye. Calm, serene and nonsense all around.'

'No one ever said.'

'When you were awake and on low dosage it didn't happen so often. I had a couple of colleagues who wouldn't work nights on your ward. Thought you were some sort of jinx. Huh.'

The 'Huhs' are a cute habit. Probably something you would grow to ignore or hate—but at the moment they're cute.

'I never knew.'

'Why should you?'

Why indeed?

'So are you staying or going?' she asks.

My beer is dead. 'One more.'

I order up another cold one and she joins me.

We shoot the breeze for a while. She's into skateboarding and watercolors. Her boyfriend was into real estate but the recession put paid to that and he's now an admin clerk with a car rental firm. They've been together for a couple of years. There is no talk of marriage and the way she skips over the detail doesn't make him sound like the love of her life.

My second beer fades into memory. I switch to soda. Adding DUI to my life might just be a bad idea.

I get the impression that there's no friend coming to meet Sharon. She doesn't make or receive a cell call and seems at ease with being stood up. When I mention it she tells me it happens all the time.

'How did you get here?' I ask.

'Car. How else? There, next to yours.'

'Mine?'

'The Corolla.'

'How do you know it's mine?'

'I saw you drive up.'

'I thought you came in after me?'

'Nope. Huh. I was in the ladies' washroom. Saw you park up.'

I decide enough is enough. 'I really must go.'

'Oh well it was nice to meet you, Craig McIntyre. Maybe we'll bump into each other again?'

'Maybe.'

I'm too quick to my feet and too quick to the car but if I'd known she had spotted me earlier I would never have spent the time chatting.

As I complete the loop and get back on the road to the high-way, I keep an eye on the rear-view mirror. A small blue Chevy zooms into view. It was a blue Chevy that was sitting next to my car in the parking lot. I reach the main junction and indicate right—hoping there's a Days Inn close by.

I join the late afternoon traffic, heading south, the blue Chevy six or seven cars behind me. I stop/start down the 19 and, as I cross into the town of Port Richey, I'm relieved to see a Days Inn on my left.

I indicate to cross over the oncoming lanes and the blue Chevy pulls into the parking lot of the Mattress Giant opposite. I park up and make for the reception. Unfortunately, the hotel is the type where the doors to the rooms open onto an outside balcony or onto the parking lot. As such I can't walk in and lose myself inside the building.

The receptionist looks up as I enter. Early twenties. Tight-cropped hair. Tanned. 'Can I help?'

'Do you have rooms that don't face the road?'

'Yes, sir. Through the large arch and the rooms at the back face the rear.'

'Could I have a look at one? I'm a very light sleeper.'

His face says what he won't. *'Why in the hell would you pick a roadside hotel in the first place then?'*

He hands me a key. I make my way out and round to the back. Slowly. Making sure that Sharon has enough time to see me.

The room is a carbon copy of every hotel room I have ever been in. I sit on the bed, counting to one thousand. I get up and exit. I stop as I reach the large arch that leads to the front. Drop to my knees, pushing my head round the corner.

The receptionist is standing in front of me. He looks down and I pretend to tie my shoelaces.

'Is the room to your liking, sir?"

'No. Too noisy.'

'Can I take the key?'

'Certainly.'

I step back and force him to walk out of sight of the highway. I hand him the key. He waits for me to leave. With me not moving it gets awkward. I stare at the ground and he stares at me. This is going nowhere.

'Look,' I say. 'I need your help. My business partner is being an idiot and he's having me followed. A blue Chevy parked across the road. I'm trying to lose it. I thought if I stopped here for a while they might leave. You couldn't check if the car is still there?'

He wants rid of me, so he walks out into the arch and comes back. 'There's a blue Chevy sitting in the Mattress Giant parking lot.'

'Thanks.'

More awkwardness.

'I'd prefer it if you were to leave, sir.'

I know he would and so would I but Sharon is giving out all the wrong signals. You don't trail someone to a hotel unless you have an ulterior motive. I step back a little more. 'I need to stay here until the car leaves.'

'I can't let you do that,' he replies.

'Come on. Ten minutes and I'll be gone.'

'Sir, I need you to leave or I'll call the police.'

Now that isn't good news.

'There's no need for the police,' I say. 'Look, she might be gone already. Have another look.'

He steps back and looks through the arch. 'The car's still there.'

'Five minutes.'

'I'm calling the police.'

'John?' The voice comes from beyond the arch. 'John, are you okay?'

'No problem, Sam. I'm just asking this man to leave.'

Sam appears at John's shoulder. They could be twins. I reckon they are gym buddies. Cropped hair and all.

'What's the problem?' Sam asks.

'I've asked this man to leave and he's refusing.' John's voice is stronger now he has back up.

'I'll go in five minutes,' I say.

'Why not leave now?' asks Sam.

John turns to his friend. 'He says the blue Chevy in the Mattress Giant parking lot is following him.'

Sam turns to look at the Chevy. I start to walk away. I need to pull them out of sight and let Sharon get bored. John isn't happy at this. 'Sir, this is my last warning.'

They both follow me.

At least they've both stepped out of view of the Chevy. The afternoon heat is turning this situation into something quite ugly. Neither John nor Sam look like they have the patience I need at the moment.

'Go phone. I'll keep an eye on him,' says Sam to John.

John nods in agreement.

'Give me a fucking break,' I spit. The swear-word seems to change the atmosphere.

'Use your cell,' says Sam.

John reaches for his pocket.

I step towards them. They tense. Two on one and I need this like a hole in the eyeball. John pulls out his cell.

I hold up my hand. 'Okay, I'll go.'

John ignores me and dials. I jump forward, slapping the phone from his hand. Sam tries to block the move but he's too slow. I step back as the cell bounces off the ground with a crack. John stares at the phone. 'What the…'

Sam moves towards me and I back off. John takes a step and I back up some more. The lot ends in a ring of brush. My head is motoring. None of this is good. 'Okay, I'll go. Just let me get to my car.'

Sam smiles. 'A bit late for that, isn't it?'

CHAPTER 25

Sam has the look of someone who has been here before. His gait has changed. His head is down, eyes to the top of his sockets. His smile is fixed. John starts to circle to my left. I back up another few feet. 'I said I would go.'

John matches my move. 'You had your chance. Maybe we should teach you a little lesson.'

'Is there anyone in the rooms?' Sam asks John.

'It's all clear.'

'Time to dance, darling?' Sam says.

'Why, I thought you would never ask,' replies John.

They're both grinning. This is not their first time. Good old boys on a mission. Probably Down-and-Out Season. A bit of bum-bashing on a Wednesday night. A few Colt 45s—'Works Every Time'—then take your partner to the head bone dance floor.

Worse still, they're both sober. Drunks can be brave but they're sloppy. Sam moves in. I'm being backed into a corner. I judge the moment and jump to my right, dummy and go left. I was the worst wide receiver in the history of our college but at least I made the team. I scrape along the wall of the hotel as Sam dives for me. His eyes are alight. This is good-time stuff for him.

I'm almost past him when he grabs at my T-shirt. You would think that a couple of bucks of material would rip easily but it holds just fine. I duck the swinging fist and try to bury one of my own in his stomach. It's like hitting the Hoover Dam. Serious six-pack going on there. He grunts but doesn't let go. John moves to grab my arm. I bring my foot up but there's no room to get a swing on and I do little more than brush his thigh.

Sam tries another haymaker, taking me high on the shoulder. I stamp on his foot, catching shin bone on the way down. This time he shouts. First blood is mine.

John is on me and we both fall to the ground.

I swing my fists and kick like I'm having a fit. Some of my blows connect but so do some of the incoming ones. I'm only going to keep an upper hand because they're not working together. The beating from the night before has slowed me down. I aim a punch straight up and catch John on the chin. He lurches skyward, giving me a chance to grab him and pin him to the ground. I headbutt him with everything my neck muscles can find. His nose explodes.

Sam shouts again, tries to stand up. I lash out with my foot. I miss and he lands an elbow on my groin. I fall back on John as my balls detonate under the blow. John wraps his arms around me. I do the only thing open to me and flip my head back, catching his broken nose. He lets go with a howl as Sam falls onto me.

I feel my head building pressure—the headache winding up— and I know what's coming when a horn sounds. We all freeze and it sounds again. An engine revs close by; the horn is now going off like an alarm. Sam turns to find the grill of a car inches from his face. He leaps up. I follow suit. John stays on the ground.

'Get in.' The passenger door of the blue Chevy is open. I can see Sharon's face through the windshield. I don't have time for questions and hobble into the car. Sam stares me down and looks at John, bewilderment in his face. He starts to raise a foot and I think he's going to plant it in John's gut, but he lowers it as my headache vanishes. I wait for the blue world but it doesn't feel close now.

Sharon reverses to the arch and through. She brakes next to my car.

'Get your car and follow me back to Fairway Oaks,' she shouts.

I hesitate.

'Now! Before they get their act together and decide to beat up on both of us. Huh.'

I still don't move.

'Charlie sent me, okay? So move.'

I leap out of the car. Sam is walking into the arch. A second later John emerges, clutching his nose. I jog to my car and pull open the Corolla door, keeping an eye on the pair as I jump in, kick the engine into life and follow Sharon into the traffic.

Cruising back up the highway, Sharon weaves her way north. At the next set of lights, I pull level and hit the window button to talk to her.

I'm slammed forward in my seat as the car is smacked from the rear. I turn to find Sam and John sitting high in a Toyota Hilux, staring down on me. Sam flips the bird and John points to his nose. Sam rolls the pickup forward, catches my bumper in its bull bars and begins to push. I stick my foot on the brake but we are three to one here in terms of horsepower. The lights are still red. The crossroads is busy. My tires squeal as the pickup shoves me across the white line of the intersection.

I glance over at Sharon. She's struggling to catch up on what is going down. Her face is creased with puzzlement. As I open my mouth to shout, the car lurches forward another few feet. I'm gripping the steering wheel so hard it hurts but it isn't going to stop the forward motion. The car jerks again as the power of the pickup overcomes the friction of my tires.

I'm only inches from being broadsided by the crossing cars.

I try to calm down. Think and act—not the other way round. The car lurches again. Why in the hell don't the lights change? How long can they stay at red?

A horn fires off as a car slashes across the front of my fender. The Corolla continues to slide onward. The pickup engine is roaring in my ear. A few more feet and I'll be midstream. A second car has to swerve to avoid my nose. I make a choice. Another car is bearing down. I whip my foot from the brake, ram the car into first and floor it.

I jump forward and catch Sam by surprise. We both shoot into the traffic. A car misses my tail but can't miss Sam and John. The sound of grinding metal falls away as the other cars signal their warning with a clutch of horns and brakes. I clear the crossing and keep my foot down.

I look in the mirror. The doors to the pickup are opening. Sam and John are leaping out—then they're lost to the distance. The next junction rears up and I almost forget to brake. As I stop I expect a crumpled Hilux to rush into my life again. Instead a blue Chevy cruises up on my right.

My window is still open.

'What the hell?' shouts Sharon. 'Just follow me.'

As the lights change I check the rear-view and pull in behind the Chevy. At the next junction Sharon hangs a right and navigates a back way towards the house. I'm not that surprised when she indicates to turn into my driveway and parks, with enough space to let me into the garage.

I hit the remote to send the garage door wheeling up.

A minute later and I'm letting Sharon in the front door. I have a bunch of questions.

Before we start I say, 'Coffee?'

She nods. I start to cook up some strong and black stuff. 'You want to tell me how you know where I live?'

'You want to tell me why you lied?'

'You first.'

'Charlie told me.'

'And you know Charlie how?'

'He used to be a patient at Hatch Roll.'

'He did?'

'Do you think he hands out cash to complete strangers? How big is your bar bill?'

'A few dollars?'

'And the rest,' she says. 'The day you walked into the bar and told him you had been at Hatch Roll he phoned me to check. When he knew you were coming here he phoned me. I moved to St Pete's two years ago and he's kept in touch. It wasn't hard for me to check on you.'

'Why did he phone you?'

'We were friends when he was at Hatch Roll.'

I place the cups on the coffee table in the sitting room, and we sit down opposite each other.

'What was he in for?'

'Same as you.'

'He was in the army?'

'Special forces.'

'No shit.'

'Good soldier as well. Just one too many missions in one too many bad places.'

'He never said.'

'He wants to forget it.'

'And you kept in touch why?'

'We were an item.'

Lucky Charlie. I sip at the black stuff. 'What were you supposed to do? Watch me? Protect me from the baddies?'

'Just check you out and let him know how you're doing.'

'You do know I'm being hunted?'

'Charlie said there were some people after you. Huh. Was that them back at the hotel?'

'No. That was a pair of idiots.'

'Just as well I turned up when I did.'

'How did you know I was in trouble?'

'I knew you weren't staying at the hotel and, when I saw the two guys walk out of sight, I thought they might be the people Charlie had warned me about.'

'You're not lacking guts.'

'Maybe you mean brains.' She smiles. 'Are you going for the job at the club?'

'Charlie has a big mouth.'

'It's my brother who hires the muscle. Charlie doesn't know anyone down here.'

'I thought this was Charlie's house?'

'Nope. Mine.'

'I thought you lived in St Pete's?'

'I do. This used to belong to my parents and when they passed on I couldn't move it. Huh. The credit crunch was on us. So I mothballed it.'

'So the house has no connection to Charlie?' Well maybe the suits won't find me just yet. 'Charlie said he would phone at seven to see if I want the job.'

'Do you?'

'Do I what?'

'Want the job.'

'No choice. I need the cash and time to get my head together. Where is it?'

'You can trail me and I'll show you. Now, do you want something to eat?'

'I do but I'm afraid your larder is empty.'

'Yes, but the telephone works and there's a wonderful Italian that delivers.'

CHAPTER 26

Charlie phones and we talk. We wander around his past, Sharon and the way to the Moon. Sharon is more than an ex from the way he talks.

An hour later I'm following Sharon's Chevy down the Suncoast Parkway with a pound of lasagna nesting in my gut. I feel better. An appetite from the wild and extra garlic bread will do that. I'm wearing the cheapest suit I have ever owned but I've been seen in worse. Anyway, bouncers need suits that are practical. Machine-washable is good.

We hit Tampa as the rush hour falls off, picking up signs for the Tropicana Stadium, passing a sign advertising the second game in the Blue Jays series.

I'm lost but Sharon weaves her way through the town with purpose. We hit a strip of bars and restaurants and she pulls up in a fire zone. I draw level. She tells me to park in the garage next to the fire zone and walk back to where she's illegally parked.

I have a sweat on by the time I get back to her.

She points to a small blue door that sits between a Mexican restaurant and a sports bar. 'Knock on the door and ask for Jake. If they give you any grief tell them Sharon sent you. I'll wait and see you in.'

The door could be a door to anywhere. There are no markings on it. I knock and it opens within a couple of fast heartbeats. 'I'm looking for Jake.'

'And?'

'Sharon sent me.' I step to the side and Sharon waves at the doorman. He nods his head and moves to let me in.

The corridor beyond is dimly lit and heavily carpeted. An airport scanner stands in front of me and, beyond this, another door. I step through the metal arch. The doorman raps on the second door. It opens and a man in a gray suit looks at me.

'For Jake,' says the doorman.

I'm ushered in to find myself in a small vestibule. A wooden table sits to the left and a stunning brunette sits behind it, protected by a computer screen. She's wearing a Bluetooth ear-piece, while pressing away at the keyboard. I'm conscious of the bruises on my face.

She looks up. 'Name?'

'Craig McIntyre.'

'And you're here to see who?'

'Jake.'

'Is he expecting you?'

'Yes.'

She hits a few more keys and speaks into the Bluetooth. Then to me. 'Go on through. He's waiting.'

There's a buzz, followed by a double door swinging inwards to reveal a large bar and restaurant, empty save for a couple of men behind the bar and a woman pushing a vacuum cleaner across the floor.

I step in. The doors close behind me.

'So you're Sharon's new man?' The voice is loud. I turn to find a guy whose eyes connect him to Sharon. 'I believe I'm supposed to give you a job.'

Jake is six feet six at least. His shoulders have the look of an athlete.

'I was told you might have a vacancy,' I venture.

'Sit down.' He throws his hand towards one of the room's large sofas. 'I haven't got much time and you have even less to impress me. Done any of this kind of work before?'

'I was on a few doors before I joined the army.'

'Army is good. What else?'

'I'm a personal security expert.'

'A bodyguard then.'

I nod.

'Better. And do you know anything about the club?'

'No.'

'Good, the less you know the better. You start tonight and you work with Clyde. You do what Clyde says. You walk where Clyde tells you to walk and you talk when Clyde tells you to talk. The pay is better than anywhere else in town and it's cash at the end of the night. You sort out the IRS. You'll find Clyde upstairs.'

He lifts his massive frame from the chair and leaves.

It appears I have the job. Whatever the job is.

A spiral staircase lifts from the centre of the room. I climb it. The next floor up is more of the same except there's a dance floor in one corner. A small man with an '80s ponytail and a taste for tight suits is leaning against the bar. He has a sheet of paper in one hand and a pen in the other.

'Clyde?' I ask as I walk up to him.

'Who's asking?'

'Jake sent me up. I've to work with you.'

'Sure. Virgin?'

'Sorry?'

'Thick too. We open at ten. That suit is crap. Far door—code is 98789. Pick out something better to wear and be back here in ten. Figured!'

'Eh?'

'Just go.' He points at a door.

I go.

The door is padded. I punch in the code to enter a small off-shoot of Saks of 5th Avenue. Suits to the left, shirts to the right, shoes at the back and ties in a carousel in the middle. A small changing-room sits in one corner. I flick through the suits and find a black Versace in my size, a brilliant white Ralph Lauren shirt, a pair of Cole Haan chukka boots and a Brioni striped tie. Total cost—probably north of three thousand bucks. What kind of club keeps this stuff as spare change?

Back with Clyde he nods approvingly. 'Any damage is out of your wages. Hand it back at the end of the night. Figured.'

I think I know what he means.

'First up. Coffee. Black.' He waves at the other end of the bar where there's an industrial coffee-making machine. I worry it for a while and he stomps over and shows me how it works. 'Thick.'

Maybe I am.

'Bar duty,' he says.

'Sorry?'

'Bar duty. Not serving. Watching. Too naïve for door or VIP club. Maybe when I see how you do.'

'What do I do?'

'You watch.'

'For what?'

'What do bouncers watch for?'

'Trouble?'

'Figured.'

It's half an hour until opening. I brew up a coffee. A couple of girls appear wearing so little that I can't keep my eye on the job. They introduce themselves as Caroline and Nell. They don't seem to be interested in the new boy. They start setting up the bar. I can't see a cash register but I'm thinking this is not a cash club.

Twenty minutes later a small alarm goes off. The girls straighten their hair and push the belts, which double as skirts, down a quarter of an inch. I drop down the spiral staircase to see the guests arrive.

Nothing happens. The door doesn't heave open and no thronging crowd fills the place. An hour crawls away and hangs itself before a man with the girth of the Louisiana Superdome walks in. He has four ladies in tow. None of them has less than five-inch heels. I climb back to my perch, not expecting the large man to make it up, but there's an elevator in the corner disguised as a mirror and he emerges.

He collapses on the nearest sofa, wet patches under his armpits despite the ice-cold A/C. Caroline takes an order. She returns with two bottles of Krug in two silver ice buckets. The man pops one and pours for the girls. He opens the other one, grabbing a straw from the silver tray that the glasses sit on. He pushes the straw into the neck of the champagne and sucks.

A hell of an expensive soda.

The night is slow to build. I should have asked when my shift finished. I should have asked what the wages were. I know neither.

At two o'clock the place is gearing up to fly. There's not a spare seat in the house. The dance floor is switched on and crammed. I can see why the A/C is so heavy—it has to fight hard to win in this atmosphere.

No one is drinking the cheap stuff. Mainly because there is no cheap stuff. Payment is through a club card. No cash. Caroline and Nell have been joined by six others and, so far, I've done nothing but people watch.

The elevator opens and a man in casual slacks and a polo shirt rolls in. I recognise his face from TV. Senator Bob Tampoline. The Tambourine Man. His surname having helped christen him when he took up a tambourine at his inauguration ball and joined in with the band. I saw it on the news.

Some say his surname is made up. That he's really called Bob Schmucker. Of course he denies it. An orphan. No mother or father save a note that said, *The son of Mr and Mrs Tampoline.* As if. But he's done well on it. There are rumors that this is also a pile of horse shit. I don't recognize the girl he's with. I'm fairly sure there is a Mrs Tampoline back at the ranch. He squeezes through the crowd throwing a few nods and handshakes as he goes.

The VIP room is at the far end of the bar and Clyde is on the door. He tilts his head at the senator as he vanishes inside. With no trouble on the horizon I walk up to Clyde. 'Can I get ten minutes for some fresh air?' I have to shout to be heard.

He looks at his watch and nods. 'Ten. No more. Go through the bar. Down the stairs. Out the back.'

I thank him.

'Figured,' he says.

The alley at the rear takes my head back to Charlie's place. A fellow bouncer is dragging a cigarette to death next to the fire door.

'Jools.' He offers a hand.

'Craig.' I shake.

'Quiet night.'

'Club's busy.'

'Club's quiet. Wait till ya get the weekend. That's busy.'

'Who owns the place?'

'Mr White.'

'Who's he?'

'Rich and ya don't ask questions like *'who's he?'*'

'Okay. Can I ask about you?'

'Sure. Born on Treasure Island. Live on Treasure Island. Went to school on Treasure Island. Had a job on Treasure Island. Got married on Treasure Island. Got divorced on Treasure Island. Ma' and Da' died on Treasure Island. You?'

'Drifting. Always drifting.' My mother's face tries to take shape in my head. A fuzzy ball that has more to do with the one old photograph that used to sit in my wallet, than from any real memory.

Jools speaks. 'Where's ya home?'

My mother's face fades. 'Nowhere really. I'm from Springfield, New Jersey.'

'The Simpsons.' He sings the words.

'Not the first time I've heard that.'

He ignores the response. 'Ma' and Da' from there?'

'No. My dad was from Brooklyn and my mother was from Glasgow in Scotland.'

'Scotland?'

'I've never been. My mother came over when she was three.'

'How did they die?'

Odd question.

'How did you know they were dead?'

'I didn't. Mine got hit by a train. Unmarked crossing. I was in the back of the car. Nine months old ya know. They tell me that the police photos show the car sliced in two but I've never wanted to see it. You?'

'Complicated.'

And it was. Very.

'I got five minutes. Don't ya?'

'I don't want to talk about it.'

'Why not?'

Because I might have killed them. I look at his face in case I have just spoken out loud. 'They died in a fire. Our house. Okay?'

'Sure.'

He finishes the cigarette in silence, and waves as he goes back to work. I inhale the last dregs of the secondhand smoke. A familiar craving creeps over me. I gave up smoking the day I left Hatch Roll but I could slip back with such ease.

I return to my post. I have no idea how you could fit in more people, but while I was away another stream of humanity has risen up the spiral staircase and we're all breathing less fresh air.

Half an hour later I get my first taste of action. To be fair, I see it coming. A young man has been leaning into a girl at the bar for a while. She has her back turned towards him but he isn't taking the hint. She's trying to blank him by talking to her friend. A couple of times she's pushed the young man away but he's drunk and persistent—a bad combination. I push through the crowd, trying not to get a drink over my wage-arresting suit. I stand a few yards away and watch.

177

It kicks off when the young man, tired of the knock-backs, grabs the girl by the shoulders and tries to turn her towards him. If I had been her I would have walked an age ago, but he would have probably followed. She tries to shrug him off. I look towards Clyde. He's spotted it. He nods his head for me to intervene.

'I think the lady wants a little space,' I shout into the young man's ear.

He flicks round to look at me. 'Fuck off.'

'Let her go.'

'I said fuck off.'

This is not going to go well. 'Look, take it easy. All I'm saying…'

He swings his fist at me, but he telegraphs it. I step back, clipping a customer, who tips his drink down my back.

Shit, that'll cost.

I grab the young man's arm, swing him round and force his wrist up his back. He squeals above the hubbub. It's too busy to march him through the club so I take him down the back way and out into the alley.

'Do you know who my father is?' He has to hold onto the alley wall to stay upright.

'No sir, I do not.'

'You will if you don't let me back in.'

'That isn't going to happen.'

I close the door but he takes a run at it. I hear him make contact.

Clyde is waiting at the top of the stairs. 'Not bad. Spell me on the VIP room. Slash time. Only go in if the bell goes. Got it?'

'Yip. Do you know the guy I threw out?'

'Colin Mark's son.'

'Is that bad?'

'No. Colin would have chucked him out first. Hates him. Figured.'

I've been promoted to VIP status. I walk to the door and

realize I have no idea who should get in. I stop Nell and ask her how I'll know.

'Black membership cards only. Blue and Gold don't count.'

Easy.

A few rubberneckers walk up but I make sure they leave with their tails between their legs.

Clyde returns. 'Stay on. Boss wants to see me. Any trouble, use this.'

He hands me a walkie-talkie with an earpiece, which I insert. I hear the doorman inform everyone that Juan Revez is in the building. I think he's the short stop for a big team up north.

The edge is off the night. The peak is past. Dawn is on its way. The dance floor has daylight and, although there are no seats to be had in the place, there's more standing room.

I check for Clyde, push at the VIP door and look in. A short corridor stretches out. There are three doors either side. All are shut. Private means private around here. One of them opens. I get a glimpse of a small room mostly filled with a bed.

Very private then.

A man walks out and I hold the door for him. He doesn't even look at me. I hear a shout from one of the rooms but there's no bell. I start to close the door and there's another shout. A woman's shout. One that signals pain. I keep the door open a crack. There's a scream.

Enough.

I step into the short corridor. I think the shouting came from the last door on the right. When another cry goes out I'm certain. I place my hand on the door handle and swing it open.

The senator is naked, standing with his flabby backside towards me. The young girl he came in with is on her knees on the bed. A rope loops her neck. The senator is holding the loose end. The girl looks at me through her arms. There's a red stain on the white duvet beneath her head.

'Stop him,' she says.

The senator turns. He has one hand round his cock. In the

other hand he has rope. Its end is red. He steps back. 'Turn around and walk out. You're history,' he growls.

I don't move. I can't move.

He isn't fazed by the situation in the slightest. 'I said turn round and leave.'

My head explodes. No warning. The pain sends me to the floor. I feel a hand on my head and then under my chin. The senator brings my eyes up to meet his and I'm inches from his engorged member. 'I said...'

He pauses, tenses and steps back. My head pounds out a new rhythm of pain. The girl is struggling but the bond around her neck is choking her. The make-up that made her look older has run with tears and sweat. She can't be more than eighteen.

The senator stands up and drops my head. Then he picks it up again. I'm frozen. Unable to think. The headache is everything.

The senator slams my head into the shag pile. It doesn't add to the pain, just to my lack of action. He pulls at the rope. The girl screams but he doesn't stop pulling, the muscles in his arms trembling with the strain. Her screams vanish as the air is cut off. There's a gurgle and she flops. Dead. Spit dribbles from her mouth.

I can't move for the pain in my head. I roll over as the senator stands up and views his handiwork. His aggression turns into a look of confusion and...boom—the world is blue—headache gone.

The door behind me bursts open and Clyde is standing there. 'Jesus Christ.'

The stop-start nature of the blue world is back and the words come out as 'Jeeeeeeeeeessssssssssusssss. Chriiiisst'. Clyde's lower jaw hangs loose.

I start to stand up. Clyde looks down on me, then at the girl and finally at the senator. He has the sort of hesitancy of action I saw in my short time as a soldier. Multiple choices but none of them solving the problem you're facing.

The senator suddenly collapses on the floor. Spent. I want to kick his head into pulp for what he's just done but I know I need to be a hundred miles from here. I turn and Clyde is blocking my way. He sees something in my eyes. Something he doesn't like. He stands to one side. I don't think it is voluntary. It's reflex.

I wonder if it would be better to wait for the police but I'm in the frame for the young girl if they want. Even if I run it will be me, not the senator, who killed the girl. If I stay it will still be me. An ex mental patient wanted by a government agency for his involvement in multiple deaths versus an elected official of the state.

I'm dead meat.

I put my foot to the floor and I'm gone. I turn so quickly towards the exit that I need to hang onto the door frame to make the ninety-degree move. I push at the padded door and fly into the club. A few faces turn to see who is exiting the VIP room. I blank them as I skirt the bar, before taking to the stairs.

The alley is empty. Déjà vu. A back alley and I'm on the run again. The only way out lies next to the sports bar. A lone ciggie junkie is drawing in the bad stuff as I sprint into the night.

The blue world vanishes.

CHAPTER 27

I climb the car park stairs three at a time. The building is a graveyard, with a few of the late-night revelers' cars in random slots. My car is on the second level. I'm sure there will be police waiting at the bottom when I exit. I'm wrong. There isn't even any activity at the club door as I pass by.

I start to put distance between the nightclub and myself.

I don't know the area and it takes a while to pick up the signs for the road north. I know the police will be involved soon. Not yet though. Not just yet. The crime scene will need to be altered to blank the senator, to put me in the picture. Only then will the police be called.

As the car bites freeway dirt I wonder what the hell to do. The miles slip away but the panic doesn't. I play out the scene in the VIP room, running it back into the previous days. It jumbles, taking on a new level of confusion and adding to my panic.

I can feel another headache beginning to build. I need to back off. A car in front flashes its brake lights. I swing out to overtake. The man in the car flips me the bird, a snarl on his face. I keep my foot down and he drifts backwards, vanishing with the headache.

The relationship between the headaches and violence is now clear to me. How it works? Why it works? None of that makes sense. Common patterns in the last few days are thin and few. That the violence is focused on others and not me seemed clear until the Days Inn duo decided to chase me down. But maybe they were just the exception that proves the rule.

The sight of the senator abusing the young girl was testament to the extremes of behavior I seem to be able to generate.

A couple of dollar tolls and I reach my turn-off. I contemplate not returning to the house. After all, the car may be tied to that address, and the police might be waiting. Maybe even the suits. But there are no blue and white flashing welcome lights. Once in the garage I take a few breaths before making for the house.

The cool air hits me and I wish I had put a few beers in the fridge.

'Hi.'

The voice makes me leap.

Sharon pops up from the sofa. 'Did you have a good first day?'

My wife has never used those words. My only job was in Iraq. 'Not really,' I reply.

'Pray tell.'

I walk her through the evening. When I reach the death of the girl she draws her feet up and gasps.

'What?' It's the only word she can find. She isn't buying it. I can't blame her. I'm ex Hatch Roll. A trained killer with a screw loose. As far as she knows the whole thing is a fantasy. Or I'm the killer?

'The police will be here soon,' I say.

'Probably.'

'And they'll be after you as well.'

'Yip. After all, I recommended you for the job.'

'They'll blame me.'

'Yip.'

'But I didn't do it.'

'Yip.'

'You believe me?'

'I should say yes and make some excuse to go to the washroom. Huh. Then run. If what you say is true, things will get messy. If you're lying I should get the hell out of here anyway.'

'But you're not going to?'

'No. I told Charlie I'd help. So let's say the senator did what you say. I'd say the chances of you staying out of jail are nil. Huh.'

'No kidding.'

'But I don't think the police will come.'

'Why?'

'A senator caught in a brothel with a dead hooker. Huh. I don't see the club being quick to dial 911. I see them cleaning up the mess or maybe phoning some guys from the FBI, CIA or even KFC first. Senators don't go down that easily. What I do see is someone else turning up here soon. If I were you I'd probably want it to be the police. Anyone else and I don't fancy your chances.'

'You seem surprisingly well versed.'

'Maybe. Five years in a military nuthouse can teach you a lot about how the world really works.'

I drop on a chair, leaning forward, placing my head in my hands. I'm so out of my depth I can't see up from down.

'I don't think self-pity is a good call. Huh.'

I lift my head up. 'What would you suggest?'

'We need space to think.'

'We?'

'I told Charlie I would look out for you.'

'You must really like him.'

'A lot.'

'Oh yeah, you two were an item.'

'*Were?*'

'You still are?'

'On the nose, Mr McIntyre.'

'But he's in LA and you're here?'

'No dodging the bullets when you're around is there? Huh. Things are bad on the job front unless you hadn't noticed.'

'So you work here and Charlie in LA?'

'I work in St Pete's.'

'Not Hudson?'

'I made that up. I've a senior administrator's job with a health company. The pay is too good to quit.'

'How long have you been doing this?'

'About a year and a half. I used to work in LA but the company closed the office. It was St Pete's or nothing and they offered me a promotion. Charlie's looking for a place out here but he can't sell the LA bar.'

'He never mentioned you.'

'Maybe you didn't ask.'

'Maybe I didn't.'

'Anyway, do you think getting my life story is a good use of time? We need to move.'

'Where to?'

'No idea.'

She gets up and I follow.

There's a thump and the window that looks out onto the front lawn shatters as a smoke bomb bounces into our lives.

CHAPTER 28

The lights die. A second smoke bomb follows the first. I grab Sharon around the waist, pulling her back into the TV room. 'Hit the floor and follow me.'

I start to crawl towards the door that leads to the garage. She follows.

'Where are we going?' coughs Sharon.

'They'll be ready for us. The garage is our only chance.'

'Who'll be ready for us?'

'Guess. Crawl, don't talk.'

There's a small gap between the back of the kitchen and the master bedroom and it's clear of smoke. Rising to a crouch, I fumble for Sharon's hand. I pull her into the laundry room, slamming the door behind us. I grab the door to the garage and throw it open.

The darkness beyond could hide an army but it seems quiet. I hear footsteps from the front and a smash as the front door is caved in.

'The car,' I whisper.

Sharon obeys. She jumps into the passenger seat. I leap into the driver's side and nearly drop the key as I try to insert it into the ignition. I miss the keyhole and miss it again. Sharon looks at me. I draw a breath and use my other hand to guide the key into its slot. I turn it enough to switch on the electrics. The dashboard lights up. I look for the garage door remote.

Shit. It's in the house. There's no time to go back. The noise from outside is now inside. I have seconds. Twisting the key, I fire up the engine, push down on the clutch, take the revs up to the limit, slide the car into reverse and wheel-spin it backwards.

Ten feet of space to cover before we hit the garage door. I'm not sure that the small car will have the momentum to punch through the aluminum shell.

Sharon screams as we hit the door. It gives—crashing from its mountings—but not enough and I'm forced to shoot forward and try again. The car makes it further on the second hit but the metal door is strong. This time we get jammed. Our rear is in the driveway and the front still in the garage. I floor it but generate tire smoke and little else.

Guns click. A million lights surround the car. I kill the engine. We're going nowhere.

CHAPTER 29

'Hands where we can see them. Don't move.'

The order is loud as men with guns appear through the door from the house, flooding onto the driveway. I lift my hands into the air, urging Sharon to do the same. Her face is white, as she stares at the men. A hand grabs the door handle, yanking it open. A gun barrel appears next to my head.

'Quick. Give it to him now,' a voice spits.

A gloved hand grabs my forearm. I try to pull away. The hand holds firm. A needle is rammed home.

There is no slow slide from oblivion. One moment I'm in the car, the next I'm in a room, strapped once more to a bed. The ceiling lighting is low and the air-conditioning hums. The restraints feel the same as the ones used in Iraq. I test them but there's no give.

'*Welcome back, Mr McIntyre.*'

The voice is way too familiar. '*Still wearing the crumpled white linen suits?*' I ask.

'*I don't know about the crumpled bit—but yes.*' He laughs. '*Mr McIntyre, you are—and I say this with the greatest of respect—a very, very dangerous man to be around.*'

'Pop in and we can chat about it.'

'*You'd like that wouldn't you?*'

'You don't know how much. Where am I?'

'*Safe.*'

'Who from?'

'From yourself.'

'Bullshit.'

He blanks me. *'So, down to business. You possess an ability that we find interesting.'*

'Do I?'

'Oh you do, Mr McIntyre. You do. And I have a lot of very excited people who can't wait to stick some probes into you, wire you up, open your head and play around inside. You're highly unusual, and in my experience—and believe me when I tell you that my experience is very extensive—I would say you are close to being unique.'

'Wow.' My sarcasm misses the mark.

'Before I let my colleagues have their fun with you, I need to test a few things.'

'Fuck off.'

'I'm not sure that this'll be as bad as you think.'

'So tying me up, torturing me, torturing my wife, hunting me down, drugging me—not bad?'

'Let me make this plain. You work with us and we work with you.'

'Or?'

'Switch on the monitor.' The words aren't for me.

A large TV monitor replaces the ceiling lights above me. The screen is blank save for a small white dot pulsing in the top left. I try to twist my head but the restraints hold tight.

The monitor fires up and splits into two images—divided down the centre. Two rooms come into view. The camera angle suggests that the cameras are high up in the corners. Each room has a single occupant. One is sitting on the floor, the other is standing in the corner.

Both are familiar. Way too familiar.

'No!' I shout and deny what I'm seeing. I close my eyes and pray, and for the first time in an eon, really pray, that what I am seeing is not real.

Energy flees my body, leaving me boneless, devoid of blood—a sack of nothing.

Lendl interrupts my panic. *'So, Mr McIntyre, here's how I read the whole game. You have a special talent for bringing out the worst in people. In your presence people seem to lose their inhibitions—an inhibition amoeba you might say. Whatever it is that you do, it takes individuals, strips them of their usual social norms and leaves them free to vent violence on others. After the event it would seem that they have little recollection or, at best, remember the incident but seem to see no wrong in their actions. Almost as if they never actually did anything. As far as we can ascertain—from interviewing our colleagues back in Iraq and the senator—there's little more that they can tell us.'*

I open my eyes and look at the TV. Lorraine is in one room. Charlie is in the other.

'So,' Lendl continues. *'A bit of deductive reasoning leads me to wonder what triggers your little incidents and—and this is key—who takes the fall. For only some seem to succumb to your abilities.'*

Lorraine doesn't look well. She's ghostly pale and a bandage covers most of the right side of her face. Charlie has his head down. I can't see his face.

'I have a theory.' Lendl is in lecture mode now. *'Stop me if you think I'm going astray. Let's take all the incidents that we know of. Iraq 2003, Iraq this week, the plane, our offices, the bus and the senator. Did I miss any?'*

At least they're not omnipresent—the Days Inn duo are missing.

'So what do they all have in common? Well the real clue was in the mess that you left in our offices. Twenty-one wounded, two dead but, when you break it down, each one was attacked by someone they knew. No stranger-on-stranger action. And then you begin to see the picture. Your two buddies in Iraq. Mr Taylor and his on/off girlfriend. The bus—well they were all old friends of a sort—and then we have the senator and his aide. She has been working for him for a few years.'

Lorraine twists her neck and looks up at the camera.

'But friends aren't enough.' Lendl continues. *'Why would friends let loose on each other? I'll put a few bucks on the fact that buried deep in most friendships is something that isn't so friendly. Something that wants to get out into the open, but the friendship stops it rising to the surface. I think that's what you set free, Mr McIntyre.'*

Lorraine lies down, curling into a ball.

Lendl keeps his foot down. *'So we have friends as a common denominator. Friends with something dark in their communal cupboard. What else do we have? What is the trigger? What sets it all off? What sets you off? I'm guessing a little stress might work, but I'm also wondering about the times you were out for the count. They're harder to figure. In every case you were under some form of stress during or not long before the incidents.'*

Charlie lifts his head. The bruises on his face suggest he didn't come quietly.

'Here's the rub, Mr McIntyre. I need to give my hypothesis a test. Run it up the flagpole as I used to say in the old days. As you see, we have your wife in one room and in room two your friendly neighborhood barman. I know they know each other and I understand that Charlie has a thing for your wife. So let's see if there's something else buried in there. Let's see if you can unlock a little secret or two, shall we?'

'You can fuck off,' I shout. 'Let them go and I'll help you.'

'Time is against me and I need some answers now. So we'll play by my rules. Put the barman in with the woman.'

A door opens in Charlie's room. A man with a gun enters—a partner covering his back. Charlie is ushered out. A door in Lorraine's room opens. Charlie flies in, landing against the far wall. Lorraine stands up.

Lendl starts up again. *'I need to know if proximity is an issue so we'll start this on a remote basis first.'*

I hear someone walk in.

They stick a knife into the back of my hand.

I scream.

They push the knife down and through the bone and into the table beyond.

Hot lead runs up my arm. It feels like someone is dipping my hand in boiling water. I scream.

They pull the knife out and drop a pad on the wound to stem the blood flow.

For a good minute I do nothing but writhe in the restraints. Above me, Lorraine and Charlie are talking.

'*Nothing.*' Lendl sounds pissed off. '*Again.*'

Same hole, same knife, only this time it's twisted as it goes in.

More screaming from me and no reaction from Lorraine and Charlie.

'*Zip,*' says Lendl. '*Okay, pull up the grill.*'

There's a grinding sound. Lorraine's voice is in the room. 'Craig. Oh, Craig.'

'Lorraine?' I try and turn to see her.

'Craig, what are they doing?'

The pain in my hand is acting like Prozac. I have no focus— no sense of what to do for the good. 'Lorraine, stay away from Charlie. Charlie, stay away from Lorraine.'

'Craig.' Her voice is followed by a gasp as the man in my room takes the knife and clips off the top of the index finger on my injured hand. This is like no pain that I have ever felt before. This is new. This is something on a different level and my scream is primeval.

'Stop it! Stop it!' Lorraine is shouting.

Charlie joins in. 'What the hell do you want?'

The kernel deep in my head cracks and, despite everything, I'm aware that this is bad news. I try to shout a warning. It comes out as a hoarse cry. The headache trumps the clipped finger. I nearly pass out.

I look up at the monitor. I see Charlie lift his head and stare at the camera. He looks at me. Not *at* the camera but *through* the camera, right at me.

I scream 'No!' as he turns to Lorraine. 'Stop him!' My shout is extreme.

Charlie grabs Lorraine by the hair. The hair I so love to touch. He takes a handful, before jumping into the air. His knees curl up as he raises Lorraine's head high. I can see the first signs of realization from Lorraine as Charlie fails to overcome gravity and starts back down to earth. At the same time, he wrenches his arm down—taking Lorraine's head with him. The combination of his fall and the pull snaps her head forward.

I'm still shouting.

At the last possible moment Charlie twists his arm and body to the left. He directs Lorraine's head towards the edge of the bed. The metal-rimmed edge of the bed.

I hear the crack. Feel the crack. Sense the crack. Bone losing out to steel. The thin layer of flesh no barrier. There is a grunt from Lorraine. A last noise from my wife? I don't want to watch but I can't stop. Her head rocks back on the top of her spine. She drops to the floor.

'Very good.' A new voice in the room. I look at my wife. Motionless on the floor.

The monitor above me flashes and dies. The grinding sound returns. No matter how hard I shout there's no response from the next room. I'm back on my own.

'Very good indeed,' says the new voice.

'Bastards.' My voice is losing power. My vocal chords scraped and worn.

'Well, Mr McIntyre,' says Lendl. 'It seems there might be some history between your wife and the barman that you don't know about.'

'Bastards,' I shout but my voice is down to a hoarse croak. 'I'll kill you. All of you. Every fucking one of you.'

'I don't think so.' The new voice is back. Smug, southern. I recognize it.

'Tampoline. You murdering bastard.'

'I don't think so.'

The word 'so' is drawn out to sound like *sow*.

Tampoline sounds calm. *'I would say that you're the murderer. You might not see it that way but think about it. All those dead people and you're the one at the centre each time.'*

'My wife. You killed my wife.'

'Wrong again. Your friend did or was it you? Hard to say but I never thought it would work quite as well—you performed like a Trojan. Her blood is on your hands. Not mine.'

I can't think what to say. What to do. The headache is still growing. There is no sign of the blue world. My vision is blurring. Sounds are fading.

CHAPTER 30

I come round. My ties have gone. I'm in a new room but the headache is too much. Too painful.

I come round again. A cool, calm, peaceful blue world. The lights are out but, with the night vision, I can see clearly. I sit up and the death of my wife is somehow distant. A thing that happened a long time ago or maybe something that never really happened.

I walk over to the door. There's no handle. I push at it but it has no intention of moving. The rest of the room is a metal cube. Bare steel floor, no wall coverings—a single panel in the ceiling that no doubt supplies the light.

I return to the bed.

The light flicks on.

'*Good morning, Mr McIntyre.*' In the blue world the voice races forward and then slows. 'Good morning' took a few seconds to roll out of Lendl's mouth, while my name was an express train. '*I need a few more answers.*'

'I need to use the toilet,' I say.

'*Feel free.*'

'Where?'

'*On the floor. We don't mind.*'

'You're joking.'

'*Mr McIntyre, given your talents I have no intention of letting you out until I know how to control you. 'Til then you'll pee on the floor.'*

'What about food?'

'There's a bottle of water under the bed. You don't need to eat.'

'What about my rights? You know, the Constitution. The Bill of Rights. The rest of the amendments. US law.'

'As was once said by Mr Spock, the needs of the many outweigh the needs of the one.'

'What?'

'I have a duty to protect the citizens of this country and you are a threat. A clear and present danger. That changes things. Think of this as Guantanamo Bay. Think of your stay here as you being a guest of this fine country.'

'What do you mean a guest. I'm a fucking US citizen. It's my country as well.'

'As you say. Anyway, to work.'

There's a hiss and I begin to cough. A cloud passes over my eyes. I try to fight the gas. I collapse onto the bed. Then I'm gone.

I'm back in the restraints. TV monitor above my head. Two rooms. Two people. No Lorraine this time. Charlie. Sharon. The blue world has gone. My finger hurts like an open wound being fed salt.

A voice crackles from a speaker. *'Okay, Mr McIntyre, let's see if we can dispense with the knife.'* Lendl is enjoying this. *'Pay a bit of attention. I want you to concentrate on the barman and his girlfriend. Do whatever it is that you do and we'll have made some progress.'*

'Fuck off.'

'You need a new vocabulary.'

I look at my bandaged hand. Neat and tidy. Must have been done when I was out of it.

'Simple really, Mr McIntyre—I don't want to send someone

in with a knife.'

'Then don't.'

'It would make things a lot easier if you were to co-operate.'

The grinding sound of the grill rolling back rings out. Charlie is led into the room with Sharon. Charlie looks cool. A man who didn't murder my wife. Sharon looks confused. A woman not aware of what's bearing down on her.

I close my eyes.

'Craig?' Sharon's voice.

'Craig?' Charlie's voice.

Rising rage at Charlie's actions builds in my gut. He killed my wife. Took her head in his hands and dropped her like a fresh egg.

There's a small beep.

'At least you're trying,' says Lendl.

'Craig, why are you tied up?' Sharon is shrill.

'Craig, where the hell?' Charlie's voice stops with a slap. On the monitor two suits have entered the room and Charlie is now lying on the floor.

'I'd appreciate some quiet,' says Lendl.

'I swear...' but I have no more words.

'You were doing well. Raised heartbeat. Good vitals.'

I must be wired up to something.

'We benchmarked you yesterday, Mr McIntyre. Heart rate one-seventy. BP elevated by ten points. Hit that again and we'll see what we will see.'

I breathe deeply. Calming myself. Fixing my head on a grass-covered hill. Looking down on a lush valley. A few white clouds dotting a perfect blue sky. Seventy-five in the shade.

'Hit him,' Lendl orders.

A hand grabs me from behind. I wait on the knife. A jab in my arm tells me that this is a new approach. My heart starts to race. I feel a rush. A solid wave of good-time rolls in. I want to talk.

So I talk. 'My mother once told me that the only way to tell a good man from a bad one is to ask him when he last told his mother he loved her. Bet you haven't told your mother that in a long while.'

I want to rant. 'I love the mother thing. I want the mother thing. Mother gone. Do you know that? Gone. Real gone. Not coming back. Whoah I need a drink. Water. Now. Can I? Would you? Dead. She's dead. Not me. Not me. Was it me? Was it? Tell me.'

My heart is flying. A trip hammer fed by whatever they've injected me with. I want up. Away from the bed. In the sky. Somewhere that isn't here.

I look at the monitor. Charlie is standing over Sharon. She isn't moving.

'*Good.*' Lendl's voice sounds smug. The grill vanishes. The monitor dies. Another needle and lights out.

I'm not sure how long I've been out. I'm not sure how often I've been back with real time. More than once. More than twice. Much more? Much less? Hard to tell. Hard to know. A strobe goes off in my memory. A flashbulb followed by a flashbulb followed by a flashbulb. Each one less distinct. Further away. Softer. Less important.

Needles are the norm. Needles to perk me up. Needles to calm me down. Needles to make me sleep. Needles to change my mood. My arm is not so much a pin cushion, as a collection of tiny little access tunnels to my ever-changing world. Liquid flowing in. Bubbling beneath my skin. Entering my bloodstream. Another delivery. Another mystery to be revealed.

The TV monitors and the restraints are no more. A soft chair sitting in front of a small stage is my world. People are brought out for someone else's entertainment and I am the catalyst. Such a good word. Catalyst. Has real grit while being round at the edges.

Tests are run. People die. Not always but most times. My

chair is moved to another room but they seem unhappy with the results and I am back in front of the stage. Proximity is a variable. So I'm told.

I don't know the people they bring. No more Charlie, and of course no more Lorraine. I want to care but the drugs never let me. I sleep the sleep of the innocent. But I'm not innocent.

The days draw out. Merge into a strip cartoon with Craig McIntyre as the central character. Never involved in the action. Never part of the story but always there. I hold sway over the world. A king upon a poor throne, dispensing my kingly duties to the tune of another.

Once there was a cast of thousands on the small stage. Too many bodies to count. But the play was cut short. The carnage too great to control. I was given an injection well before the curtain came down.

I know I'm being used to bring pain and suffering to others. I know I'm being primed like a pump. Ready for something in the future. I know they are working out the kinks. Finding out ways to make me jump through the right hoops at the right time. Tuning in to me. Creating a cocktail of drugs and instructions that will act as a remote control when they require it. Press *Play* for the action. *Pause* to check things are going their way. *Stop* to put me away for another day.

I never see the same person twice, not on the stage, not in the wings. Faces are random. The suits are the most random. I'm sure they must be running out of new people to administer the drugs.

They're careful. The restraints are released in stages. Each time testing that I have no influence over the suits. Once, a suit tried to inject another suit. Now they only come alone. It seems that in my world two is the magic number. Solo and I'm no threat.

Friends, acquaintances, knowing. These are variables as well. Lendl says that proximity and friendship are key. The prime variables. The two locks I have the key for. Close and personal.

A deadly combination. Don't underestimate what I can do if I'm in the right mood and the victims know each other.

There is a third variable. Lendl hitting another home run. Moments in the past that run sour in the good blood of friends, sometimes hidden, rarely talked about—but always there.

Moments that need out and want out. And, one day, even without me there, they would have leaked. A drunken argument. A slurred set of words dredging the river the cohorts swim in. A minor indiscretion or maybe a major one. Something from the past spilling out into the daylight. The friendship taking up the strain. Often surviving but never as it was before. Maybe weaker, maybe stronger. Never the same though. I just nudge things along. Amplify it. Give it permission to breathe. Then it stretches its rotten wings and people die. Sharon. Lorraine. People.

The tests continue.

There is no day. There is no night. There is but pre, during and post needle. I need the needle. I can feel it calling in the morning. I desire its few milliliters of liquid. Wish them into my system. I adore the rush. Crave the world in overdrive. I book an appointment in my head each time for the next time. For the upper, for the downer, for the sleeper. Three needles. Three points in my life to look forward to.

The stage is long since gone. They now take me outside. Never the same people. Often more than one, but they don't know each other. It's essential in my drugged-up new universe. I walk among others, ripping inhibition from their souls. Exposing old wounds.

We drive through the suburbs of Tampa. Fights break out as I pass. Road rage makes *Eyewitness News*. I'm harder to control in the open. They experiment with new drugs. Looking for the switch. On and off. It's all they want.

Then they find it. A rush and I am live. A fall and I am neutral. I suspect I am more artificial, synthesized fluid than plasma now. You could sell me to the junkies downtown and they would auction off my blood. I don't know what they are giving me. Nor do I care. I just want more and they're happy to oblige.

New targets are found—in the park, in the mall. Trial and error as I'm dropped in as many places as they feel fit. Always figuring out the master plan. How to control me, direct me—make me work for them.

I have no idea what people see when they look at me. There are no mirrors in my world. No dressing rooms. I am the white T-shirt and blue jean man with a beard and eyes that scare. People look away. I've lost weight. A lot. I can circle my upper arm with my forefinger and thumb. My hard-earned muscle is gone. I am wasting away. Deep down I know this is a one-way trip. Much more and there is no coming back.

My teeth are loose and occasionally clumps of hair fall to the floor, and my head now feels smooth. Walking is hard. My feet blister with surprising ease. My skin splits at the slightest of contacts.

Soon I'm moved around in a wheelchair. Soon I will die. I am a drug addict with no way back. I cannot stop, nor would they want me to. I am being primed for one last act. One major event. They won't tell me what or when, but it has to be soon.

My body tells me this.

CHAPTER 31

'Craig?'

I want the voice to stop. I want the needle to begin.

'Craig?'

The slap does little to penetrate the mist. My nerves are fried. Useless wires, dead to the touch.

'Craig?'

A needle. I'm happy.

Then I'm not. No rush. No welcome high-voltage planet. Just awareness. Frightening awareness. Lights too bright. Sound too loud. The real world knocks hard and I don't want it to come in.

'No.' It's so long since I've used my voice that it sounds alien.

'Craig. You need to come back to us.' Lendl is standing over me. I'm Craig to him now. So nice.

'No. Take me away.'

'Give him another shot,' he says.

I try to pull away but there's no strength in my arms.

'Craig.' A bullet in my ear. 'Craig, are you with us?'

'Yes. Please stop it.'

'I can't stop the real world, Craig. This is where most of us live all of the time. Time to wake up. No more Oz for you.'

'Just one shot.'

'Not going to happen.'

I want to scream and shout. I want to vomit up the words that will make them obey but the old world is crowding out my senses—what's left of them.

'How long before we can get sense out of him?' he asks someone.

'Hard to tell. I'm amazed he's still here.' An unknown voice. 'But he is and he's primed.'

'Yes, but much more and I think he'll be history. Once more up the hill. Once more down and then he's gone.'

'I only need one more turn,' says Lendl. 'Craig, can you understand what I'm saying?'

I nod but I'm not sure if this means yes or no.

'We leave in twenty minutes. You're about to meet two old and dear friends. Friends with a dreadful yesteryear that they share. Just do your stuff and we're all home free. After that you can have as many shots of uppers and downers as you want.'

I like the last bit.

'But I need you to act normally for a little while. Best bib and tucker. Shave. The works. A suit. Five minutes on your feet and then it'll all be over.'

I am violated in this new world. Scrubbed and I bleed. Shaved and I bleed. New clothes and they cut me. The creases in the shirt staining red.

I cry. I can do nothing but cry.

Hands lift me. I'm dropped into a wheelchair. Strangers take me to a car. Black. Another SUV. My buttocks split as I sit on the leather. I leak fluid into my pants.

A drive. Not long but full of pain. We stop at a ball of fire. Lights dance around doors and I'm spat from the car into the pit of hell. People around me stare but the suits rush me to the stairs and up. We plunge into a box overlooking a stage. Two chairs and a lectern sit in the centre.

The theater fills. I wonder when the needle is coming. The sound of the crowd hurts my ears and they bleed. Silence as the lights dim. Two men walk onto the stage. Both are dressed in suits that try to hide their fat. Both men speak and both sound African. One black and one white.

The crowd applauds at words that mean nothing to me. The men sit down. A third man walks on. He talks to each and they answer. Questions lead to questions and more applause.

Then a suit leans towards me. The needle is back. My world returns to normal. I embrace the charge. I grab the charge.

Chaos descends. The black man rises from the chair and leaps on the white man. They fall to the ground. A roar goes up from the audience. I don't care. I just wrap my arms around the electricity running through my body. Sucking it in.

Beneath me the theater begins to boil as fights break out. Violence and violence meet violence and violence. I'm a conductor in a world of pain. Directing the electricity. Sending it to the seats. Watching the people as they dance to my tune. Fists, legs, heads. Handbags, pens, hairbrushes. All weapons.

I spray the electricity in larger waves. The noise becomes one of death. Voices way beyond the norm. Sounds that belong in a war, not downtown Tampa. People doing unto people the worst they can. A storm of hate rolling across the seats. There's no hiding place in the hurricane. No one is untouched.

I revel in my isolation as blood flows, blows fly and teeth bite. On the stage the black man has reduced the white man's face to pulp. He has no intention of stopping.

The guards—no doubt expected to intervene—have little interest in stopping the black man's pumping fists. They're too busy with each other. As the electricity burns bright one of them reaches out and snaps his colleague's fingers with the ease of pulling a dead branch from a tree. He holds on to the hand, pops it into his mouth, bites down and starts chewing on the fingers.

There's movement from behind me. Panicked, quick movement. A needle is pressed home. I stop rising and fall back. Caught in the smooth hairless arms of the downer drug. I'm lifted from the chair and dragged down the stairs into the night. The door to the SUV is open. I'm flung inside.

We take off, as the narcotic tells me all is right and nothing is wrong.

'Fucking mess.'

I don't know the voice but it's coming from the front passenger seat.

'I thought he had this shit figured.'

I can guess who he is.

'Did you see what the hell was going on?'

'The whole place went crazy. God knows how many are dead.'

The words stop as the world moves sideways in an instant. The car spins and mounts the sidewalk. I'm flung against the door and bounce back, my head coming to rest on the seat.

Warm evening air invades the car's interior as the door is ripped open. A hand reaches around my leg and pulls. Even if I wanted to there's nothing I can do to stop myself being hauled from the car.

The suit next to me is trying to react but with a pop his face explodes. He bounces back, his head bursting into the car's interior like a rotten firework. The hand keeps pulling. My skin rips.

I bounce off the running-board and fall to the sidewalk.

'Help me.'

I recognize the voice but I'm in no position to help anyone. Arms cup under my armpits and I'm lifted. I try to place some weight on my legs but the drugs have softened my bones. I dangle.

I see the SUV, hard against a shop window, a giant pane of glass crazed but not yet collapsed. Another car is welded to the side of the SUV. Nose in. Creating an L-shaped vehicle. The second vehicle is a pickup. Loaded into the back is a mud-splattered trail bike.

The hands drag me to the back of the pickup and let me fall to the road. The tailgate drops above me before the bike is tugged across my line of vision. A second pop and there's a scream. I see a gun in the hand of the man heaving the bike.

He bounces the bike's rear tire to the ground and guides the front tire down, inches from my head. Another pop from his gun as the engine fires up.

'Can you hold on?' I still can't see his face.

Hands lift me to the bike and onto the back. The man struggles to keep the bike upright, holding me by the waist as he leaps on in front. I start to fall. He reaches round and pulls my arms around his waist. I try and snuggle in but I need his hand to keep me upright.

'Shit, Craig. You need to help.'

I realize that it's Charlie and I grab his stomach. I don't want to help. It's not on my agenda. I live in the needle world and in that world people do the work. I do nothing.

The bike leaps forward and I start to fall back. Hands whip round my arms to pull me tight. The driver lets go to change gear and grabs me after flexing the clutch. He does this three times, then he hits top gear. A set of lights flick red as we approach but he keeps on the speed and we zip through. Five blocks down he slows, taking a left—the engine moaning at the lack of gear change. If he lets me go I'll be roadkill in seconds.

Another turn. Another, and we hit the interstate, roaring up the on-ramp. Four junctions later we're off and into a small town. A couple of rows of shops flicker by. Charlie forces the bike down a small road. Open fields ride beside us. A small wood drifts into view. We take a dirt track into the trees and out the other side.

The field beyond is barren. At the edge sits a trailer. At one time it was someone's pride and joy, now it's slumped at an angle—silver aluminum faded to gunmetal grey.

The man parks the bike behind the trailer and lifts me off. He carries me to the trailer door and fumbles for keys. Once inside he drops me on a foam-covered bench seat.

I look up as Charlie leaves me on my own.

CHAPTER 32

I don't sleep. I don't think I can without my 'out' drug. The trailer is dark. I hear movement outside and the door opens. I try to smile as Charlie walks in. 'Craig, you're a mess.'

I need some more liquid in my veins. Up, down or out—I don't care. 'You killed my wife.'

'No I didn't.'

I want to argue but I also want drugs. 'Got any of the stuff?'

'What stuff?'

'You know. Needles. Drugs.'

'Ain't none of that shit in here.'

'Need it.'

'I'm sure you do.'

'Can't do without.'

'You'll have to.'

Cold turkey is a phrase that means nothing to me. Words from a novel or a TV show. 'Can't.'

'Sorry, you have no choice. Not unless you want me to take you back to your hosts?'

I don't and I do. 'Something?'

'I can give you Coca-Cola, food, a blanket and sympathy. How much shit have they been pumping into you?'

'It's not shit.'

'Coke?' He fetches a can and I drain it in three gulps. 'Again.' He hits me again and I need a third before I can talk. 'Charlie, what happened?'

'You tell me. Last I know I was running my bar and then whack, and I'm being bundled into a car and driven across most of the USA.'

'Not to you. To me?'

He sits on the bench seat opposite. 'I've no idea. I'm not even sure what you are. Other than bad news.'

'How did you escape?'

'Carelessness. After the thing with Sharon I was taken to a new block. I'm not sure they knew what to do with me. I asked for fresh air and they assigned someone to watch me. One day they let me walk round the compound on my own. Then they stopped accompanying me. The pound was chain link and razor wire but I've been there before and it didn't take much to use the metal on the bed to make a cutter. Once I had that I just picked my time and one night I never came back.'

'How did you find me?'

Charlie sits back. 'I knew where you were. Same place they had me. I just sat it out. Took a while. I had nearly given in when you appeared. Once you hit the theater I waited. Chaos rolled out. Then you. I knew they were taking you back so I took a chance.'

'Thanks.'

I slump to one side. The craving for the drugs is building. I have no idea how bad it will get but it doesn't feel good. Normally I'm gone by now.

Charlie takes a blanket from an overhead cover and places it on me. It smells of damp and dirt.

'Please.'

He ignores me.

I curl up into a ball.

CHAPTER 33

I'm bathed in sweat. My trousers are slick with urine and something else. Charlie is gone. Cans of Coke stand in a line and are backed up by large bags of chips. I'm shivering despite the warmth inside the trailer. I have a single thought. Needle world. It is all I can focus on. I try to stand up but my legs won't carry any weight. I stuff the blanket into my mouth and bite down hard.

I have no breath to scream. I have no way to move. I want a needle in a way that my heart needs blood. I'll die without the drugs.

A large packet of own-brand headache pills stands next to the Coke cans. I pick it up to discover only four pills sitting in the box. I eat them all. Crunching and chewing with the few teeth I have left.

I curl up tight as a wave of shivering flows through me. Ice cold one moment—burning hot the next. My stomach churns and a blowtorch is lit. I vomit and the painkillers mix with the small puddle of yellow fluid as it drips from my bed.

I stick my head into the bench seat. Driving my skull hard against the wood that lies beneath the foam. Wanting pain that will distract from the pain.

The door opens. Charlie walks in. I see his nose wrinkle. A young woman and young man trail in after him. They seem less bothered by the smell. Both are fresh-faced and vaguely familiar. The girl has short red hair and a set of diamond-white teeth.

The boy is no more than twenty. Curly hair and the same teeth as his partner. They could be the Osmonds' grandkids.

They get to work on me. I'm stripped and cleaned with a bowl of water and a collection of damp cloths. My wounds are bandaged. I'm given pills to swallow. The sick feeling falls away. The girl makes broth on the trailer ring and they force-feed it into me. Five glucose tablets are dessert.

'What did they have you on, man?' asks the boy.

'No idea.'

'Not good. It's hard to help when you don't know what you've been into.'

Not good when they take it away either.

'You look as bad as I've seen and I've seen plenty,' says the girl.

Great.

'Take these.'

I swallow more pills and the world starts to dull.

Days start to crawl away. Twenty-four hours—each hour full of too many minutes—each minute full of too many seconds and each second lasting a week.

The girl and boy appear twice a day, but they don't chat much. Charlie thinks I might not die. So does the boy. The girl is not so sure. I'm with the girl.

'Do you do much of this sort of thing?' I ask them both one day.

The girl and the boy are called Tina and Gary. Stage names.

'More than we would like to. We work in a rehab clinic in Laguna Beach. You're quite the privileged one getting house calls.'

Long way for a house call. 'Charlie must pay well.'

A smile. 'Not really his style, paying.'

'You're doing this for free?'

'Kind of.'

You have to love someone who'll clean up your shit for free.

Broth, pills—then solid food. The pills to dull the craving. But the craving is strong. The solid food helps. I can't remember the last time I had any.

'I want to get up.' It's been a few days since I asked about the pay.

'On you go,' says Tina. This time she's alone.

'Just like that?'

'Just like that.'

'I could run away.'

'Who cares?'

Nice.

I swing my legs onto the trailer floor. I don't recognize them as my own. Stick-thin and white as chalk. They don't look like they could support a balloon. I press down. Tina catches my arm as I push up. My emaciated body is less of a burden than I thought. My legs hold. Then the world spins. I fall back before I faint.

'Still feel like hitting the road?'

Funny ha ha she is.

By the end of the week I'm on my feet and able to go to the toilet for myself. Which makes Tina and Gary happier. Charlie has been noticeable by his absence.

'Where's Charlie?' I ask Tina. I'm sitting on the edge of the bed. Shoes on. Dressed. Ready to take some air.

'He calls but he doesn't say from where.'

'Tell me again why you're doing this?'

'We love the job.'

'Bullshit.'

'You asked.'

'I need some air.'

I step out into the evening and the cool air feels like it has just leaked from heaven. I draw in a deep one and cough myself into a sitting position on the stairs that lead to the trailer door. The trees sit close by, the leaves fighting their last round against nature. Winter is nearly here. I miss not having an autumn but that's LA for you. Then I remember I'm not in LA and that brings back Lorraine.

'Can I have a mirror?' I shout.

Tina comes out of the trailer, rooting around in her purse. 'Are you ready for this?'

'Just give me the thing.'

She hands me a compact. I flick it open.

The man in the mirror is not me. My face has no substance. My cheeks look like they should meet on the inside. My eyes are sunk so deep that a baseball cap won't be needed to keep the sun out of them. Wafer-thin parchment paper has replaced my skin—all the color of weak tea. A few tufts of white hair cling to the cratered moon that is my head. I was thinning before I met the suits but at least I could still style my hair for a night out. Now I'd be better with Pledge.

'Not exactly your strong handsome type,' I say.

Tina smiles. There's something familiar in the smile.

'You're doing well. You're lucky to be here.'

'What were they giving me?'

'I've no idea. Describe what it felt like.'

I tell her.

'Hard to tell. A mix. Something to get you up. Something to bring you down and something to make you sleep.'

'I still want it.'

'Of course you do. You had an express course in becoming an addict. Most people slide into it slowly. You had front row seats by the sound of it.'

'Aren't you interested in what this is all about?'

'In our business we don't ask. Discretion is writ large upon our front door.'

'Tell me again why you're doing this?'

'No.'

I dream for the first time in an age that night. Not a long dream. A simple dream of standing on the edge of a lake. Water lapping at my ankles. The lake is warm and inviting. The wood behind cold and far away. I want to walk into the lake.

I don't need Freud to decipher this one for me.

I wake, drop to the floor and try a press-up. I fail but feel good that I tried.

I'd kill for a burger.

CHAPTER 34

'Charlie, I want to kill them.'

The sun is low in the sky. Charlie hands me a beer. I sigh. 'Are you sure this is good for me?' My arms are still thin but I'm up to three press-ups today. I could have done four if I'd pushed.

'If we're going to talk about Lorraine, essential.'

The wind blows leaves around, and a dust-devil picks some up, wheeling them under the trailer.

'Why would we talk about Lorraine?' I crack the tin and sip at the liquid. I'd still prefer a needle but the beer mixed with a few of Tina and Gary's tablets helps keep the craving at bay.

'Craig, what did they do to you?'

I look at him and, instead of avoiding the question, I offload. The whole shebang.

When I'm finished he looks at me. 'Brings back the old times. Me serving you beer. You wringing yourself dry.'

'This is cheaper.'

'For you, maybe.'

'Charlie, why the hell are you helping me?'

'Hatch Roll.'

'Garbage. Thousands of people cycle through there. I'm nothing special.'

'You want to know about Lorraine?'

I don't want to know about Lorraine. I don't want to remember the sound of her skull cracking like a busted snail shell. This is the man who took her away from me. And now I'm sitting on the stoop sipping suds and chewing air with him.

'I know that you didn't mean to kill her. Let's leave it there.'

'No.'

'My rules. We play by my fucking rules. Okay?'

'My beer. My rules.'

'Charlie, this isn't the time.'

'It's exactly the time. You know what it felt like?'

I don't answer.

'Like nothing. Like the biggest nothing on earth. That's what. I didn't even believe I'd done it. Not right after. It was a blank but the suits played me the tape. Again and again. At first I thought it was a James Cameron moment. CGI and all that. Not me. Not me with Lorraine. But they had it on tape and I have to accept it. I didn't want to believe it but it was me. I still don't want to believe it. I loved your wife.'

'I know.'

'I mean I really loved her. Ever since the day you walked into the bar. I saw her and I didn't see you until an hour after you sat down. There was Lorraine and there was everyone else. Except you had her. Not me. The joke about the money. A thousand and one dollars! I would have given you every cent in my bank if I thought she would have chosen me. But it was never going to happen. She loved you. And that was that.'

'So why did you kill her?'

'Because you made me. Isn't that the way it works?'

'All I know is that I'm somehow responsible for you killing her.' I stop. The words are harsh and too real. 'I pushed you to do it but there was a reason. I haven't figured out all the angles yet but I only set off people with bad history. Something nasty in the past that I bring to the surface. Not bad blood. Something hidden. Something that's rotten at the core of the apple. All rosy on the surface but deep down? Buried. So what happened with you and Lorraine?'

Charlie sits back. He drains the can he's holding. There is

something. The pause is enough to tell him that I know there's something.

He leans away from me. 'You know what, maybe it doesn't matter.'

I shake my head. 'You wanted this. You dug me from the grave and decided I was worth saving. You wanted this conversation and now I want to know what happened between you and my wife.'

'I tried it on with her.' He lets the words hang in the evening air and I watch them blow around our heads.

'What?'

'I tried it on with her. One night after closing. You were back at Hatch Roll for a check-up. She had come down for a late-night chat. She didn't even have a drink. Just coffee. I, on the other hand, had been drinking. Stupid. I pushed, she pushed back. I pushed too hard and she ran.'

'How hard did you push?'

'It was enough. I overstepped the mark. I tried to kiss her.' Pause. 'And then a little more.'

I hit him square on the chin. Then I'm on top of him. Raining down blows. But I'm weak. He pushes up and rolls me off. I try to stand up. He pushes me back down.

I shout. 'Bastard. Is that why you're helping me? Is it? You kill my wife and then tell me you tried to rape her. So this is your Get Out of Jail Free card is it? Save poor Craig and bang goes your guilty conscience.'

The power in my voice feels good. 'Is that *IT*?'

'I never tried to rape her.'

'But you weren't far away.'

He drops his head.

'Fuck you,' I say. I stand up. He backs off. I spit in his face, turn away and begin to walk towards the woods.

'I'd never have hurt her,' he shouts after me.

I turn. 'You killed her.'

He takes a step towards me. 'Craig. You killed her and you

know it. I might have been there but, without you, it would never have happened.'

I start to run. It hurts but I need to be away from Charlie. I hit the edge of the wood. I feel dead leaves slap me in the face. It feels good. I take another twenty steps and fall to the ground. I struggle to get up. I want to run. I want Lorraine back. I want my life back. My legs won't support me and I start to crawl. Anything to keep moving. I fall to my stomach and slither forward a few feet. I scream in frustration.

I'm not going anywhere. The scent of the dying leaves buries itself in my nose. I roll on my back. Charlie is standing over me. He reaches out. I flip my face away. I try to crawl but I'm spent. Charlie's hands grab my waist. I try and wriggle free. Charlie lifts me clean from the ground, wrapping me over his shoulder.

Tears flow as I thump on his back. He walks to the trailer. His back is damp by the time he lays me in my bed.

He walks out. I try to get up, fall back and slide into sleep.

CHAPTER 35

'I really do want to kill them.'

Charlie is sitting next to me on the bed.

My anger with Charlie comes and goes. It's been two weeks since I tried to run. Two weeks of tearing my head apart. Trying to figure what to do. 'What you did to Lorraine was wrong.'

He says nothing. I want him to say sorry again. Just to let me have another pop. But there is no mileage in this. I need to make a decision.

'I'm going to kill them. Lendl, Tampoline—then maybe you.'

'Food and rest first.'

I pass thirty press-ups in the next week. Sixty in two weeks. I go for a walk each day. On the day I do one hundred press-ups and walk two miles, I'm on the way back.

I shave my head each day. My dream of thick, offensive hair has gone for good.

Tina and Gary are like clockwork toys. They arrive every day at eight in the morning and then again at six. Conversation is random but never useful. Baseball scores. World news. Small requests—I'm back reading again. Charlie is in and out. I ask what he's doing. Where he goes? He tells me he has sold the pub and is tidying up a few things. He tells me how hard it is to do stuff when you have a government agency trying to track you down. And then he tells me if the Unabomber could evade the FBI for seventeen years then a few months should be easy.

I'm not sure I care and I'm not so sure he's right. The suits don't seem to dance to the same tune as the FBI.

I've worked through a thousand scenarios in my head. All involving the death of Lendl and the senator. None hold water. For a start I'm not sure where Lendl is. I have a rough idea of where I was held, but it was a secure facility and wouldn't be easy to get into. Anyway, he could be anywhere on the planet. I first met him in Iraq after all.

The senator is easier. He has a public diary but I want both and, given my talent, I know if I can get them in the same room, things may well take care of themselves.

Charlie comes into the trailer. 'Time to move on.'

'Why?'

Tina and Gary are just finishing breakfast around us. I won't need them much longer. I'm still a shadow of my previous self but I'm in no need of babysitting.

'I caught sight of a couple of suits.'

Charlie has refused to tell me where he's staying. All I know is that it isn't Hudson or Sharon's place.

'Where?'

'Too close for comfort.'

'So where do we go?'

He throws a paper on the table. It's the *Tampa Tribune*. 'I thought you might like to see this. Try the sports pages.'

I flick through. The Devil Rays are at home tonight. The second in a series against the Boston Red Sox. 'What am I looking for?'

'Look who's throwing the first pitch tonight.'

I read. 'Tampoline.'

'Thought you might like to know.'

'Pity that Lendl won't be there.'

'Won't he?'

Charlie drops a small leaflet on the table to join the paper. It's an invitation to buy into the Tampa Bay Devil Rays. At the bottom there's a bunch of faces and names of current shareholders.

Lendl's face is dead centre.

'He has a share in the baseball team?'

Charlie nods. 'Clive Lendl's one of the minor players.'

Tampoline and Lendl. Tonight. In the same place. Assuming Lendl attends.

But of course he'll attend. He knows Tampoline. He might even be funded by him. After all, Tampoline was there the night they started my experiments.

I look up at Charlie. 'When is the first pitch?'

'8.00pm.'

'Tonight. I'm going after them tonight.'

'And what are you going to do once you get there?'

'Let nature take its course.'

'Great plan.'

'Best I have.'

The window shatters, something bounces off the far side of the trailer and smoke pours from the object. Charlie looks at it, at me and then to Gary and Tina. I drop to my knees, shutting my eyes. These bastards are nothing if not consistent. In the confined space we have seconds before the gas forces us from the trailer.

'Gary, Tina—get out.'

I hear Charlie push Gary and Tina to the door—his eyes must be streaming. There's a scuffle, coughing, then the door opens. Charlie joins me on the floor.

'Under the bed,' he coughs.

I want to point out that this is useless, just as a second missile flies in. I don't see it—just hear it smack off a surface and start hissing.

Charlie drags me under the bed. He fumbles around. There's a click and I fall into a hole. He joins me then reaches up to close the trapdoor we've just fallen through.

'Here.' He hands me a mask with small metal bottle attached. 'Oxygen.'

I strap the mask to my face. I fiddle with the bottle until I start the oxygen flow.

We are lying side by side in a metal box maybe eight feet long by four wide. At a couple of feet deep the tip of my mask touches the top of the box as I lie on my back.

'What is this?' My voice is muffled and amplified at the same time. Muffled from the mask, amplified in the metal coffin.

'A back-up plan. You can't see the box from the outside. I had it installed when I decided I was coming for you. A modern-day priest's hole.'

'It won't take five minutes for them to find us.'

'This is only part one of a three-part plan.'

'What's part two?

'This.'

I hear a click in the dark. There's a few seconds' silence, followed by a dull whoomph from above.

'What was that?' I ask.

'It's going to get hot in here. Stay with it. The trapdoor has a strip of Pyroblanket on it.'

'What?'

'To give protection from heat.'

'What heat?'

'I've just set the trailer on fire.'

CHAPTER 36

Charlie coughs as the fumes he breathed in still rattle around his chest. I feel him shudder with the effort.

I turn to him. 'What do you mean you set fire to the trailer?'

'I set up a firebomb in the trailer. I'm betting that once the trailer is a molten mass they'll assume we're dead.'

'Are you kidding? We *will* be dead.'

'Not if I've thought this through correctly.'

'Have you?'

'If you're asking if I've ever done anything like this before— the answer is no.'

'Great.'

The temperature is rising. Whether this is because of our body heat or the fire above I can't tell. I try to move but there's little room. As I wriggle, I feel the metal box bend beneath me.

'Charlie, the box is moving.'

'Metal one-o-one was never my strong point. Had to guess at what was needed. This is hardly in the Home Depot manual.'

There's a roaring sound from above. Light leaks in from the edge of the trapdoor. I turn my head. Charlie is coming into view.

'Not good,' he says. 'I thought the seal on the trapdoor was airtight.'

'Charlie, this is insane. We'll bake to death.'

'There's still part three. But we need to wait.'

'For what?'

'Just wait.'

Something shatters above us. There's a crash as an object falls to the floor. Another crash and the whole trailer rocks. The box-floor dips a little more. The light around the trapdoor is bright—a constant glare. I can now see the inside of the box. It's made of the non-slip metal sheets that started life in industrial complexes and are now used as a shorthand by theme parks to indicate danger. The raised surface is a crisscross of short strips. The welding that keeps the whole thing together would fail a freshman's first exam.

Heat is coming in waves. Each wave hotter than the last. The air has been sucked from the space. My exposed skin is starting to smart. I try to draw slowly on the bottle of air. It doesn't look like it holds much and without it I'll be dead in seconds.

'We can't take much more,' I yell.

'A couple of minutes. Just hold on.'

'For what, Charlie—for what?'

'Just hang on.'

An explosion from above suggests that the fire is having fun. The noise is now making it difficult to hear. A series of mini bombs go off as my home for the past few weeks is reduced to little more than ashes and bent metal. Each bang, each explosion, each sound vibrates in the coffin. All the time the heat is rising.

We lurch downwards. I roll into Charlie as we settle at an angle. I hear a faint grunt and realize Charlie is shouting. 'I can't get to the release.'

The words are a whisper against the hurricane. I lean over to try and press my ear to Charlie's mask.

'Lever. Pull the lever,' he shouts.

I reach around but all I can feel is the rough texture of the metal. We lurch again. A blast of heat flows in as the corner of the trapdoor bends towards us.

'It's under me,' shouts Charlie.

I push beneath his back. I feel a rubber-tipped object. I wrap my hand around it and pull. Nothing happens.

'I can't pull it up while you're on it,' I scream.

Charlie arches his back. I try again, but nothing happens. He rolls on to his side and the handle is free. I pull hard.

We fall.

We land in dirt. Charlie pushes me away and a blanket flies over my head. I can feel the cool, damp sensation of lying on moist earth. The blanket kills the light, dulling the sound of the fire at the same time.

'Is this part three?'

Charlie coughs. 'Yes. I dug the pit before I moved the trailer in. I'd hoped we wouldn't have to use it. Anyone watching the trailer might have seen us fall.'

'I doubt it. The whole trailer must have settled a couple of feet. Coupled with the fire we'll have been invisible. What now—part four?'

'I was lucky to get to part three.'

'Well at least they won't have to dig our grave.'

'The blanket is the same stuff I used on the floor. As long as something large doesn't fall on us we should be okay.'

'What, like a trailer?'

'That could happen.'

I want to laugh. 'Charlie, if we survive they'll still find us. Tina and Gary will tell them we were inside.'

'Not a problem. They both know what to do.'

'They're kids. The suits will make beef-chuck out of them.'

'They may be kids but they're my kids and they'll do the right thing.'

'Your kids?'

'Well, kind of mine.'

I knew there was something familiar about the pair.

'Look Charlie, we need to get out. This is fucking serious. They know we aren't David Copperfield.'

Above the roar of the fire I hear sirens.

Charlie rolls onto his side. 'I told the kids to phone the authorities before I joined you.'

'The police and fire won't make any odds. The suits are way beyond them.'

'Station twenty. I just hope they're on call.'

'What?'

'Station twenty. A couple of friends.'

'What are you on about?'

'I chose this place because it's in station twenty's area. I have some friends who work there.'

'Station twenty?'

'The local fire station.'

Sirens are closing in.

'And they know about us?'

'Kind of.'

I'm at a loss. Charlie has put his own kids on the line for me with the ropiest of 'outs' if things go wrong.

'You know the suits will search for us?'

'I'm counting on it.'

'Then what?'

'Trust in friends.'

The fire is starting to die down. The noise is falling away. I can hear some voices where there had only been a din before.

Water starts to flow in from above. In seconds the hole starts to fill with it as the hoses are turned on the fire.

'We need to get out. We'll drown.' Charlie nods and pushes the blanket away. We're faced with a metal ceiling.

The floor of the priest hole has fallen and sealed us in tight.

CHAPTER 37

'The trailer has collapsed on us!'

Stating the obvious is not a trait I admire in Charlie.

The water is running through a small gap between the trailer floor and the earth. Only the narrowness of the entry has prevented the hole filling with water already.

'Dig at the opposite end from the water,' Charlie shouts.

'But the trailer might be sitting there.'

'Yes, and if we dig where the water is it'll flood in and we'll drown quicker.'

I reach up and start to pull away at the earth. It comes free in clumps. Charlie squeezes in next to me and starts to claw. We hit metal and need to start again further along. This time my hand breaks through. The fire is all but out above.

I start to widen the space. I am kneeling and beneath me the water is up to my waist. Charlie is stronger than me. I push him forward. I take up the rear. He tears into the earth. I reach up and help with one hand.

Water cascades down the opposite wall. The fire is out. Why are they still pumping?

The gap is now big enough to stick a head through. The water is up to my chest and I can feel the icy cold drawing away my strength. We're losing this battle.

'Charlie, faster.' A useless thing to say. He's burrowing like a mad mole. The earth may be damp but it's still hard to shift. Each handful has to be pulled free and thrown into the rising water and this takes time. Time we don't have.

I reach over, grab at the dirt and pull. My hand yanks away a few ounces and I slam my fist in frustration. 'This isn't working. We won't get out in time.'

I wade across the hole to where the water is pouring in and reach up. Charlie turns to see what I am doing and shouts. 'Stop!'

I grab the edge where the water is flowing hardest and pull. The mud falls away, turning the water into a torrent.

'Jesus, Craig, don't!'

I grab another two handfuls and pull down. The water cascades into my face. I fight against the flow to grab some more and succeed. I dig deep—burying my fingers up to the third knuckle. My bandaged finger screams at me. I ignore it.

I close my fingers as much as I can and lean back—putting all my weight on both hands. Pressing my feet against the wall of the hole, I pull. A large slab of mud slides free. I fall back into the water and I'm engulfed.

The mask is ripped from my face.

The surface of the water recedes as I fall to the bottom of the hole. My head is spinning. My nose fills with filthy liquid. My eyes sting. There can only be four feet of water but I can't tell up from down. I push and my head rams the metal roof. There's no space left for air.

Charlie is behind me. I grab his hand and push him to the point where the water is coming in. He slides past me and I follow. My lungs are already burning.

I see light in the corner and Charlie seems to be climbing. I hold onto his leg. He raises it, then he's yanked from my grip. I push forward trying to find the edge of the hole. The mud is slippy and my mind starts to fog as the lack of air bites.

A hand grabs my wrist. I grab back, holding tight. I'm yanked up and, as my head breaks through the surface, I suck in air— just keep sucking.

Another hand takes my arm and I'm pulled out of the hole. I emerge from under the wreck of the trailer.

Charlie is lying next to me. Two firemen are slouched beside us. Both are rubbing their upper arms. I might have lost a lot of weight but it took effort to pull me from the hole.

Charlie spits up brown water and I join him. He grasps the hand of the nearest fireman. 'Thanks.'

'Always digging you out of a hole. Always.' The fireman's accent is thick with New York.

Charlie turns to me. 'Craig, meet Ryan. Ryan, meet Craig.'

Ryan reaches over and shakes my hand. 'You ex-army as well?'

I nod.

'I thought you guys were supposed to be saving *our* skins,' he says.

'You're the ones with the dangerous job,' I say. 'They gave me a gun when the going got tough. They give you an axe and a hard hat.'

He smiles at his colleague and heads for the fire engine.

'Who are the men in black?' asks Ryan.

'Bad men,' says Charlie. 'They want to talk to us and we're not in the mood for a chat. Understand?'

'Perfectly.'

He signals to the paramedic, who jogs over, bag in hand. 'Both for the hospital I think.'

'The guys over there say they're in charge,' says the para. 'They want to talk to the survivors.'

'See the fire still raging in the trailer?' says Ryan. The paramedic looks at the trailer. A small line of smoke is drifting into the sky. The aluminum shell is burnt black. There are no flames.

The paramedic looks back.

'Smoke,' says Ryan. 'While there's smoke, I'm in charge. If they want to discuss it then fine, but in the meantime get these two to hospital.'

Three suits start to walk over. Ryan points the para to the ambulance and stands up. 'Hospital.'

He walks towards the suits, meeting them as they reach halfway. Voices start to rise and Ryan stands like a human road-block, hat under arm, legs slightly apart.

One of the suits tries to walk round him. Ryan reaches out and blocks him. The suit tries to free himself. A second suit intervenes.

The firemen who are rolling up the hoses drop what they're doing and walk over. They take up positions either side of Ryan. Six of them in a line, facing down the suits. There must be another twenty suits standing next to a clutch of black SUVs but they don't move. To be fair, neither would I.

The paramedic signals for the ambulance to back up, and Charlie and I are stretchered into the back. As the door shuts, Ryan turns, giving us a thumbs up. Next to him, Tina and Gary wave. The ambulance sets off. I lie back for a few moments as we bump over the rough ground and, as we enter civilization again, I turn to Charlie. 'Who the hell is Ryan?'

Charlie smiles. 'My ex-wife's first husband. Tina and Gary's father.'

'I thought you said they were your kids?'

'Kind of. When I married Susan they moved in with me, but they're really Ryan's.'

'Susan?'

'My ex-wife.'

'And her ex-husband is on our side?'

'Yip.'

'Did he know what was going on?'

'Probably. He's still close with the kids.'

Whatever familiarity I saw in the kids was coincidental.

'And you get on with your ex-wife's ex?'

'You know what they say. The enemy of my enemy is my friend.'

This time I smile.

The paramedic steps into the cab to talk to the driver. I tap Charlie on the shoulder. 'Ryan might be our savior at a fire but ten will get you twenty that the suits will be camped out at the hospital.'

'And?'

'Time to ask this taxi to drop us off.'

'And how do we do that?'

'Next set of lights.'

'Are you up to it?'

I'm not. 'Yes.'

The ambulance isn't on the siren. We're hardly emergency material. As we slow down I sit up. Through the gap into the cab I see an approaching set of lights as they flick to red.

'Now.'

We slip from the stretchers. I grab the handle to the back door, swing it open and jump out. Charlie follows, pushing the door shut as he hits the road.

The couple in the car behind stare wide-eyed. The ambulance accelerates on the green, before slamming to a halt.

We jog to the sidewalk, walk into a diner and head for the washrooms. I turn as we enter. The paramedic is out on the street—scanning—trying to find us. I walk on.

The washroom is empty.

'What now?' says Charlie.

'Tropicana Field tonight. After that I don't care.'

'They'll be over the place like a rash. They know what you can do and now they know where you are, it won't take long to put two and two together.'

'I'm still going.'

'It won't solve anything. In fact, it'll make it worse.'

'Worse. How the hell can it be worse? My wife's dead. I've no job. No cash. I'm being hunted to be used as some sort of fucking assassin. How can it be worse?'

'You could be caught. They'd have you back on the happy juice in no time. Maybe one more gig and then a bullet in the head. That's worse.'

'And what do I do instead? Run?'

'I've got some money. We skip the country and find somewhere to let things cool.'

'Charlie, much as I like you, I'm not going to retire to some tropical paradise with you. What about your kids? Are you just going to leave them? And then there's the fact that you killed my wife.'

He looks away. A low blow and I know it. Charlie no more killed my wife than he killed Sharon.

'Look,' I continue. 'Let me have one crack at this tonight. Then I'm done. Anyway, nothing might happen. It took the combined expertise of Pfizer and the US government to find a way to trigger me. Even then it went south in a big way. What's the odds that anything will happen?'

'I've no idea.'

'Tonight, and then I'm with you. You don't even have to come to the game. I'll fly solo.'

'Sure you will. You can hardly stand as it is. You might feel a bit better than you did but you're a country mile from being right.'

'I'll make it.'

'Not without me.'

'Okay, so are you out or in?'

Charlie sits on the washroom's only sink. The door opens and a man in a jogging suit walks in.

'Can you give us a minute?' The man looks me up and down as I speak to him.

'I need to use the toilet.'

I step forward. 'Can you give us a *minute*.'

He looks at me. He backs out.

'Scary,' says Charlie. 'And you think nothing is going to happen tonight?'

'We'd better move. The guy might report us.'

'We need to change out of these clothes.'

'You any friends left you haven't used up yet?'

Charlie shakes his head. 'But I know where we can get a fresh set of clothes and hang out until tonight.'

He pushes up from the sink. 'I just need to lose some of the water I swallowed.'

I exit the washroom and wait until he's finished relieving himself. There's no sign of the ambulance. The man who had entered the washroom is standing talking to the waitress. He's pointing in my direction.

Charlie walks out and we leave the diner with two pairs of eyes burning holes in our backs.

Charlie waves down a taxi. 'The Village Motel, 4100 East Hillsborough.'

The taxi driver gives us the once-over and decides we're not carrying the plague.

'Where are we going?' I ask.

Charlie closes his eyes and stretches. 'My home from home for these last few weeks. You'll love it.'

The taxi driver settles into the journey.

I don't.

CHAPTER 38

The Village Motel sits next to a used-car lot in a dodgier end of town. On the opposite corner sits another used-car lot. We are in sub-two-grand-auto land. The motel is a collection of mismatched buildings. Charlie pays off the taxi driver with a wet twenty.

'Nice,' I say.

'Don't knock it. Very reasonable. Clean, and the owner is very discreet.'

We walk to the back of the complex. As we enter the room I find myself in a spacious, well-kept bedroom. The bathroom is off to the right and a wire-meshed window looks out the back onto a small road. I look through the window. Four men in hard hats are chatting as they stroll by.

'Okay, so I was wrong. It seems quite nice. Who has first dibs on the shower?'

Charlie doesn't answer and walks into the bathroom.

I lift a newspaper from a pile, placing it on the chair next to the vanity table. I'm still soaked through but I'll wait until Charlie is finished before stripping off—I don't have anything to change into and hanging around in another man's bedroom in my birthday suit just feels wrong.

When I hear the shower kick in I walk over and switch on the TV. I take a minute to locate the remote and jig it around until I find the local news channel. A dark-haired stunner is giving the gossip and intelligence the once-over. A car smash on the 275, an emergency landing at Tampa International, a child abduction—all in all, a normal day in wonderland.

The sports reporter is introduced to preview the upcoming game with the Red Sox. There's no mention of the senator, but the Barenaked Ladies will be playing a gig after the game.

The shower stops.

The newsreader picks up on the next story. *'And now for some breaking news. Police are anxious to interview a Mr Craig McIntyre in connection with a fire near Lettuce Lake Park.'*

My military snapshot sits on the newsreader's shoulder as she speaks.

'The fire engulfed an illegal trailer, and, in a police statement, we are informed that loss of life was only avoided by the swift action of the Fire Department. If you see Craig McIntyre, please call the number on the screen or contact your local police station. The police are advising not to approach him.

'And now to the story of a dog that wanted to fly...'

I realize that the bathroom door is open and Charlie has taken in the news.

'Look on the bright side. *You* weren't mentioned,' I say.

Towel wrapped around his waist, Charlie nods at the statement as he crosses to sit on the bed. 'You'll never get into the stadium now the police are looking for you.'

I stand up. 'Let me take a shower and think on that.'

I close the door and wind up the hot water. Once it starts to pour I grab Charlie's shower gel. I get to work on my still-thin arms. Thirty seconds in I jump from the shower, grab a towel and stick my head out of the door.

'It was an old photo,' I say, dripping on the carpet. 'They used an old photo on the TV.'

Charlie is pulling on a pair of pants and looks up. 'So they did.'

'Well do you think I look like myself?'

The photo was of a lean but muscled man, a hint of a five o'clock shadow, dark curly hair and bright eyes. Not a drugravaged skeleton with a shiny pate and eyes with a sheen of dust over them.

'Strange that,' says Charlie.

'They won't have new photos of me. I don't remember them taking any. Although I was so out of it they could have put me in a movie and I wouldn't have noticed.'

'I can't see the point in using the old photo.'

I nod in agreement, drip back to the shower and try to clean out the dirt. Teeth brushed (fingers only—I draw the line at using someone else's toothbrush). A rough shave (chin and head) and I feel a touch more human.

'What about clothes?' I say as I hang out the bathroom door again.

Charlie hands me a stack. I retire to realize that we're not the same height, width or mass. The jeans are too baggy. The T-shirt is voluminous and I skip the boxers—preferring to go commando. My shoes will do once they've dried out, and Charlie's socks will suffice.

I take the belt on the jeans to the last hole. Even then I'm a yard shy. A few minutes with a fork, and the belt holds the trousers up. They are flying at half-mast. The T-shirt hangs like a kaftan but the look isn't that bad. With my new baldness I have an air of rebellion about me.

'Nice.' Charlie laughs as I re-enter the room.

'Food?'

'On its way. The wonders of pizza delivery.'

The TV is still on but the sound is down.

'So, to tonight.'

Charlie sighs. 'Craig, is it really worth it?'

'I'm not having a debate. I'm going. Full stop.'

He shrugs. 'I don't think it'll be hard getting close to the stadium but it will be a bitch getting in. If these guys are half as connected as we have seen so far they'll be fully loaded when it comes to tech. Face-recognition software, mobile CCTV, access to city-wide cameras, maybe even aerial reconnaissance.'

'Come on Charlie, I'm not the leader of the resistance.'

'Are you sure?'

He reaches into the pile of newspapers and throws me a *USA Today* from the day after my escape. It details the carnage at the theater. In the intervening weeks I hadn't been ready to view my handiwork.

Thirteen dead, fifty-two in hospital—a riot with no reason is how it is described. The two on stage had been the President-in-waiting for Nigeria and his rival for the role. Twenty years as enemies—the event at the theater had been a symbolic burying of the hatchet. Neither had died but both were hospitalized.

I sit back. 'Hell.'

Charlie sits on the bed. 'The good news—if there is any—is that the riot overshadowed what happened on the stage. In fact, if you read the detail you would be forgiven for thinking that the two politicians tried to intervene to help.'

'So I didn't kill a future world leader?'

'The suits underestimated what they had turned you into.'

I remember the electricity flowing from my fingers. Of playing it across the theater. The feeling of hate sweeping across the building. Driven by me. 'I was drugged to the hilt.'

'And you think you have it under control now?'

'Strangely I do. Not in a way that I can explain. Hell I can't explain the half of it but there's been nothing since you rescued me. Your kids would have been prime candidates. The firemen. The suits. All were in proximity when I was in the hole with you. If it's stress that brings it on then it sure as hell should have happened then.'

'So, is it gone?'

'Not gone. Just a bit more predictable. I think. I can still feel it buried in the back of my head. Waiting. But I think it needs my permission now.'

Charlie looks doubtful. 'Are you sure?'

'I'm not sure of anything.'

'So what will you do tonight if we get in?'

'I told you. Let nature take its course.' I lie back in the chair. 'So how *do* we get in?'

The newsreader is sitting in front of a picture of me again. Only this time it's a grainy shot from a CCTV of me in my full baldness. It's a crop from the theater. My eyes are glazed but it's clearly me.

'Shit.' We both say it at the same time.

CHAPTER 39

The pizza boxes lie. Fallen soldiers to our appetite. We're two large bottles of Coke down and a couple of Babe Ruths to the wind.

'I'm stuffed.' Charlie rubs his stomach to prove the point.

I stand up. 'Me too. Now to work. It's baseball night and I feel like a bleacher moment. We should get there early. Before the police and security get into full swing.'

'Won't it be easier to lose ourselves in the crowd?' Charlie asks. 'After all, they don't know you're going to the game.'

'I wouldn't bet on it. The senator, Lendl—it has to be a risk for them. I'd be betting on me being there.'

'Where the hell will we hide if we do get in?'

'Good question.'

'And we need tickets.'

'Cash only. They'll have your cards marked.'

'I'm low on cash. I need to use an ATM.'

'You can't. They'll be onto us in minutes.'

'We can't get in without money. And we sure as hell can't go on the run with loose change.'

'True. Any thoughts?'

Charlie scratches his head. 'I know where there's a wedge.' 'Where?'

'In the house in Hudson. Ten grand to be exact.'

'That's some nest egg.'

'As long as Sharon hasn't used it at some point.'

238

It's the first time he's mentioned Sharon since the escape. He pauses mid breath.

'I'm sorry.' I say.

'It doesn't seem real. They showed me the tape but it wasn't me.'

'It wasn't. It was me. Both times it was me.'

'Let's not go there. It won't help.'

'You can't go to Hudson. They'll be watching. Anyway, why the hell didn't you tell me you had ten grand? I wouldn't have needed the job.'

'It's the only source of cash I have and I'm not a complete charity case. Anyway, I'm betting the suits will be watching the front. Remember the house backs onto a golf course and I have the key. If I'm lucky I can be in and out before they know I'm there.'

'Charlie, they're not stupid. They'll have the house covered from all angles.'

'Have you any better ideas?'

'I'll come with you. Two heads are better and all that.'

'Will you hell. You're dead weight and anyway it's you they want. I may not have a two hundred IQ but taking you up to a house we know they're watching is dumber than a dumb thing. I'll get a cab. All being well I'll be back before five. That'll give us plenty of time to get downtown.'

Charlie stands up and heads for the door.

'Take care.' My words sound weak.

'Stay put. Don't answer the door. Don't leave the room. Watch the adult channel if you have to, but stay put.'

I nod.

As the door closes on him I slump onto the bed and wait for my face to reappear on the TV.

My mind turns to the night ahead. I have no plan and no idea what will happen—but it *will* happen. How the hell do we get in? The place will be alive with cameras and, even if we go early, security won't just let us wander through.

I go back to my training. Occam's Razor. Not exactly a grunt's phrase but my platoon leader liked it.

'Occam's Razor. Keep it simple. Complexity leads to complexity. The easy way is often the best way. The more obvious the less likely they'll see it coming.'

I relax on the bed. Sometimes you just have to give your mind a chance to take a break. A little lateral thinking time. Wait for the rabbit to pop from the top hat.

An hour rolls along. I'm starting to fear the worst for Charlie. He would hardly have reached Hudson by now but my mind is a dangerous thing when given nothing to do. I take to checking the windows on a rota basis. Looking for signs of suits, SUVs or police.

I switch off the TV. My face is annoying me. I also wish I'd thought about picking up some pre-paid cells. Then I remember that I haven't any cash.

There's a knock on the door and I freeze. A drain fly flaps in front of me, its large wings in slow-mo as the sound of flesh on wood settles in the room. I watch the fly circle the main light as a second knock breaks the silence. There's the sound of a key in the lock. I move across the room and into the bathroom. I shut the door and flip on the shower. I'm at the small window turning the latch when I hear a Spanish accent. 'Housekeeping.'

I relax a little but push the window out. At a squeeze I could get through.

'Housekeeping.'

A prelude to an attack or a genuine call to scrub up the room? Hard to tell.

'I'm in the shower.'

'Okay,' comes the reply.

I hear the door click shut. If they're going to come in, it'll be quick. I push my head through the window. No one in sight but that means little. I check I have the room key in my pocket and clamber out. I'm better out than in.

I drop to the ground, tensing for whatever it is that I am tensing for.

Nothing.

I stand up and walk to the edge of the building. I take a breath before poking my head out. The rear of the maid catches my eye. There are no suits. No cars. No nonsense. I walk to the main road and all is clear.

When the door opens I'm half asleep back in the room. Charlie stands in the doorway like a returning hero. His face is filthy and his clothes are ripped. If he looked bad after our episode in the hole he looks worse now.

'Trouble?' I enquire.

'You might say.'

'The suits?'

'Yes.'

He flops on the bed.

'They were waiting. Two car loads. One in front of the house and a second round the corner. No SUVs this time. Old battered Cutlasses instead.' He brushes some dirt onto the floor. 'I spotted them easily enough but they had the house well covered and I didn't have the luxury of waiting for dark. I skirted the golf course and came at the house from behind. I was lucky. The car covering the back had two in it but they were more interested in chatting than watching and I got in okay. I grabbed the cash and was on my way out when the door burst open.'

'They saw you?'

'I think the house was wired.'

'What did you do?'

'I ran. Straight out the back and across the golf course. I had no time to avoid the bushes and trees and I figured it would make it easier if I took them through rather than round. I feel like I've torn half my skin off.'

'But you lost them?'

'Only because I stole a golf buggy. You should have heard the owners. They were just teeing off when I grabbed the thing and put my foot down. They're faster than you think. It was all I needed to get a lead. I abandoned it a couple of blocks away. Spent an hour working my way back to the main drag.'

'If they had cameras inside they'll know what you were back for.'

'All the more reason to cut and run.'

'No. We're going to the game. I've had a change of mind on the plan. Clean up. I need you to run an errand for me.'

Charlie takes his second shower of the day, and, once he's wearing clean clothes and fifty Band Aids, I tell him what we're going to do.

'Let's not make this complicated. There will be thirty or forty thousand going tonight. So let's dress the part. Full Devil Rays kit. Baseball cap. Tops, the lot. We simply merge in with the crowd. They're never going to check everyone, and with a cap pulled down, collar up and head down we just walk in.'

'We just walk in?' Charlie doesn't sound convinced.

'Yip. I need you to get two home plate tickets, or as close as you can. You also need to strip the nearest seller of a lunatic-fan's-worth of Devil Rays gear. We leave at six-thirty.'

Charlie is back in less than forty minutes. He looks like the Devil Rays' best ever customer. 'I hope the hell that the suits aren't looking for odd patterns in the sale of baseball gear. The shop will stick out like a sore thumb.'

After we dress I look in the mirror. Head to toe in Devil Ray's gear. With the cap down I doubt anyone would know who I am.

I lift a knife from the table and put it in my pocket.

'What do you need that for?' asks Charlie.

'Stimulus. What's this?' I hold up a cowbell.

'Seems the fans use them. Usually on the three and two count.'

'You're kidding?'

'Nope.'

I ring the bell. 'I reckon a taxi to within a half mile of the ground. Then we walk.'

My optimism was misplaced. A mile out and we're down to a crawl. We pay off the taxi, taking to the sidewalk. We fall in behind two large families and in front of six teenagers. As we close in on the stadium the throng swells. I begin to believe this is not going to be difficult.

The Tropicana Stadium sits in St Petersburg, despite being the home to the Tampa Bay Devil Rays, and is a closed dome. It looks a little worn at the edges but the fans don't care. The Rays are in the hunt for a pennant. A win tonight will put them a game up on the Yankees.

We need to cross the parking lot to get to the stadium and people are threading their way through the cars—passing tail-gaters who are in full beer-and-BBQ mode. The buzz is good, the noise one of hope.

We squeeze between two compacts and then we hit a line. We join it. I step out to get a better look at what the hold-up is.

A temporary fence has been set up. It stretches around the stadium. There are gaps every ten feet or so, each one manned by police, security or suits.

They are asking everyone to remove baseball caps. They aren't searching bags, just checking faces. As such there's only a small delay. I pull Charlie out of the line by pretending to tie my shoelace. We're next to a large van. I slide behind it, out of sight of the checkers.

'The checks have to be for me.'

'Probably.'

'We wait.'

Charlie shakes his head. 'They have people working the lines. Two are on their way up this one.'

'Back, then?'

He spins to look behind us. 'More. Coming the other way. We have a minute at most.'

I turn. A second line is snaking up on the other side of the van. 'Anyone working that one?'

'Not that I can see.'

'Come on. We'll join it.'

'But you'll be on the police in a couple of minutes.'

'Better than one minute.'

We join the new line to do the traditional line shuffle. Around us the crowd are griping at the delay.

'Checkin' for bombs.'

'Escaped prisoner, I hear.'

'Police killer.'

'Terrorist.'

Charlie is eyeing me as we approach the fence. I reach into my pocket. I take out the knife I lifted from the motel room. We're six from the front and there are two young police officers manning our gap.

'Hats off. All hats off. We need to see faces.'

The smaller of the two officers repeats the phrase and the people in front pull off their baseball caps. I keep mine on. I place the knife, point first, into the side of my thigh.

'Hats off, sir.'

We are at the front of the line.

'Hat off, sir.' The smaller officer is speaking to me.

I shove the knife into my thigh and twist. A living pain train shoots up my leg and I drop to the ground. Charlie bends over me as the policeman steps towards me. I give the knife another twist and nearly pass out.

'Sir?' The officer leans down.

One more twist and my head explodes as the kernel cracks.

I look up and remove my cap. He recognizes me in an instant and stands up. Turning to his colleague he opens his mouth. My headache rolls up and he stops, turning to me, tipping his head

244

to one side.

'Problem, Jim?' His colleague is stepping forward as he talks.

Jim's fist is already travelling when his colleague reaches him. The punch is a good one and takes the other officer by surprise. Jim follows up on the punch with a kick.

'Move,' I say to Charlie.

The world drops blue. The pain is gone. We push through the gap as the second officer retaliates. I cut to the right, dragging Charlie with me. Weaving through the crowd. The fighting police officers are lost to the rear.

'Did you just stab yourself?' Charlie asks.

I nod. When the blue world goes the wound will hurt like hell but, at the moment, I can move and that's all that counts.

'We need to get to our seats,' I say. 'The suits will put two and two together and be after us.'

Charlie checks the tickets. He points to the main entrance. 'We're in there. At the back of home plate. Best seats I could get.'

The entrance swallows us up as we enter a concourse lined with food concessions and merchandise areas. The place is alive with people behaving like ants. Scurrying around. Charlie counts down the entrances before leading me up a set of stairs and through a tunnel.

We emerge into a filling stadium. A vast empty space sitting below a dome roof that seems to float high above. Three sides of the diamond are attended by seats. The fourth is a wall of advertising and glass. Charlie checks with the ticket girl and we're shown to our seats.

We have to squeeze by a few people to find our allocation but Charlie has done well. We are less than a dozen rows back, slightly to the left of home plate. The Red Sox pitcher is loosening up. We're a lot closer to the start of the game than I had bargained for.

The mike is out for the National Anthem and the teams have already been introduced. I look for the senator and Lendl but there's a lot of ground to cover. A lot of people to check. 'See if you can spot the senator.'

Charlie starts to look. The blue is fading. The knife wound takes this as a cue to start bitching. I feel blood on my leg and wonder why it's only starting now. I ask Charlie for the pennant he's carrying and, to the disgust of the lady next to me, wrap it around the wound.

'Got him.' Charlie grabs my arm and points. The senator is talking to some players in the tunnel. There's no sign of Lendl but he can't be far away. 'You realize they'll be scanning the crowd.'

I nod as Charlie says this. 'I know.'

I keep my head down.

'Keep your face out of sight,' I say. 'We'll know when the first pitch is due. Let's try and not give them anything to work with.'

The National Anthem starts up. I don't stand. The disgusted woman next to me spits at me. 'Stand up.' I ignore her. The anthem stops and everyone sits. The announcer calls for the first pitch. I look up and see the senator walking across the infield, ball in hand. The catcher is standing—ready to receive. There is no sign of Lendl. I bury my head in my lap, playing with the knife in my pocket.

The senator pitches and a weak cheer echoes around.

'What now?' asks Charlie.

'We wait. Where's Tampoline now?'

'Five rows down, in the VIP seats.'

'Lendl?'

'Can't see him.'

The game gets underway. I keep my eyes on my lap. We hit a three and a two on the Rays' pitch and the crowd go nuts with the cowbells. I look up and a hand taps me on the shoulder. I start to turn and a familiar prick hits me in the arm.

'Just sit still, Mr McIntyre. No need to get worked up.' The voice is not one I want to hear behind me. I feel the drug take me down.

'You too, Charles. Just take in the game.'

Charlie slumps onto my shoulder.

'I'm afraid your bar friend may not be quite so used to our hospitality as you are.' Lendl is oozing confidence.

Treacle flows through my veins and candy floss plays with my head. 'I'll fuckinhish, bashdard. I'll fuchsin.'

'We'll talk later. Save it for then.'

There are a hundred things I want to do and say but the drug is strong. Not the ones I'm used to. This is a new sensation. Not so much chilled as just cool. I'm cool with the world. I want to tell Lendl we're okay. He and I. Really okay. He's just doing his job. I understand.

I look at the game and I see men trying too hard. Running too fast. I want to tell them to take a drag on a Jamaican Marlboro. Inhale a little of that Caribbean slow time.

Lendl speaks softly. 'Just watch the game and we'll all have a friendly cup of coffee at the end.'

A few innings in I can feel some of the mist beginning to clear but, on cue, another dose is administered. There are worse ways to watch baseball.

Two more shots and the Rays are Happy Larrys. Three— one. Top of the pile now. The stadium should empty but they're gearing up for the concert.

Lendl leans forward. 'Time to go.'

A couple of suits are making their way down the stairs. They don't look happy. I wish I could make their day a bad one but the drugs are an anchor on my abilities. They remove Charlie from my shoulder and lift me from the chair.

'A touch too much drink, I fear.' Lendl is talking to those around me. Another shot and I'm close to passing out.

Soon we are wandering through the maze that makes up the innards of the stadium. I'm bundled into a closet. The smell suggests it was recently used to store cleaning equipment.

Lights out. Another cell.

I hear a door close nearby and wonder if Charlie has just been dumped in his own cell.

I fall to the floor as the light fairies play with my eyesight. The feeling of helplessness is not quashed by the narcotics. I know I need to act. There will be no second chances. Lendl knows what I can do. The drugs running around my system are designed to keep me under control. They can't know that it will work but they are smart enough to keep me awake. I suspect—and I think they suspect—that the two incidents in Iraq were down to me—even if I was lost to the world. An afterburner of my ability.

Limbo is the best way to describe my situation. I feel for the knife but at some point in the journey it has been removed. I roll onto my front. This alone takes an unbearable amount of effort. I flop around with one hand, hearing the distant beat of music and a cheer as the band start up.

The floor is smooth. Masonry paint smooth. I shuffle my knees to make some headway but they slip around and I go nowhere.

Time is not a friend. The suits will be back. For some reason I've been dumped here but once I'm away from the stadium I'm finished. I reach down to the blood-soaked pennant and work it loose. I push my finger into the hole in my trousers and find the wound. I clench my teeth and push my finger into the cut. The pain is there but still too far away. I curl up the finger, rolling onto my side—forcing the digit deep into the muscle.

The pain grows nearer. My hip rises. All my effort into raising it. A few inches, then back to the ground. I ram my finger home.

The pain is suddenly very real. I gasp. The kernel in my head flashes. The headache rises and falls and the blue world appears. The drugs seem to fly from my body and the stop/start blue planet engulfs me.

I stand. My finger looks bent. It might be broken.

In the night vision I take in the closet. There's a single door and three walls of shelves. I try the door handle. I'm not surprised to find it locked. I give it a tug but it stays firm.

Then the handle turns of its own accord under my hand. I step back, flattening myself against the wall.

The door opens. The corridor is dark but it makes little odds to me. A hand holding a flashlight appears and, when the body follows, I chop down on the wrist. The flashlight goes flying. I grab the arm and pull. Caught off guard, the man flies into the closet. I push him to the floor and I'm out the door.

A second man is standing in the corridor beyond. I launch myself at him. No time for subtlety. My head connects with his and he starts to fall. I keep the momentum up, crashing him to the ground beneath me. I slam my fist into his face. He grabs at my head. With my new bald look his hand slides off. I bounce another fist into his face.

I stand, leaving him on the ground.

The corridor is narrow and bends in a curve. I follow it and reach a junction. It looks like a main serviceway. To my left is clear but to my right a clutch of suits are in conversation.

'Look!' The shout comes from the nearest suit. I try to break into a run but even with the blue world at my disposal I'm short on stamina. I stop, turn, place my finger into my wound and push.

'Fuck!' I shout as the pain bursts inside me.

The blue world vanishes. The headache is back. I lose the night vision. The first man is almost on me before he stops, turns and catches the man behind him in the groin with a foot. I don't wait to see how it pans out, instead I hobble along the corridor.

The sound of a fight fills the space behind, as the suits start to tear each other apart.

The corridor stretches out before me. I'm not sure I have the energy to make it far. Without the blue world my leg is screaming at me to stop—blood is running like a small river.

I stop to draw breath and realize that the music is a lot louder. I pick my way along the wall to find a door. The crowd is cheering as I open it. A set of stairs lie ahead.

Up.

So many stairs.

Up.

At the top another door. This one swings open to reveal the stadium. I am at the extreme end of the seats—up in the gods. The band members have their backs to me. The stadium is rocking. The group are singing about having a million dollars.

I start down towards the pitch, using the wall as a support as I drop. I am maybe ten rows from the outfield when a security guard spots me. I change tack and thread my way along a row of empty seats. A few blocks along the crowd are dotting the edges. The security guard is watching me, keeping parallel on the bottom row.

My footsteps are slowing. I want to sit but I need to keep going. I reach the first of the crowd and I'm forced up to the next passageway. Flicking my head back I see the security guard starting up the stairs. I cut along, trying to put some distance between us.

Shuffling along the back of a row, I'm being sucked into the crowd. The band is doing well and people are bouncing around me. I'm just a view-blocker to those on the row next to me.

Head down. I'm starting to run on empty. There is no escape plan in my actions. Just movement. The exits will be sealed by now. I'm also expecting a bullet. Valuable as I am, they won't risk me staying free. Maybe not a bullet. Maybe a tranquilizer dart. A man in a safari suit sitting high up. Taking a bead on me now. Waiting for the kill shot. Finger pressure light on the trigger. Tracking me. Breathing controlled. Waiting to exhale. Settle the sight. Squeeze. And, like a hunted animal, I'm on the floor.

I look up. There are two suits at the bottom of the next set of stairs. The passageway I am on runs out. More suits are emerging from doors right across the arena. Behind me the security guard is on my level but he's on his walkie-talkie and not moving in. Under orders from the suits. Dangerous. Don't touch.

The blood flow down my leg is increasing and my head is feeling light. I have nothing to stem the flood. My headache vanishes. A woman is shouting at me to get out of her line of vision. She's waving a Devil Rays flag. I grab it from her—wrapping it around my leg as she goes off on one. I ignore her. She steps forward. I turn and look her in the eye. She stops and backs off. The man next to her doesn't even move.

I change direction, doubling back towards the security guard. My vision is going and my legs have the strength of fire-damaged twigs. Each step is becoming an effort. I stagger against the handrail. A woman in the row below turns round to see what I'm doing.

Lorraine?

I freeze.

Lorraine?

I mouth the words. She stares at me.

'Lorraine?' I say.

Quiet. Too quiet for the noise around me.

She shakes her head, turning away. I reach out and tap her on the shoulder. She turns back round.

It's no longer Lorraine but some woman wondering who I am. I start moving again. It's taking everything I have left to stay upright. I reach the stairs I climbed and, with the security guard a few yards away, I start down.

My eyes focus. Just for a second. Lendl is at the bottom of the stairs. He's on his cell. I close my eyes and open them again in case it too is an illusion; but, unlike the woman, Lendl stays as Lendl. Next to him is Tampoline. They're now both on their cell phones. Lendl is pointing at me.

A hundred stairs between me and my targets. A hundred steps that I don't have in me. And yet Lendl and Tampoline are there. Together. The reason my wife is dead. The reason my life has imploded. A man with no conscience and a man with blood on his hands.

A hundred steps.

The image of the young girl in the club floats up—blood gushing from her mouth. She morphs into Taylor and his girlfriend in Iraq. The two bodies rising from the dusty road. Both pointing at me. The air stewardess and her boss appear. Fighting each other.

My hand slips on the rail.

Then I'm back in Iraq. Only now I'm way back. My first patrol. Clegg and Johnston on point. Arguing. When they aren't having a pop at each other they're having one at me. I'm tired. The heat and fear are eating me alive. I want to stop but we have our orders. Then there's an explosion and something hits me in the head. I go down. Something opens inside me. I feel it crack wide and spill its guts. Something alive crawls around inside my skull. Exploring. Then it settles at the back. Curls up and wraps a hard shell round itself.

I scream and keep screaming.

When I awaken, Clegg and Johnston are dead.

Then I'm back in the stadium.

I tip my head to one side. I can feel the hard thing rolling around. Inside. The crowd around me go wild as the group winds up for a finish. Lendl is still at the bottom of the stairs. Tampoline is walking away. Around me I can sense the suits closing in.

I push upright and make a decision.

Breath.

Step.

Breath.

Double step.

Breath.

Triple step.

Down.

Out of control.

Feet trying to find steps.

Feet failing.

And I'm falling.

I bounce off the handrail and I'm down. I hit the concrete stairs, tumbling forward. I push with one foot and I'm out and into the arena air.

I arc and come crashing back. My shoulder taking the hit. Up again. I veer to the left, clipping someone. They give under my weight and I fly into someone else. My stomach crashes into the back of a man's head. We both fall forward.

I can feel myself coming to a halt. I push out with my leg, catching some thigh, and I launch myself forward, over the crowd. There are no empty seats. On my return to earth I take to violent crowd-surfing.

Logic suggests that I should stop soon. Fall to the floor in a bundle of limbs. But I don't. Instead I flip onto my back. I see Lendl looking up. Tampoline has stopped in his tracks. He's watching me fall.

I smash into another body and I'm thrown up. Each time I touch down I feel a lift as the people shove me back into the air. Hands, elbows, heads—it makes no odds.

I'm sliding down the seating—closing the gap to Lendl. No deviation from the path. A straight line. As if everyone in the crowd has agreed in advance that I have somewhere to be and it's their job to help me get there.

I can still feel blood leaking. If I had a giant bottle of Luminol and sprayed it behind me, you could track my progress through the spatter. Two old women shove my legs. A young man pushes at my head. I flip over and a large fat man, stuffing a hot dog into his mouth, reaches up to thrust me forward.

Pain has now passed me by. Left somewhere in the bleachers. The hands and the heads should hurt but they don't. The people should be complaining but they aren't. I feel my weight drop away. Ounce by ounce. Each drop of blood taking ten times its weight with it.

Halfway to Lendl a pretty girl looks up at me. She smiles as her hand flicks me onwards. I smile back. Her push lifts me twenty feet into the air. I reach the apex of the climb and look down on a thousand eyes. A spray of blood follows me like a contrail. I return to the crowd and the next heave lifts me to a new height.

The stadium is now spread out beneath me. The band is finishing its set—oblivious to my acrobatics. Lendl has his mouth open as I rise once more. Tampoline is edging back to Lendl. I can see the questions beginning to build on his lips.

I turn my head. Suits are lining the passageways. All eyes are on me as I return to earth. The next shove takes me in an arc that will cover the remaining distance to the stadium floor. I curl up to brace for the impact.

I land with the lightest of bumps, open my eyes. Lendl is above me. I have no energy left to stand. I can't even lift my head from the floor. I feel the rough texture of the artificial surface against my cheek. I dig for the kernel. For the headache. For the blue world.

In vain.

Suits begin to arrive. Lendl is shouting. I know he wants someone to pump me full as soon as possible. Tampoline is also looking down at me.

A flicker. A small cranial ember begins to burn. I watch a suit unzip a bag and pull out a syringe. The ember is dull but the living thing in my head blows on it. The man breaks the seal of the small vial he's holding—piercing the rubber and plunging the needle into the liquid.

The breath in my head is oxygen-rich. The ember starts to glow. The man with the syringe tips the needle to the roof and shifts the plunger, pushing out a few drops. They sparkle in the stage lights. One lands on my face as the air in my head rises from a breeze to a hurricane. The headache builds. I open my arms to welcome it in. I realize that my arms have responded to the mental image. The man with the needle is caught off balance and slips.

The headache arrives with the force of a diesel locomotive. I look up at Lendl but he has nothing on his face other than contempt. The man with the needle regains his balance and reaches for my arm. I try to pull away but the last of my energy is spent.

The band finishes. The music stops. The crowd go into overdrive. The roar of approval is a wave around my head. A chant goes up. They want more.

The note of the crowd changes. A subtle change. From adoration to something different. The cheer from the front is being modulated. Adjusted.

I flop my head to one side to look. The man with the needle also turns to look. Something is making its way towards us. A Mexican wave of sound and action. Screams are audible as the atmosphere phases from good to bad.

Then the wave hits me and the people nearest turn to their neighbors and lash out. One man takes his index finger, plunging it into the eyeball of the person next to him. An older lady lifts her purse high and tries to drive it into the skull of a girl in the front row. Hate washes over me. A giant ball of hot revulsion spreading across the floor.

Thirty thousand people are responding to my signal. Each individual finding a vent for a long-pent-up fury. A moment of hurt, shame, selfishness, fear, recklessness—a moment of payback.

I can't see past the front row but I know what's unwinding. This is the theater on a grand scale and there is nothing I can do to stop it. I'm no longer the conductor.

A girl—hardly out of her gym slip—leaps the barrier to the outfield. She's being chased by a young lad. Probably her boyfriend. He's missing an arm and a gusher of blood is running him dry. She has his arm in her hand—waving it high, taunting him with it. He slows, stumbles. The arm is placed in her mouth and she bites—taking a chunk of forearm in her mouth, ripping at it until the flesh comes free. The boy collapses to the floor. Not understanding what is happening. Dying.

A pair of men tumble over the barrier. Locked tight. Each trying to deliver a blow. One lands on top and the other's grip is lost. The victor takes his enemy's head and smashes it into the ground. Behind him a girl is cheering him on.

I want to turn to look at Lendl but my muscles no longer

respond. A screech rises from the direction of the stage. The band are joining in the fun. A guitar being used as a weapon.

Around me the sound is guttural—base human noise—attack and defense. Life and death. It spins around me. A cacophony. Wet mist is dropping on me. I can recognize the smell of copper as the blood-letting creates a cloud. Plasma rains down.

Somebody kicks me in the back. Air rushes from my lungs. Then a foot in front of my face. A patent leather shoe, its shine spotted with blood. I lift my eyes. Tampoline is standing above me. His face is one of calm. He's not part of what's going on. The look of someone who considers himself superior in more ways than make sense. His hair is perfect, tie superbly knotted—double Windsor of course. The suit jacket cut low to give him the impression of height.

He bends down and is joined by Lendl—now a man in a blood-created, leopard-spot coat. Lendl talks but in the din the words are lost.

Lendl has the syringe in his hand. He doesn't need it. I'm no threat. I can't move. Whatever lives in my head is out on its own. He drops to the floor and places the syringe in front my face. The fluid is darker than earlier.

He leans into my ear. 'This will hurt.'

My resistance is spent.

Tampoline joins him.

'What a waste,' he shouts. 'Just look at what you can do. Think what we could have done with you when it came to America's enemies.'

Lendl's face is inches from mine. The heavy scent of drink mixed with the sour smell of garlic. His eyes are red and sweat peppers his brow.

'Time to die, Mr McIntyre. Time to die.'

CHAPTER 40

I close my eyes. My last act of defiance. I'm not giving him the satisfaction of seeing my fear. I may not even feel the prick of the needle. Sensation is fading. The world collapsing around me. I am the calm eye at the centre of my own hurricane.

Nothing.

Not quite.

Almost nothing.

Background sound. A distant portable radio trying too hard with small speakers. A faded reproduction of what had been going on before. I force my eyes open and Lendl is still there, his head cocked to one side. The syringe is an inch from my neck—frozen in his hand.

He rises up, the needle recedes, he lets it go. It tumbles to the ground. Tampoline is walking away and, with movement that comes of training, Lendl closes the gap and wraps his arm around the senator's throat and drops to his knees.

Lendl propels himself forward to land square on Tampoline's back. He reaches for Tampoline's head. His hands start to explore the senator's face. Searching for softness. The senator squirms but years of inaction and overindulgence weigh against his chances. Lendl knows what he's doing. This is not about killing. This is about pain.

Lendl leaps to his feet. Tampoline is holding his head and rolls over. Blood is pouring between his fingers. Lendl steps back. He double-steps towards Tampoline and launches a sixty-yard, three-seconds-to-go, last-ditch, fourth down, Hail Mary. He takes Tampoline in the crotch and there is no way he hasn't broken a few toes. Tampoline—airless—spasms in agony. His hands fly from his face as his body concentrates on the area under attack. His eyes are gone.

Lendl limps back a little, hopping on his good foot. He kneels to pick up the syringe. He looks at me but there is no recognition. His eyes are blank. He circles Tampoline who is curled into a ball. With a flourish he lifts the needle into the night air. High above the curled ball of the senator.

Then it starts down.

As it falls I watch it. A single drop of dark fluid flies into the air. The needle descends and then, at the very last instant—the very, very last instant—it veers away from the senator and Lendl thrusts the needle into his own leg and stabs down on the plunger. He empties it.

Something goes off inside his chest and he's dead before he starts to drop.

I can no longer keep my eyes open and, as Lendl dies, my head flashes, the blue world gone.

The crowd noise takes on a new dimension.

Stunned silence.

CHAPTER 41

Charlie speaks. 'Dead?'
  He's probably right.
  Another voice. 'Not yet.'
  Not right. I'm dead.
  Charlie responds. 'Amazing.'
  My arm bristles as it's brushed.
  Smell.
  Bad taste in the mouth.
  A beep—regular.
  I open my eyes and the hospital engulfs me.
  'Welcome back.' Charlie is sitting next to me, a nurse standing above him.
  I try speaking but I'm out of spit. The nurse reaches over and fills a cup from a jug of water. She passes it to me. I swallow enough to produce sound.
  'Hi,' I squawk.
  'Hi yourself,' she says.
  I drift off and drift back. I note the drip feeding me nutrients and drift off again. I lose count of how many times I do this. The time between each sleep stretches. But every time I waken Charlie is always there.
  This time it's dark outside. 'Any chance of some food?'
  Charlie hits a button and the nurse appears. He points at me. 'Your patient wants some sustenance.'
  'I'll see what I can do.'

I ask Charlie to help me sit up.

Once up I slump back a little. 'Okay, so why am I alive, what happened to Tampoline and Lendl, did they lock you up, how did you escape, what went on in the stadium, where are the suits, why are you here, do they allow JD and Coke in this place?'

'Hang on soldier. One thing at a time.'

Charlie pulls his chair a little closer, checking that the door is closed. I'm not sure why I'm in a private room. I'm fairly sure my health insurance doesn't cover this. 'And?' I want some answers.

'The stadium was a mess. Biggest story in years. One hundred and twenty dead, thousands injured and no reason found.'

'Me!'

'Yes but the media don't know that. They're having a field day. Mass hysteria. A terrorist plot. Something in the water. Drugged hot dogs. A government experiment. No one knows. They are calling it the Tropicana Terror, or the TT.'

'Yeah but the suits know it was me.'

'Maybe.'

'Yes.'

'So why are you lying here and not in some cell?'

'I've no idea.' I'm hoping Charlie has an answer. 'Lendl?'

'Dead. Tampoline is alive but in a bad way. Both victims of the TT.'

'No suits sitting outside my door?'

'I can't figure that. My best guess is that Lendl and Tampoline kept you a secret. Your trip to the theater was a black op of the blackest type. Need to know only.'

'Need to know? There were endless suits involved.'

'Grunts I would guess.'

'And they don't talk to each other?'

'No idea. All I know is that I've been here over a week and there hasn't been a single suit.'

'Has it been that long?'

'Longer. They didn't find me for two days. No one thought to check broom closets while they were trying to sort out the TT. I had a few days in hospital before I was let go. It took me another few days to find out you were alive. The health system was swamped.'

'Tampoline knows I'm alive and he knows what I can do.'

'Sure, but he has other things to worry about. From what I read he's blind and won't be beating off while abusing girls anytime in the near future.'

'Good. I wonder what the history was between Tampoline and Lendl?'

'Do you care?'

'No.'

'I think you should get on the road as soon as you can.'

'Charlie, I killed all those people.'

'Maybe. Maybe not. There isn't a court in this land that would find you guilty.'

'They will. Whatever it is that I do is not going away. Laws are for re-writing and they'll re-write them for me.'

'Hard one to prove. At the moment it would be their word against yours.'

'All they have to do is drug me up again, video it and show the authorities what happens. I'll be dumped in the deepest hole for the rest of my life.'

'What do you want me to say? You need to move on.'

'That won't stop them looking for me.'

'I know but what else can you do?'

I say nothing.

CHAPTER 42

Outside, the wind is slicing through the trees. A constant keening sound as a backdrop to the silence in the backwater cabin I'm sitting in. The log fire is doing its best to fight the sub-zero temperature that wraps the building. Charlie is sitting as close as he can to the flames, reading a novel. I'm watching the fire dance.

We crossed the Canadian border a week ago and Charlie found the cabin while I was lying in my thirtieth hotel bed in as many days. It's a summer retreat for some family living in Toronto. It had been shut up for the winter. As Charlie points out, it's cheaper than a hotel and, if our luck holds, it may be weeks before someone spots the smoke from the chimney and decides to investigate.

Charlie flicks a page as a log spits an ember onto the hearth. I'm thinking about Lorraine and the simple fact that Tampoline is still alive. I think about that a lot. Charlie tells me I should leave well alone but a life on the run is no life. For all I know we may not even be wanted. No suits on the road looking for us. So why run?

But that feels wrong. Tampoline knows what I can do and he knows I am responsible for what happened to him. A few days ago we caught an article in *USA Today* about the return of the senator to the floor of the Capitol. He received a standing ovation.

Charlie sighs. I add my sigh to the night. I know I can't keep running. I stand and walk over to him. I squat next to the fire.

He looks down. He smiles and I know that somehow this has to be sorted.

But for now the road will need to be my friend.

I hope it's a friendship with a happy future.

ACKNOWLEDGMENTS

Thanks to Keith Charters for his help in drafting and editing and to Eric Campbell for his continuing belief in my writing.

GORDON BROWN has been writing since his teens and has six crime thrillers published—his latest, *Darkest Thoughts* being the first in the Craig McIntyre series, is out now in the US. A founder member of Bloody Scotland—Scotland's International Crime Writing Festival—Gordon lives in Scotland. He's married with two children and he once quit his job in London to fly across the Atlantic to be with his future wife. He has also delivered pizzas in Toronto, sold non-alcoholic beer in the Middle East, launched a creativity training business called Brain Juice and floated a high-tech company on the London Stock Exchange. He almost had a toy launched by a major toy company, has an MBA, loves music, is a DJ on local radio, compered the main stage at a two-day music festival and was once booed by 49,000 people while on the pitch at a major Soccer Cup Final.

GordonJBrown.com

BOOKS

On the following pages are a few
more great titles from the
Down & Out Books publishing family.

For a complete list of books and to
sign up for our newsletter,
go to DownAndOutBooks.com.

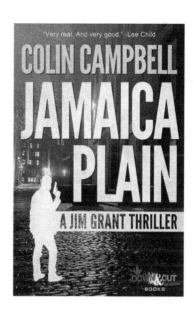

Jamaica Plain
A Jim Grant Thriller
Colin Campbell

Down & Out Books
978-1-948235-87-7

Jim Grant is in Boston to interview a prisoner, but when the prisoner is blown up at Jamaica Plain he stays on to investigate.

With the help of a veteran detective and a troubled ex-marine he soon discovers the truth behind the prisoner's activities. A truth that leads to a deadly race against time and an explosive climax.

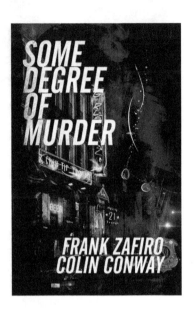

Some Degree of Murder
Frank Zafiro and Colin Conway

Down & Out Books
March 2019
978-1-948235-76-1

A young woman has been murdered in River City. Police Detective John Tower is assigned to the case but there are few clues to go on. As he digs further, he's soon picking up hints that this murder may not be the killer's first...or his last.

Virgil Kelly lives in the shadowy world of the criminal underground. He's just arrived in River City with a single-minded mission: find his daughter's killer and bury him.

Virgil Kelley and John Tower are on a collision course...and somebody is going to die...

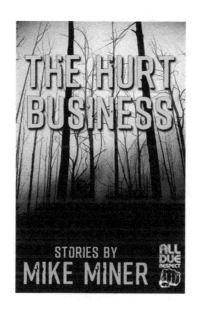

The Hurt Business
Stories by Mike Miner

All Due Respect, an imprint of
Down & Out Books
March 2019
978-1-948235-75-4

"We are such fragile creatures."

The men, women and children in these stories will all be pushed to the breaking point, some beyond. Heroes, villains and victims. The lives Miner examines are haunted by pain and violence. They are all trying to find redemption. A few will succeed, but at a terrible price. All of them will face the consequences of their bad decisions as pipers are paid and chickens come home to roost. The lessons in these pages are learned the very hard way. Throughout, Miner captures the savage beauty of these dark tales with spare poetic prose.

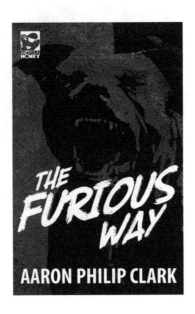

The Furious Way
Aaron Philip Clark

Shotgun Honey, an imprint of
Down & Out Books
May 2019
978-1-64396-003-6

Lucy Ramos is out for blood—she needs to kill a man, but she has no clue how. Lucy calls on the help of aged hit-man, Tito Garza, now in his golden years, living a mundane life in San Pedro.

With a backpack full of cash, Lucy persuades Garza to help her murder her mother's killer, ADA Victor Soto. Together, the forgotten hit-man hungry for a comeback and the girl whose life was shattered as a child, set out to kill the man responsible. But killing Victor Soto may prove to be an impossible task...

CPSIA information can be obtained
at www.ICGtesting.com
Printed in the USA
BVHW031651180521
607630BV00006B/889

9 781643 960135